JEA
WARMB

THE *white* HAND

Inspired by, and dedicated to the Christic Institute,
in its ongoing efforts to expose our 'Shadow Government'
and bring justice to bear.

'Educate Crows and they pluck out your eyes'
An old Spanish proverb

Published by VIRAGO PRESS Limited 1990
20-23 Mandela Street, Camden Town, London NW1 0HQ

First published in the United States by
The Permanent Press, Sag Harbor, NY, 1988

*A CIP catalogue record for this book
is available from the British Library*

Printed in Great Britain by
Cox & Wyman Ltd, Reading, Berkshire

San Rodino, California
December 25, 1987

Christmas morning—5 a.m. And I was mired behind the wheel of this rented Toyota, popping peppermints and waiting for the 'Mad Bomber' to pay a call. There was no point in complaining. I had asked for the damn assignment, hadn't I? If for no better reason than to get away from San Francisco this holiday season. Away from the numbing loneliness that had been hounding me there. But it wasn't working. The loneliness had followed me down here, gotten worse, compounded by the strange hours I'd been keeping, the alien surroundings, the fact that this misguided stakeout was going nowhere at all. Six nights running, I had been casing this family clinic with Eddie's infrared Minolta in hand. And six nights running, the Bomber had been a no-show.

Another two hours and four peppermints slipped by. Dawn pushed over the horizon. And the only action in town was the young woman standing at the bus stop down the street. She was short and fat, and buried in a huge red parka, a clashing purple scarf trailing down to her feet.

The longer I watched the woman, the more I realized she was more pregnant than fat. Good and pregnant. And impatient enough, as she stepped on and off the curb, to make me wonder if she wasn't on her way to the hospital at this very moment. She certainly couldn't be waiting for the clinic to open its doors? Not on Christmas Day?

She turned and stared straight at me. Or so it seemed. But it wasn't me she was staring at. It was the mailbox some distance in front of the car. She dug a long white envelope out of her coat, crossed the street, and proceeded to scribble something onto the envelope, using the mailbox for support. Then held the envelope up to the early morning light for a moment or two before dropping it into the mailbox and starting back across the street.

What happened next, happened as if in a dream. Or a nightmare. Two men in black stepped out of a side alley, lifted rifles to their shoulders, and took measured aim at the woman. A frantic scream stuck in my throat as I watched her take one step back, and another, spinning low to the ground and wrapping her arms tightly around her waist.

My God, I murmured, squeezing under the dashboard as gunfire cracked meanly through the air. My God. My God . . . Then silence. A sinister, eerie calm. Had they seen me sitting here? Were they making their way across the street at this very moment to bump me off? I felt nauseous, limp, staring up at the window as my entire life flashed before me, amounting to nothing more than a dissipated and inconsequential blur.

Time passed, at least four or five minutes worth, before I finally risked checking out the scene. The gunmen had disappeared. The young woman lay in a pool of her own blood in the street, her arms flayed out at her side. Was it my imagination or had she moved slightly? An infinitesimal fluttering of a hand? I steadied my own hands and opened the door. Then gently closed it again, slumping low in the seat as a black and white police van eased around the corner and up to the curb.

Two more men, this pair younger in appearance and dressed in uniform, stepped out of the van. My camera finger didn't fail me this time around, as the driver approached the body and the second officer withdrew a stretcher from the rear of the van. Very impassively, and without a word spoken between them, they lifted the body onto the stretcher, covered it with a blanket, and deposited the dead woman in the back of the van. The vehicle took off again, leaving behind the pool of blood and her black woolen hat as the only material testimony to the butchery that had been done.

I sat there, frozen to the seat, trying to make some sense out of what I had seen. And asking myself what the hell I was going to do about it. Call the police? But the police had already been here. And left. Without calling homicide to the scene or even bothering to check the area for witnesses or clues. There seemed little more reason to trust those two cops than the two gunmen who had come before them.

Two kids barreled around the corner on bicycles and pedaled down the street. A wino of indeterminate age weaved up to the bus stop and stood over the pool of blood, studying it for some time. At last, he bent over and scooped up the woman's hat, removed the baseball cap from his head, pulled on the woolen hat, jammed the baseball cap over the hat, and headed on his way.

It was 7:35 by my watch when I risked getting out of the car. I stepped gingerly into the street, dipping a toe into the already drying blood. It was real, all right. A cool chill moved up my spine. I looked up, around, behind me, struck by the palpable impression that I was being watched. But the streets were empty. Too empty. Taking a few halting backward steps, I turned and raced to the car, beating a hasty retreat back to the motel.

Safely ensconced in my room, I stewed in place for several hours, mulling over the star-crossed inevitability of this morning's scene. That young woman had been expecting those two gunmen or others like them. Maybe not today. Maybe not tomorrow. But sometime, somewhere, she had been expecting them. Of that I was somehow convinced.

I considered the idea of calling up Deb Wilson, my main contact on the clinic staff. Then changed my mind. Any connection between a flurry of bomb threats aimed at the clinic and the murder which had just taken place outside its doors had to be tenuous at best. So why get Deb involved, on today of all days? For that matter, why get myself involved? The situation looked very professional and very ugly.

But there were the pictures in my camera to be taken into account. And the fact that I had seen the murder take place. To wash my hands of the entire incident would be no easy matter. I soaked in a hot tub, then tried to get some sleep. But the murder scene kept playing through my head; those eerie futuristic rifles and the offhand manner in which the two gunmen and their apparent accomplices had carried out their task.

I was convinced that the young woman, by turning her back to their fire the way she did, had hoped to save her baby. It was the futility of that gesture that continued to haunt me throughout the afternoon and evening and well into the night.

December 26, 1987

When I awoke next morning, the episode was as vivid as ever in my mind. I dressed and headed over to the motel's coffee shop, picking up a copy of the *San Rodino Times* outside its doors.

"Have yourself a groovy Christmas?" the congenial young waitress asked me, setting me up with the usual black coffee and cinnamon twist.

"Could have been better. And you?"

"Yeah. Same here," she said, snapping her Juicy Fruit and winking at the elderly gentleman to my left. "It comes and it goes, right?" she announced to no one in particular, slapping the counter top and sashaying on down the aisle. "It comes. And it goes."

I took a quick look through the paper, finding what I was looking for in a brief paragraph at the bottom of page nine:

> *Pregnant woman shot by unknown assailant*
>
> Miss Diana Stevens, a twenty-eight-year-old divorcée and seven months pregnant, was found dead Friday morning on the corner of Ferndale and 14th Street. She had been shot four times by an unknown assailant. No valuables were found on her person and robbery is the suspected motive.

Robbery? A cold-blooded execution would be more to the point. A big-league, mob-style hit. I reread the paragraph a second time. She had been twenty-eight? I wouldn't have taken her for a day over twenty. And divorced? So who had been the father-to-be, and what connection might exist between the man and the young woman's brutal death?

I checked out the funeral notices at the back of the paper, but no Stevens was listed. Tossing down my coffee and paying my bill, I returned to the room to place a call to the family clinic, on the off chance they had some file on the woman. But the clinic was closed. All I got out of them was a recorded message wishing me Happy Holidays and reminding me that they would be re-opening their doors on January 2.

I tried Deb Wilson at home, which only got me another cheery message from another cheery machine. Now what? Hauling out the half gallon of Gallo from under the bed, I poured myself a glass. A little on the early side for such indulgences, but what the hell. And with glass in hand, I settled at the desk to make a half-hearted stab at my 'Terrorism at Home' piece, as my editor had tentatively called it. But I didn't get very far. Yesterday's horror show kept intruding into my thoughts.

Digging the address book out of my suitcase, I thumbed through it once. And again. Then tossed it aside. There was only one person I wanted to talk to at the moment. And that person was nowhere around.

More wine, more thoughts. Damn if I wasn't missing Stanley again. Settling back on the bed, I conjured up his image, the one that came the easiest: the first time I ever set eyes on Stanley, some six and a half months ago, as he approached my table in Verdi's front room. Lean, tall, a look of permanent bemusement in his face, in his eyes, behind those horn-rimmed glasses. Attractive in an unassuming way that was to grow on me over the weeks and months. The more time I spent with the guy, the more I came to know him, his wryness, his easy laugh. That was my first memory . . . And my last?

I poured out a bit more wine and fished out our last few hours together, just over a month ago . . .

The evening had started off pleasantly enough, with dinner at Verdi's, followed by an impromptu going-away party for Stanley in the restaurant's back room. The usual crowd in attendance, in our usual inebriated and convivial mood. Including Stanley. Including myself. And after all, why not? He was only leaving for a brief six months. Hardly a lifetime. And we had already made plans for a little R&R in Paris come April or May.

It was only later in the evening that my spirits soured. And it was Chuck Laskey, one of Stanley's fellow columnists at the paper, who did the honors, informing me in the middle of one of his well-oiled soliloquies that Stanley had more or less created his appointment in the Middle East. That he had, in a manner of speaking, gone begging for the job on hand and knee. How very interesting. And how very unexpected. Since to hear Stanley tell it, he had been coerced into the assignment from the very start.

This little discrepancy, this little white lie, sizzled for the rest of the evening, fueled by one too many Manhattans, and exploding in a blitzkrieg of recriminations when I finally got the man alone.

"Goddamn it, Sarah!" Stanley interjected into one of my juicier lines, kicking a loaded ashtray halfway across the room. "This could be one hell of a story for me. So what's the point in begrudging me my chances?"

"Begrudging you your chances! And just who the hell is begrudging you your chances? You're missing the entire point, Stanley! It's the lies I'm begrudging! The sham! Why go around pretending you didn't want the damn assignment all these weeks, when you really did? Would have climbed over your own grandmother to get it, to hear Chuck tell it. So what's the point in—"

"It wasn't all sham, Sarah," he said, interrupting me again. "You don't think I relish the idea of leaving you behind, do you?"

"Whoa. Let's get one thing straight, Stanley. Nobody is leaving anybody behind. All right? Now—did you or did you not create this spot for yourself in Haifa?"

A pause. "More or less, yes."

"Then why didn't you just *say* so?"

He walked over to the sofa and sat down, placing one foot and then the other onto the cocktail table in front of him. Then he looked up. "Maybe I didn't want to hurt you, Sarah."

"*Come on,* Stanley. If that isn't the tiredest excuse for lying that's ever come down the pike . . ."

"Okay. So let's just say—let's just say that I was hoping to avoid exactly the kind of ugly confrontation we seem to be getting into right this moment. Where's the gain in—"

"But Stanley! If you had been straight with me from the beginning, there wouldn't be any ugly confrontation. Don't you see? What's wrong with you wanting to take this assignment in Israel? What's wrong with you wanting to get out another book? Absolutely nothing. It's great. It's one of the things I find so fascinating about you. So why start in with the lies, Stanley? Because once the lies start in, it's the beginning of the end."

"I see. And you've never been guilty of these 'lies' yourself, Sarah. Is that what you're saying?"

"Damn right. Whatever other faults I may have, I've always played it straight with you. You have to give me that much."

"And that episode with the Martinelli kid, last July?"

"Jesus, Stanley. We're not going back to that, are we? How many times do I have to tell you that *nothing* happened."

"Doesn't that depend on one's interpretation of 'nothing'?" he suggested, clasping his hands behind his head. "And how did I learn about this murky affair? From 'Honest Abe' Calloway herself? Unfortunately, no. I had to wait for George to give me the lowdown, didn't I? Why, Sarah? Why did I have to hear it from George instead of getting it straight from the horse's mouth? Can you answer me that?"

"There was no 'lowdown'. And this is very old ground, Stanley. Last July, for Christ's sake."

"Not for me, it isn't. To my way of thinking, you lied to me, Sarah. Plain and simple."

"I didn't lie, Stanley. I just omitted telling you something. There's a difference there," I added weakly.

"I see."

"I mean, it was such an inconsequential—there just wasn't any point in causing any unnecessary . . ." I stopped right there.

"What was that, Sarah?"

"Nothing. I can't believe we're rehashing this thing, again."

"Unnecessary what? What were you about to say? You didn't see the point in causing any unneccesary—what?"

"Any unnecessary ugly confrontations," I said, unable to keep the smile off my face. "Okay, so I admit it. I'm as guilty as you are. But that doesn't make either of us right, does it?"

He peered at me over his glasses.

"Come to Israel with me, Sarah."

"I'm in the middle of a story, for God's sake."

"All right, then. Finish your story. Then come. We'll get married over there. Tie the knot. Or better yet, we'll meet in Paris, as planned, and get married over there. How does that sound?"

"Don't you think one ex-wife is plenty enough for you to handle?" I suggested, joining him on the sofa. "You sure as hell don't need two of them. Besides, we're doing just fine the way we are," I added, moving into his arms. Marveling at the way the louse could always bring me around.

Neither of us got much sleep that night. And he left on the 8 a.m. flight for Jerusalem, the following day. I hadn't heard a word out of him since.

December 27, 1987

I awoke this morning with one hell of a hangover, and under a very cold shower added three more New Year's resolutions to my list. Then dragged body and soul over to the coffee shop for a morning hit of caffeine.

The young waitress was bubbling over with high spirits. Whatever had 'come and gone' in her life yesterday morning must have come back again. Either that, or something else had come in its place. I sipped my coffee and thumbed through a copy of the *San Rodino Times*, making my way inexorably back to the lineup of funeral notices on the very last page.

It was there, all right. The second to last listing on the page:

> Stevens, Diana K.—December 25, 1987 in San Rodino, California. Native of California, age 28. Survived by her

mother, Maude Ella Stevens. Friends are invited to attend memorial services at 10 a.m. Sunday, at St. Benedict's Church, San Rodino.

Sunday? But that was today. So much for New Year's resolutions. I decided to attend.

A small notice tacked onto the front doors of the church informed all interested parties that the Stevens funeral was taking place in the East chapel. I followed the arrow around to a side entrance and slipped into the darkened oratory. In time, my eyes adjusted to the flickering candlelight enough to make out five other persons in the room: the church organist, three women huddled together in a front pew, and a single gentleman seated in back. I settled across the aisle from the man and stayed put for the next 30 minutes as the organist ran through his gloomy repertoire. The women up front were weeping. The gentleman to my left persisted in crossing and uncrossing his legs and turning in my direction. I confronted one of his many obtrusive, rubber-neck glances and locked eyes with a surprisingly attractive man in his early thirties. The ex-husband, perhaps?

It was some time after eleven when the organist finally rose to his feet, and with a slight bow in our direction left the room. The three women followed suit.

"Mrs. Stevens?" I called out from the top of the stairs.

All three women turned to face me.

"Mrs. Stevens?" I repeated, joining them on the sidewalk below.

"Yes?" It was the shortest and heaviest of the three women who spoke up. Under the circumstances, her manner of dress was on the unusual side: a black shawl draped over a bright purple knitted dress, long dangly earrings and heavy liner around the eyes. But in spite of the gypsy-like trappings, the pain was clearly written across her face.

"I wanted to tell you how very sorry I am about your daughter. It was a terrible, a vicious thing to have happened to her."

She nodded mutely, twisting the ends of the shawl in her hands.

"Would it be possible to speak with you some time soon?" I added, glancing back over my shoulder to find the grey-eyed gentleman watching us from the top of the steps. "About your daughter?"

She hesitated, looking from one companion to the other and then back at me.

"Who are you?" she finally asked.

"My name is Sarah Calloway. I'm a—I'm working here in Rodino for a few days."

"Were you a friend of Diana's?"

"Might we talk sometime, Mrs. Stevens? Alone?"

"Couldn't you let this wait?" one of her friends suggested testily.

"Where did you know Diana?" Mrs. Stevens asked, putting a hand on her friend's arm.

"It's a complicated story. Look here," I said, foraging through my purse for one of the motel's matchbooks. "Why don't you get in touch with me when you feel up for a little talk? Do call soon," I added, following the three of them over to a Pontiac station wagon parked at the curb.

She nodded, looking from the matchbook back up to me. Under the shroud of sorrow, a nascent curiosity had been aroused. I could not say the same for her friends, shooting me icy once-overs as they herded their charge into the front seat of the car.

I headed for my own automobile, parked directly across the street, uncomfortably aware of Grey-Eyes' continued surveillance from the church steps. Should I stop? Have a word with the man? On second thought, I decided to continue on my way, satisfied with the idea that I had done all that could be expected of me under the circumstances. Mrs. Stevens would make the next move, or there'd be no more moves made at all.

Back in the room, I settled before my notes and cassettes, and for the first time in three days made some real headway on my piece. A short coffee break at four, then more work until 9:30 or 10 p.m. when I headed across the lot for a grilled cheese and french fries to go. No sooner had I returned to the room, than there came a muffled rap at the door. Peering through the venetian blinds, I caught sight of Mrs. Stevens in profile on the balcony, attired in the same black shawl and purple dress she had been wearing earlier today.

"I'm so glad you have come, Mrs. Stevens," I said, settling her into the only comfortable chair in the room. An upholstered rocker which made the woman look tiny and pathetic, her handbag clutched tightly in her lap and her feet barely touching the floor.

"Tell me, Miss Calloway," she said, clicking her handbag open and shut and squirming to the edge of the chair. "How did you know my daughter?"

I hesitated, wondering how to put this.

"I didn't know your daughter, Mrs. Stevens."

"You . . . ? Then what is the meaning of all this?" she demanded, getting back to her feet.

"If you will just sit down, I will explain everything."

She edged toward the door.

"Mrs. Stevens. I saw your daughter murdered."

"What?"

I took a breath and went on. "I was parked just down the street from where it happened. It was no robbery, Mrs. Stevens. It was more of an execution. She was standing there at the bus stop when these two men came out of nowhere, gunned her down, and disappeared. Not a word was ever exchanged. Neither of them ever touched her from what I could see. Neither her or her purse."

"Sweet Jesus," she whispered, hand over her face as she sank back into the chair. Wrapping her arms around her waist, the woman rocked slowly back and forth as the tears rolled freely down her cheeks. I headed into the bathroom for a clean glass and filled it with what was left of the Gallo.

"Drink this," I said, shoving the glass into her hand. She continued to rock back and forth, holding the glass in her hands like a small child holding a glass of milk.

"Did she see them coming?" she murmured.

I shook my head, reluctant to give the woman any more of the details than I already had.

"But why didn't you go to the police with all this?" she finally asked in dazed bewilderment.

"Because, Mrs. Stevens. It is just possible that the police are involved."

"What?"

I went on to tell her about the uncanny timing of the police van and the cool efficiency of the officers involved.

"But it's possible they were only doing their job, isn't it?" she said, blinking at me.

"It's a most unorthodox way to treat a homicide, Mrs. Stevens."

"This is all a horrible dream," she moaned, staring into the glass. "A terrible, horrible dream."

"Have a bit of the wine. It might help."

She shook her head and put the glass aside. Then she brought out a handkerchief from her purse and daubed at her eyes. Spotting a gob of mascara on her hanky, she excused herself and headed into the bathroom.

"Tell me something, Miss Calloway," she said, upon returning to the room. "Just who are you? How did you happen to—to—"

"I'm an investigative reporter," I said, digging a card out of my bag. "It was purely an accident that I happened to be there when she was—when it happened."

She took her time reading over the card, mouthing each word silently with her lips. "And this morning?" she said, looking up at me. "How did you happen to find me at the church?"

"The funeral was written up in this morning's paper."

"Yes, of course," she murmured, turning to look out the window and biting her lower lip.

"I thought you would want to know, Mrs. Stevens. Know how your daughter really died."

She gave me a pathetic smile. Then gazed out the window again. "It was a baby boy," she said, drawing circles on the window pane.

"Or—well, would have been." A pall fell over the room as she continued to trace circles onto the dirty glass.

"Mrs. Stevens, who was the man attending the funeral this morning?" I asked.

She turned to face me, a vacant look in her eyes.

"The gentleman sitting in the back pew," I added.

"Why I—I never saw such a man."

"Mrs. Stevens! The man who came out of the church just after we did. The one watching us from the top of the church steps?"

She shook her head and drew the shawl more tightly around her shoulders. "You must forgive me. I really haven't been myself these days."

"Could it have been her ex-husband?"

"Philip? Why no. He's dead."

"I see. Well then tell me, Mrs. Stevens. Who was the father of the dead child?"

She stiffened, her hands clasped tightly around the handle of her purse. "I have no idea, Miss Calloway. Now I really must be going. Thank you for—for thinking to contact me," she added, moving toward the door.

"Did you receive the letter?" I asked, taking a shot.

She turned and stared at me, a hand at her throat.

"The . . . What letter?" she asked hoarsely.

"Your daughter sent you a letter, Mrs. Stevens. Isn't that true? You see, I saw her mail it only moments before she was gunned down."

"I—I really must be going," she repeated as if to herself, shaking her head and slipping out the door.

"Mrs. Stevens!"

She stopped midway down the walk, turned.

"Mrs. Stevens, you must realize something. It is just possible that those two gunmen saw your daughter mail that letter. If there's anything of an incriminating or controversial nature in there, then you too might be in danger. Do you understand?"

She blinked, and without another word, turned and headed on

her way. Leaving me behind with a lot more questions than answers. Evidently the woman *had* received the letter? If so, what could it have contained to make her react the way she did? And what possible connection might there be between that letter and the young woman's death? Could it be possible that she *hadn't* noticed the grey-eyed gentleman at the funeral? Highly unlikely. Then there was the question of her relationship to her own daughter. How remote must it have been if she couldn't even identify the father-to-be? Or did she know the man and simply wasn't saying?

I turned off the lights and crawled into bed, nagged by the suspicion that behind the murder of one young and pregnant woman loomed a much larger and bloodier story. It was a cold and restless night of sleep.

December 28, 1987

7 a.m. and Maude Stevens was back at my motel room door.

"Did I wake you?" she asked, peeking around me and into the room. The dangly earrings were gone. So was the makeup. But the dress was the same. Had the woman even gone to bed?

"I've been—well, I've been thinking over our conversation," she said, rocking in the chair. "I mean, about how it happened and all." She looked into her lap, then back at me. "I suppose I should start at the beginning, she suggested, the sad smile flitting across her face.

"I suppose you should."

"You see, Miss Calloway. I—" She paused, biting her lip and gazing down at her hands. "This isn't going to be easy to talk about. I haven't—well, you're the first person—" She paused again, taking in a deep breath and blinking up at the ceiling.

"What is it, Mrs. Stevens?"

"Well you see, I . . ."

"Yes?"

"As silly as this may sound, I . . ."

"You *what*, Mrs. Stevens?"

"I—I didn't even know my daughter was pregnant. For that matter, I didn't even know she was in town. I had imagined her miles away. Perhaps in San Francisco. Or—or up in Seattle. Or, goodness knows where. I still can't really take all this in. That she was right here in Rodino. Right here under my nose all this time!"

"The two of you had been out of touch?"

"My daughter left home four months ago, Miss Calloway. That would be August 25th. I never heard from her again."

"I see. Was there any particular reason that she left?"

"Well, I—that's just it. I mean, I didn't—well, obviously my daughter had met someone. A man. Goodness, the pregnancy tells us that much."

"So you assume that she ran off with this man?"

"Well, yes. I should think—I mean, it does seem to be the logical—though of course there were other—other signs, if you will."

"Signs?"

"You know—changes."

"In Diana?"

"That's right, yes. Do you read the Bible, Miss Calloway?"

"I—no, I don't."

"Well now, I have nothing against the Good Book myself. But those last few months she became a fanatic about it. About the Bible, I mean. When she wasn't at work, she was home reading her Bible. Even now as I speak, I see her there, hunched over the—the kitchen table and . . . Oh my," she murmured, closing her eyes as a hand flew up to her face. Moments elapsed. "You must forgive me. I . . ."

"Take your time, Mrs. Stevens."

"Where—what was I saying?"

"About Diana's Bible study?"

"Yes. Well that—that wasn't all. Her entire nature seemed to change before my eyes. It was almost as if—as if she were possessed. I don't mean that literally, of course. But there were times . . ."

"Could you be more specific?"

"Specific? There was her diet, for one. She had nothing to do with meat at the end. The child was living on macaroni and cheese, I swear it. And vitamins. You cannot imagine how many vitamins that child would consume. Thirty to forty at a single sitting. But it was more an overall—well, she became so secretive at the end. So aloof. Diana had always been one to keep to herself. But this was something entirely different. There was no question of my learning what was going on. It wasn't, well it wasn't a very happy time for us, need I add."

"You have no idea what might have caused these changes?" She shook her head.

"It's a terrible thing for a mother to have to admit. But my daughter became a stranger to me those last few weeks. I no longer understood the child at all."

"And you never heard from her again?"

"That's right. That is, not until—" She paused, eyeing me guardedly as she clicked her purse open and shut. Open and shut. "Well, you were right, you see. About the letter, I mean. I didn't bring it up yesterday evening because—well, I'm sure you understand. After all, it was to her mother that Diana turned to in the end, wasn't it? It was to me that she entrusted her letter. And nobody else. Which makes me responsible for seeing this through. When I got home last night and thought over what you had told me—about Diana's death, I mean—then I had to ask myself if—well, you suggested the possibility last night, didn't you?"

"Suggested what?"

"That there might be—you know—some connection between the letter and my daughter's death."

"Do you have this letter with you?"

She nodded, fidgeting in place a moment before opening her purse and bringing out the envelope. The address was written in a childish scrawl and mailed to 'Mama.' "I received it just yesterday afternoon. After the funeral. It was a terrible, a horrible experience to see her handwriting like that, having just buried the poor child only hours before. There's no stamp," she added, pointing out the obvious as she handed it to me. "I see that as a sign from God, if you will. Don't you? I mean, that it got through the mail without being stamped. Go on, dear. Open it."

Inside I found a single piece of white paper bearing some twelve lines of unintelligible coded script. "This was it?" I asked, skimming down the page. "No message? No note?"

She shook her head, scooting to the edge of the chair. "What do you suppose it could be? A secret message of some kind?"

"Who can say."

"Yes. Well, it's obvious that Diana sent it to me for a reason. But why? And what on earth should we do about it?"

"We?"

"Well, yes. I was hoping you might—I mean, I can't very well go at this thing on my own, can I? An old lady such as myself."

"Not so old," I corrected her, my eyes still riveted to the paper—to the bizarre lines of script—as the chilling ramifications of its existence began to sink in.

"Well now, you're an investigative reporter, aren't you? That's what it says on your card. Sarah Calloway—Investigative Reporter. All right then—investigate."

"Mrs. Stevens, it isn't always that easy."

"I see."

"For starters, I happen to be involved in another story. And I don't even live here in San Rodino. My home's up in San Francisco."

"Well, if it's a question of money," she murmured, fumbling in her purse and bringing out a prodigious-looking roll of bills.

"It's not a question of money, Mrs. Stevens. At least, not yet. But you're aware that if you—or we—were to get involved in this case, we would be dealing with an extremely dangerous situation."

She gazed into her hands, then back at me. "I feel I owe my daughter this much. But if you would rather—I don't mean to force you into any—" Her voice faded out. We sat in silence as I took another look at the jumble of numbers, punctuation marks, asterisks and dollar signs before my eyes.

"Where did you say your daughter worked, Mrs. Stevens? Before she left?"

"I didn't say."

"And where did she work?"

She shook her head, shifting in her seat. "I contacted her place of employment the very day she ran off. They knew no more about her whereabouts than I did."

"And where *was* her place of employment?" I tried again.

There was another pause, as she clasped and unclasped her hands in her lap. "Diana worked at the Interlude Salon."

"So she was a hairdresser?"

"No, Miss Calloway. Diana was a masseuse."

"I see."

"I'm not sure that you do see! I'm not sure that you see at all! My daughter was a lovely child. Warm. Good-hearted. I think you should know that. She had her faults. We all do. But she was a wonderful, wonderful girl."

"I'm sure she was. Mrs. Stevens, hasn't it ever occurred to you that your daughter might have been kidnapped?"

"Kid—? No, I'm afraid that is quite impossible."

"But why? Let's just imagine—for utilitarian purposes—that Diana got herself mixed up with some religious cult or another. From what I gather, those kinds of kidnappings are going on all the time."

"But you see, my daughter left me a note when she, well when she went on her way."

"I see. Would you mind telling me what she said in this note?"

"Nothing that you need know, Miss Calloway. Nothing that bears on this case. Simply—her good-byes."

"No hint of where she might be going?"

"Just what do you take me for? If there had been a hint, I would have told you of this *hint*. There were no *hints*, Miss Calloway," she added with an indignant toss of her head.

"Fine. And this Salon she worked at—I assume it's located here in San Rodino?"

"That's right, yes. But as I've already told you, I contacted them the very day my daughter disappeared. And they knew no more about her where—"

"Look, Mrs. Stevens. Do you want my help or don't you?"

She clasped her hands again, biting at her lower lip. "I do."

"Fine. Now it seems to me that there're two ways we can go about this thing. One, is to try and get to the bottom of this strange sheet of symbols. Which might well prove impossible. The other, is to trace back your daughter's recent past. Find out where and with whom she spent time these last few months of her life. What I could suggest for the time being, is that you leave this paper with me for a few days. See what I can make of it. Then we'll get back in touch."

She nodded, stuffing the roll of bills under the rocker cushion as she got to her feet.

"I do appreciate this, Miss Calloway," she said, turning toward the door.

"Sarah."

"Sarah. My mind rests easier to think that something is being done."

"No promises, Mrs. Stevens. But I'll give it a try."

Alone again, I dug the roll of bills from under the cushion and counted it. There was five hundred dollars here, all of it in twenty dollar bills. Guilt money, perhaps? I stuffed the bills into my suitcase and settled at the desk for a serious look at the coded page of script.

9 5 (6 m 9 8 * t m $ 5 , - 4 6 - 5 3 m

2 8 * * : - m * ¢ 5 : ,) 5 * % m) 8

(8 & % 5 9 8) 9 - * 5 o o : , (6 & 8 ( ) 6 t 8

t(18o6.8%?5(8$,95*45;;5*

(?28*)3?8((5,96596

t(1(5*-6)(m98(m,)5*t683m

963?8o)5*;m),%8()8:-6;:

%811(8:;5o6*,96596

t((6-45(t2(53m,1m(;o5?t8(t5o8

t(m)-5(om.8$,.5)5t8*5

38m(389m)),96596

(m*5ot¢6o!6*)m*,)5*t683m

-5(om)9m(5o8),om)5*38o8)

If it was a secret communiqué, as Mrs. Stevens had suggested, then intended for whom? And how had Diana gotten her hands on it? And had it indeed been the reason behind her death?

I placed a call to Roger Costello in New York. If anyone could help me unlock this code, Roger could. But he wasn't home. I left a message on his machine. Then I headed over to the public library, on the other side of town.

The only book available on the subject of cryptography was a small volume by Henry Lysing, entitled *Secret Writings*. I settled at a back table and read through the opening chapter, learning that there were two basic code types: transpositional and substitutional. Transpositional codes deceived the reader by re-positioning the letters. In such a code, CAT might read ACT. Or CTA. Or TAC. Substitutional codes, on the other hand, deceived the reader by substituting other symbols for the intended letters. In such a code, CAT might read *&!. Or 275. Or E3T. Obviously, Diana's script was based on just such a substitutional code.

According to Lysing, the basic strategy in breaking through any substitutional code—and a deceptively simple one—was to break down the symbols in the cryptogram according to their frequency on the page. And then to compare the frequency patterns of the symbols with the frequency patterns of the English alphabet. From such a comparison of frequencies, I should be able to deduce which symbols were standing in for which letters of the alphabet.

I proceeded with a lengthy analysis of the thirteen lines. Out of a total of 25 different symbols used on the page, the number 5 cropped up most frequently, appearing a total of 32 times. According to Lysing's alphabet frequency tables, the letter *e* was the most frequent or common letter in the English alphabet. I was therefore to assume that the number *5* in Diana's code was standing in for the letter *e*. The second most frequent symbol in the code was the number 8, appearing a total of 29 times. Since the letter *t* is the second most common letter in the English alphabet, I was to assume the number 8 was standing in for the letter *t*.

And so it went, back and forth between the frequency patterns of Diana's symbols and the frequency patterns of the English alphabet, until I had an entire hypothetical decoding of Diana's cypher at hand:

5	= **E**	-	= **U**
8	= **T**	4	= **M**
(	= **A**	3	= **F**
*	= **O**	?	= **W**
m	= **I**	.	= **G**
6	= **N**	2	= **Y**
o	= **S**	1	= **P**
)	= **R**	$	= **B**
,	= **H**	¢	= **V**
9	= **L**	!	= **K**
t	= **D**	%	= **X**
;	= **C**	&	= **J**

: = Q

Using this hypothetical decoding, I translated the first line of script into:

LEANILTODIBEHUMNUEFI

Not particularly promising. The second line translated into:

YTOOQUIOVEQHREOXIRT

And it didn't get any better as I moved down the page. It got worse.

What had gone wrong? According to Lysing himself, there were any number of explanations for the failure. I could be dealing with another language than English, in which case his alphabet frequency tables would no longer be holding true. Or I could be dealing with a combination substitutional-transpositional code, which would entail an impossibly complex approach to the cipher. But a third, and more probable reason for the failure was simply the margin of error one had to expect when trying to gauge accurate frequency patterns from only thirteen lines of script.

What now? Lysing had other suggestions. But I had been moored to this table for well over three hours by now, and needed a break. It seemed as good a time as any to pay a visit to the Interlude Salon.

The parlor was located some eight blocks from the library, a drab two-story affair flanked by a seedy flophouse on one side and an upscale Cambodian restaurant on the other. The obligatory curtains were drawn across the front windows and a sign on the door announced that 'Walk-ins' were welcome. I walked in.

This being my first experience with massage parlors or their ilk, I had no idea what to expect. But this wasn't it. The erotism quotient of this place was about as high as my dentist's waiting room, right down to the tacky aluminum wreaths decorating the walls. I helped myself to a chair, while the blonde behind the desk—a plumper, harder version of the blonde Venus in their Yellow Pages ad—wound down her conversation on the phone.

"Can I do anything for you?" she asked, dropping the receiver into the cradle and getting to her feet. A very tall woman.

"I'm inquiring after a Miss Diana Stevens?" I said, getting to my feet as well. "She worked for you a few months back?"

"That's right."

"Yes, well I was wondering if you might have any information as to her present whereabouts?"

"If I did, honey—which I do not—I don't suppose I'd be passing it along to any stranger off the street, would I now?" she said, the forced smile still holding in place.

"I'm a friend of her mother's," I explained, moving closer to the desk.

"You don't say? 'Bye, Harry," she added sweetly, for the benefit of the well-dressed businessman sidling past us and out the door. "Same time next week?"

"Mrs. Stevens hasn't heard from her daughter in over four months," I went on. "Naturally, she's very concerned."

"Mrs. Stevens? Mrs. Stevens is very concerned? Mrs. Stevens happens to be a royal pain in the butt. And if Diana wants to live her own life, what business is it of yours or your Mrs. Stevens to be saying any differently?"

"You talking about Diana Stevens?" murmured a voice behind me. I turned to find a young slender black woman standing in the inner doorway.

"Would *you* happen to know Diana's whereabouts?" I asked, taking a few steps in her direction.

"Who are you?"

"I'm a friend of the family. Mrs. Stevens hasn't heard from her dau—"

"I'll take care of this, Cory," Blondie said curtly, moving from behind the desk.

"Okay, sure."

"Wait now, please. Both of you," I said, looking from one to the other. "Diana has been murdered. It happened last Friday—Christmas Day—right here in San Rodino. No one knows yet who did it or why. I was hoping you could—"

"So what are you? Some kind of cop?" Blondie demanded.

"Like I said. A friend of the family. She was seven months pregnant at the time . . . Were either of you aware of this? Of Diana's pregnancy?"

"Cowboy?" the young woman murmured uneasily, looking past me to Blondie.

"Who's Cowboy?" I asked.

"A former client," Blondie spoke up. "Why don't you let me take care of this, Cory," she repeated, bearing down on us and closing the inner door in the woman's face.

"What's going on?" I asked, turning on the receptionist.

"Cowboy's no murderer," she muttered, settling back down at the desk. "He's a poor dumb schmuck who had a thing for Diana. That was all there was to it. A schoolboy crush. Got it? Nothing more."

"Did this 'Cowboy' continue to patronize this place after Diana left?"

"Not to my knowledge," she said, bringing a small atomizer out of a drawer and spraying a mist of heavy perfume about her head.

"Well then, isn't it highly likely that the two of them took off together?"

"Beats me."

"Would you be able to give me this Cowboy's real name?"

"Beats me."

"You're saying you don't even register your clients?"

"Only when they use plastic. Our cash customers go by any name they damn well please. Now if you don't mind, Miss. I have some things to attend to."

"Don't you care at all? Doesn't it faze you one iota that a former employee has just been murdered?"

By the look on her face, I had hit a raw nerve. With slow deliberation, she rose to her feet again. A very tall woman, as I said.

"Just who do you think you are?" she demanded hotly, moving towards me, hands on her hips. "Barging in here and playing your little games?"

"I wouldn't want to bring the police into this," I said, edging toward the door.

Her lips curled into a rather nasty smile. "If that is intended to be some kind of threat, sister, you're barking up the wrong tree. This happens to be one of the cops' favorite hangouts. Now I strongly suggest you removing your carcass from the premises before I do it for you. Am I making myself perfectly clear?"

You win some, you lose some, I told myself sourly, hiking back out to the car. What the situation obviously demanded was a little finesse. With that in mind, I moved the car into an illegal parking space kitty-corner to the parlor and bided my time, waiting for the young black woman—Cory—to finish her shift. Three hours and a good ten to fifteen clients passed by, most of them of the salesmen variety, but no female masseuses emerged. By eight o'clock, I was half starved, and sprang for a couple of jumbo hot dogs at the hole-in-the-wall a couple of doors down. No sooner had I settled back in the car and taken my first messy bite, then Cory appeared on the sidewalk across the street.

She was accompanied by another woman, the two of them walking three blocks west and lingering a few minutes at the corner, saying their good-byes, then parting ways. I followed Cory down the street, calling out her name.

"It's you," she murmured breathlessly, her hand at her throat. "I'm not supposed to talk to you."

"Says who? Blondie?" She didn't answer me, shifting the grocery bag in her arms and continuing on her way. "Look, Cory," I said, sticking to her side. "A woman you used to work with has just been gunned down in cold blood. With a seven-month fetus in her belly. Couldn't you help us find out who did this to her?"

She stopped walking and turned to face me. "I don't know anything. Honest."

"You could fill me in on this Cowboy character, for starters."

"I don't think Cowboy killed Diana."

"That's not the point. He's a lead, isn't he? We have to begin somewhere."

"Okay, lady," she said, handing me the grocery bag. "If you want to talk, we'll talk. But not out here," she added, digging through her purse for a set of keys. She turned into a battered apartment complex a few steps further down the street. The stairwell was lit by a single bare lightbulb that hung from a long black cord. I followed her up five flights of stairs, past a pungent array of cooking odors which seemed to lean heavy on garlic and grease. It got worse the higher we climbed. Her place was on the fifth floor, at the end of the hall.

"Mummy! Mummy!" A little girl in overalls and spiffy patent leather shoes came tearing into the room and grabbed one of her mother's hands.

"Hi, Pumpkin," Cory said, bending over to kiss the top of her daughter's head. "Let Mommy get out of her things."

"Isaac says I can't watch TV," the little girl announced with a practiced pout. "And I'm hungry," she added, taking note of my presence and edging under her mother's arm.

"Didn't you eat supper? Where's Marci?"

"She went away."

"Went—? Where's Marci?" she asked the young boy who had just stepped into the room, his arms folded across his chest.

He shrugged. "She had to go."

"Go where?"

Nobody seemed to know. Cory eased her children back into the TV room with a couple of glasses of chocolate milk. Then she returned to the kitchen and snatched up the phone.

"Where the hell is Marci?" she demanded of the person on the other end of the line. Nobody there seemed to know either. As the woman fumed into the receiver she darted about the room, hauling a bottle of Seagram's out of the grocery bag, wrestling some ice cubes out of the refrigerator, uncapping the bottle and pouring a healthy dollop into each of a couple of mugs hanging over the sink. Slamming down the phone, she handed me one of the mugs, tossed down her own allotment, and refilled her cup. Then she kicked off her heels and settled cross-legged on the linoleum floor.

"So?" she said, looking up at me. "What is it you want to know?"

"Anything you can tell me," I said, joining her there on the floor.

"I just—you know—can't believe she's really dead. She was such a—a real sweet kid. Wouldn't hurt a fly. You know the type?"

I nodded, waiting.

"A year or so back my boy was sick, right? Real sick. And Di started in visiting him there at the hospital. Just like that. I didn't ask her to or nothing. She just started in doing it all on her own. Can you dig that? She'd be there in the afternoons when I couldn't come—you know—'cause of work. And the nurses told me how she used to just sit there, holding Isaac's hand and never saying a word. Just like, sitting there. Really something, huh? . . . And now she's dead. Kind of hard to believe."

"Yes, it is."

"You a friend of Diana's?"

"Of her mother's, actually."

"Yeah? No shit. Well, excuse me for saying, but that woman bugged the hell out of us after Di took off. Phoning every day, making all kinds of looney accusations, things like that. She had it in her head that we were hiding Diana out or something. Or keeping secrets from her. It was real weird. She even came by one day. And the lady was sloshed. I mean, real tanked, right? It was kind of a bad scene. But you can hardly blame the poor lady. I suppose Di was the only family she had? That right?" she asked me. I nodded, trying to tally the impression of Mrs. Stevens that Cory was giving me with the impression I already had. "Anyway," Cory spoke up again, "she stopped all that a long time ago. Guess she got wise. Gave up. Something."

"You think there could have been anything to her suspicions?"

"What do you mean?"

"You think someone—Blondie or anyone else at the Interlude—might have known where Diana had gone?"

"Jesus, I don't think so. I mean, she didn't give us no warning or anything. One day she was there. Next day she wasn't. Just like that. Course, it did occur to some of us that she might have run off with Cowboy. You know, cause he never showed up again neither."

"What can you tell me about this Cowboy?" I asked.

She rubbed her back up against the refrigerator door, wrinkling her nose in distaste. Then shook her head. "Not a whole lot, really. He was sort of on the old side, if you ask me. Middle-aged and hard looking. Hulky. And Diana was so kind of—you know—soft. But the guy sure took a liking to her. Wouldn't see nobody but Diana whenever he came by. Which got to be pretty often near the end. I suppose—I don't know, I suppose that Di kind of dug him, too. Different strokes, right? Not that she ever said so in so many words or nothing. That woman never talked very much. She had a—you know—a kind of stutter. But they were always having these private bull sessions in back. Jesus knows what they found to talk about all the time. We used to kid Di about it. That he'd be shelling out all this dough, these silver dollars—that's all he ever paid in, silver dollars—that he'd be shelling out all these silver dollars just to go back there and talk."

She wrinkled her nose again, shrugged, took another swallow of whiskey. Then stretched out her arm to her little girl, who had returned to the kitchen to try to wheedle another glass of chocolate milk. Cory gave her what was left in the carton, then suggested that she rejoin her brother in the other room. But Tammy preferred staying put, holding tightly onto her mother's arm and flirting with me from across the room.

"You got any more questions?" Cory asked. "'Cause, well it's getting kind of late and the kids gotta, you know . . ."

"You wouldn't know where this Cowboy hangs out, would you? Or where he works?"

"He drove a cab. Yeah! Yeah, right. Cause he was always—you

know—leaving the damn thing parked in front of our place when he dropped by. Funny I didn't think of that before."

"Yellow Cab?"

She shook her head. "Blue and white. At least I—yeah—that was it. Some kind of blue and white cab. Come over here, sugar," she added, as Isaac wandered shyly into the room.

A blue and white cab? DeSoto? I had more questions. But it was obvious that I had preempted enough of the woman's time for one evening. Passing her one of the motel's matchbooks, I encouraged her to get back in touch should anything come to mind. Then I headed back to the car.

By the time I hit the motel room, a discomfiting curiosity had turned into an obsession. And the more I played back Diana's murder, or toyed with the page of coded script, or tried piecing together the few facts I had on hand, the fiercer the obsession became, bleeding into my dreams that night in the form of a grotesque scenario that borrowed all too heavily from the movie *Alien*, and ended with Diana's unborn child crawling towards me down a long dark hall.

December 29, 1987

Sometime after 5 a.m. I gave up on sleep, rolling out of bed and settling down before Diana's cipher once again. It had been nagging at me since yesterday morning; the fact that four out of the thirteen lines began with a small t, followed by the opening half of a parenthesis. Why would this particular pair of characters be starting off four lines, when no other consistencies seemed to exist on the page?

As I continued to toy with the dance of scribbles before me, a not unfeasible theory began taking shape. Suppose—just suppose—that this piece of paper was in fact a coded list. A list of names. Which would explain the varying lengths of every line. It would also explain why Lysing's frequency patterns hadn't helped. Even more important, it could explain the presence of this *t(* combination at the beginning of those four lines. The pair of symbols could be standing in for a title. Mr. perhaps? Or Dr.? Or much less likely—Ms.?

Working from the premise that the two symbols were standing in for Mr., or more specifically, that the *t* was standing in for the letter *M*, and the *(* was standing in for the letter *R*, I superimposed accordingly down the entire page:

95**R**6m98***M**m$5,-46-53m

28**:-m*¢5:,)5*%m)8

R8&%598)9-*5oo:,**R**6&8**R**)6**M**8

M **R**18o6.8%?5**R**8$,95*45;;5*

R?28*)3?8**R** **R**5,96596

M **R**1**R**5*-6)**R**m98**R**m,)5***M**683m

963?8o)5*;m),%8**R**)8:-6;:

%811**R**8:;5o6*,96596

M **R** **R**6-45**R** **M**2**R**53m,1m**R**;05?**M**8**R** **M**5o8

M **R**m)-5**R**om.8$,.5)5**M**8*5

38m**R**389m)),96596

Rm*5o**M**¢6o!6*)m*,)5***M**683m

-5**R**om)9m**R**5o8),om)5*38o8)

No revelations emerged. I abandoned this experiment and went on to the next, hypothesizing that the *t(* combination stood for *Dr.* rather than for Mr. After superimposing the letter *D* over every t, and the letter *R* over every (, the cipher now read:

95**R**6m98***D**m$5,-46-53m

28**:-m*¢5:,)5*%m)8

R8&%598)9-*5oo:,R6&8R)6D8

DR18o6.8%?5R8$,95*45;;5*

R?28*)3?8RR5,96596

DR1R5*-6)Rm98Rm,)5*D683m

963?8o)5*;m),%8R)8:-6;:

%811R8:;5o6*,96596

DRR6-45RD2R53m,1mR;o5?D8RD5o8

DRm)-5Rom.8$,.5)5D8*5

38mR389m)),96596

Rm*5oD¢60!6*)m*,)5*D683m

-5Rom)9mR5o8),om)5*38o8)

Something meshed around the first nine characters in line 9. The pattern DR R_ _ _ _ RD if I saw it as such, could easily be the makings for a Dr. Richard Someone. And if this were to be the case, then I would have broken through the code for four more characters on the page:

6 = **I**
\- = **C**
4 = **H**
5 = **A**

I superimposed accordingly, obtaining the following results:

9ARIm98*Dm$A,CHICA3m

28**:Cm*¢A:,)A*%m)8

R8&%A98)9C*Aoo:,RI&8R)ID8

DR18oI.8%?AR8$,9A*HA;;A*

R?28*)3?8RRA,9IA9I

DR1RA*CI)Rm98Rm,)A*DI83m

9I3?8o)A*;m),%8R)8:CI;:

%811R8:;AoI*,9IA9I

DRRICHARD2RA3m,1mR;oA?D8RDAo8

DRm)CARom.8$,.A)AD8*A

38mR389m)),9IA9I

Rm*AoD¢Io!I*)m*,)A*DI83m

CARom)9mRAo8),om)A*38o8)

I continued to stare at the lines of script, willing more telltale patterns out of the maze. But no matter how long I sat there studying the damn thing, no new patterns came to light.

The telephone rang, jarring me out of a daydream that had nothing to do with coded scripts, substitutional or otherwise. It was my editor, 'Crazy Eddie' as we not always so fondly called him.

"That's the breaks, right?" he said, starting off in the middle of a thought, as was his habit.

"What are you talking about, Eddie?"

"Hey kid, pick up the paper. It made the front page of the Chronicle this morning."

"*What* did?"

"The Mad Bomber, as you like to call him. He made a hit last night. Right here in San Francisco. Torched a clinic out on Third Street. So I would suggest you get your tail on up here and—"

"But how do we know it's the same guy?"

"They caught him. He fessed up to everything. Four clinics back East. And the four that have been hit here on the Coast. Some kind of LaRouche looney, as it turns out. So we're going to have to come up with a novel slant on this thing. Otherwise, it's going to look like yesterday's news, if you see the problem. I've got an interview set up with the guy for tomorrow morning, just before he's arraigned. Then they're sending him out to San Bruno. I figure we can—"

"Eddie, listen. Can you find someone else to do that interview tomorrow? Something has come up."

"What are you saying, babe? Don't do this to me, okay?"

"What about Mel? Or Karen? Really, Eddie. I need to stick around here a few more days."

"It's Christmas, for Christ's sake. How the hell am I going to pick anyone else up now?"

"I think I might be on to something down here. I mean it, Eddie."

"You couldn't be a little more specific about this, could you?"

"Not over the phone. Look—today's the what? The 29th? Give me until New Year's. See what I can dig up. All right?"

Silence.

"Eddie?"

"I'll be expecting you in my office first thing Friday morning. Understood?"

"Make it Monday," I said, and hung up before he could get in another word.

What the hell did I think I was doing? I asked myself, stepping under a cold shower. I may be in the act of trashing four weeks of solid investigative work, not to mention my working relationship with Eddie Connors and *Probe*, by insisting on staying down here. And for what?

A dead woman. A coded list of names. The complicity of a city's police force. The components were beginning to add up.

I dressed, stuffed the roll of film into my purse, and headed out the door. My intention was to hoof it to a quickie film-processing joint I had noticed a block down from the motel. But when a DeSoto cab came cruising by, I flagged it down.

The driver was a burly gentleman in his early thirties. I directed him to a shopping center at the edge of town.

"Cowboy still driving a cab?" I asked him, a minute or two into the ride. He checked me out in the rearview mirror.

"You a friend of Cowboy's?" he asked, twisting in his seat for a better look as we waited out a red light. I nodded. He nodded, in turn. Then shifted into first and lurched down the road.

"But we haven't been in touch for months," I finally added. "He still driving for DeSoto?"

"Nah. Cowboy's long gone."

"I see."

"What's your interest in the guy, if you don't mind my asking?"

"It's not me, actually. It's his sister. She's pretty sick. Been asking for him."

"Yeah? And she don't know where he is? Her own brother?" he added, giving me a toothy grin in the mirror. A sleazy William Devane. "Well now, you just better tell that sister of his that Cowboy didn't leave no tracks. Least, not that I know of," he added, swinging the cab into the parking lot and shoving down the red flag. The meter read $5.45. $5.45 for nothing.

"Well, thanks anyway," I muttered, paying the man and fumbling with the car door.

"Here, doll," he said with a laugh, leaning across the seat and springing the lock. I watched the cab disappear around the corner, cursing my second-rate performance, then headed into the mall.

As chance would have it, there was a Presto-print shop just inside the door. I turned over the film, then went in search of breakfast. An hour later, to the minute, I was back in the shop. The pictures were ready, for whatever they were worth. Which wasn't much. Three out of the four shots caught nothing but sky, telephone poles, and billboards. The fourth shot, sliced in half by my car window, was of one of the cops in profile, in the act of hauling the stretcher out of the van. I handed that particular negative back to the service clerk, requesting a blowup of the man's face. It would be a three to four hour wait. In the meantime, I backtracked to a phone booth in the center of the mall and looked up the address for DeSoto cabs. 1138 6th Street. That was about a mile and half from the mall. I decided to give it a try.

The cab company's dispatcher's office, unlike the massage parlor, was exactly as I would imagine a dispatcher's office to be. I approached the skinny, middle-aged woman working the switchboard up front. She waved me into one of the cold metal chairs lining the wall. I took a seat and passed the time studying the local fauna, from the funky fifties calendar and crucifix hanging over the rotting sofa, to the *Popular Mechanics* and girlie magazines piled on the table by my side. There were a couple of empty feeding bowls in one corner and dog hairs all over the damn place. That was what this room reeked of: dog.

I started to jot a few impressions into my notebook, then stopped short at the sight of Willie Boy coming through the side door. Of all the rotten luck. He spotted me immediately, grinning that toothy grin of his as he tossed a clip board onto the front desk and made his approach.

"You planning to pull that sick-sister routine on some other sucker?" he asked, standing over me, one hip propped against the wall.

"Look, Mister. I'm serious," I said, shutting the notebook and squinting up at him. "This is a matter of life and death. I mean it."

"Yeah? Whose life and death?" he asked, settling into the chair next to mine.

I didn't answer him, stuffing the notebook back into my purse and moving further down the row of chairs. He moved down with me.

"*Whose* life or death?" he repeated, bending his head down far enough in his lap to catch my eye. Something about this man made me want to laugh.

"I already told you. His sis—"

"Hey, look. Try anything but that. Cause it just won't fly. See? You know if you play it straight with me lady, I just might be able to help you out. So what's the problem?"

I looked from him back into my lap. "Let's say that I'm pregnant," I said, looking back over at him. "Let's say that's the problem."

He stared at me a long moment in silence, shaking his head. "Hard to figure you dames out," he finally said. "All us good-looking hunks around and you chase after the old men." He was kidding. And he wasn't. "Okay, so let's say I hook you up with Cupcake."

"Who's Cupcake?"

"One of the operators. Been with the company longer than any of us. So how's that?"

"Why are you turning so obliging on me, all of a sudden?"

"Hey. 'Cause I'm a nice guy. Yeah, really. You don't believe me?" He was grinning again, but it was a lot more palatable this time around.

"Anyone ever tell you you're a dead ringer for William Devane?"

"Yeah," he said, slamming a heel into the floor. "My ex-wife. Think that's why she married me," he added sourly, shoving to his feet. "Tell me, lady," he added, leaning over me, his hip back against the wall. "Cowboy some kind of spook?"

"Spook?"

"That was the rumor going around, yeah. That true?"

"I'm afraid I wouldn't know about that."

"Yeah? Anything you say, lady," he said, shaking his head as he pushed off the wall and crossed the room, heading behind the dispatcher's cage to speak with a very large woman attired in earphones and a brightly flowered muumuu. Cupcake, I presumed. They took turns sending me surreptitious glances as he talked into her ear. Finally, she removed her earphones and waved me back to her desk. I followed her into a rear office. She settled before a file cabinet in one corner and blinked up at me, fingering the pair of glasses which hung from a black velvet ribbon around her neck.

"Davy tells me you're interested in the whereabouts of a Mr. Kelsey?"

"That's right, yes." Kelsey?

"Well now, we don't generally give out information on our employees, past or present. It's company policy."

"Yes, I know. But this is somewhat of an emergency."

"So I hear." She slipped the glasses onto her nose and peered up at me a moment longer. Then maneuvered herself around to face the cabinet and began thumbing through the files. "There isn't much here. Nothing more than a next of kin. His parents, I expect."

"Better than nothing," I said.

She blinked at me again, pushing the glasses further up her nose.

"Look, Ma'am. It's just that—well, I think Cowboy has a right to know. Don't you? I mean, before I make any rash decisions, if you see what I mean."

"All right, kiddo. You win. It's a Mrs. Phoebe Kelsey, 200 Church Road, Weatherby, California. That ought to do it for you," she said, slamming shut the drawer and heaving herself to her feet. With a nod, she ushered me out of the room.

According to my California road map, Weatherby was some thirty miles northeast of here. I walked back to the motel, picked up the car, and headed on my way, arriving at my destination just after noon. The town looked like another in a long line of casualties of this administration's 'farm program,' the windows showing more plywood than glass. The most attractive building on the entire stretch was the funeral parlor at the far end of the street.

Locating Church Road should have been an easy matter, but it wasn't. After three dry runs, I parked the car in front of a Hibernia Bank and walked across the street to Sparky's Luncheonette. There was a fair-sized crowd in this place, and it was a long walk from the door to the counter as heads turned and conversations hung in midair. Bad Day at Black Rock.

"Busy," I commented to the spare, elderly woman who flipped a menu my way.

"No busier than usual," she said, turning back to the grill. In something under sixty seconds, the woman slapped together two bacon, lettuce, and tomato sandwiches, quartered them, slipped them onto two plates, yanked a basket of fries out of the oil and dumped a heapful onto either plate. "Billy Joe!" she snapped, shoving the two orders aside. "What'll it be?" she snapped again, jutting her chin in my direction as she cracked three eggs into a stainless steel bowl lodged in the crook of her arm.

"One of those BLT's would be just fine. And a cold beer."

"We don't serve no alcohol here, young lady," she said, whipping her eggs.

"Diet Pepsi?"

"That neither." Ducking under the counter, she resurfaced with a can of Coke and a plastic glass. I sipped at the Coke and watched the woman work.

"Fast hands," I commented, when she skated the BLT my way.

"Been doing it long enough," she muttered, turning to nod impatiently at a new batch of orders 'Billy Joe' was yelling into her ear.

One o'clock came and went. I asked for my check and directions to Church Road.

"Why you be wanting to know?" she asked, exchanging looks with the elderly gentleman two stools down.

"Any reason why I shouldn't?"

"Them folks don't take too kindly to strangers, case you're interested."

"What folks?"

"There's only one set of folks living out on Church Road," the old man piped in, slipping a quarter under his cup and getting to his feet.

"The Kelsey family?" I confirmed, looking from one to the other.

"That's right," she said, pushing out a plate of fries. "Just who're you looking for out there?"

"Cowboy," I said.

"She means Howie," spoke up the freckle-faced young man with the carrot-red hair sitting to my left.

"That boy's not in town, is he?" she asked him. The young man shrugged. "Is he?" she repeated, squinting back at the old man.

"Don't know. And I don't much care," the old man said, snatching a toothpick off the counter and popping it into his mouth. "See you tomorrow, Betsy," he added, hitching up his belt and heading for the door.

"How *do* I get to Church Road?" I tried again. But old Betsy turned back to the cash register without saying a word.

"It's just a mile west of town," Carrot-top offered up. "Follow the main road to the first stop sign and hang a couple of rights. Can't miss it."

I thanked him for the information, left some change under my plate, and headed back to the car. Coming out of a U-turn in front of the bank, I caught sight of Carrot-top jogging down the walk.

"You know they're Brotherhood out there, don't you?" he said, sticking his head through the window.

"Brotherhood?"

"Got themselves a regular compound on that farm. Bunkers. Target ranges. Underground tunnels. The whole shooting match," he added, looking over his shoulder. "Kooks. They don't come into town much, but when they do they're usually packing."

"I see. And there's more than the Kelsey family living out there? Is that what you're saying?"

"Kind of hard to say just who's living out there and who isn't. Locals, most of them. Farmers, losing their shirts. Don't know how much sense it makes dropping in on them like that. More than likely, Cowboy won't be out there, anyway. He's away more than he's ever here."

"But he was driving a cab in San Rodino only a few months back."

"So I heard. You still settled on going out, are you?" he said, nodding on down the road.

"I assume his parents can tell me where he is?"

"They ain't his parents. They're Aunt and Uncle. His Ma died a long time ago . . . You might try addressing Old Man Kelsey—that'll be Cowboy's uncle—you might try addressing him as Reverend. He kind of eats that crap up."

"He's a minister, is he?"

"Self-ordained, you might say," he said with a grin, pushing off from the car. I thanked him for his help and started on my way, taking a right at the stop sign and right again. Any further progress was blocked by a makeshift wire fence that stretched across the road. A sign posted over the gate read:

Government agents and others: No trespassing. 10,000 dollar fine. 10 years in prison. Title 18, Section 241 242 U.S. Criminal Code.
Warning: *Survivors Will Be Prosecuted*. Signed:
Reverend Ralph Kelsey

The man had a real way with words.

I got out of the car and settled against the fender, rereading the sign and considering my options. At which point a middle-aged man in camouflage fatigues came around the bend of the road, a rifle resting on his shoulder and a second gun strapped around his waist.

"What can I be doing for you, Ma'am?" he asked, strolling real casual-like up to the gate and sticking a foot through the fence.

"Are you Reverend Kelsey?"

"No Ma'am, I ain't."

"Well, I need to speak with his nephew, Cowboy."

"'Fraid that won't be possible, Ma'am. Cowboy's away on a little trip."

"I see. Then I'll have to speak with his uncle."

"What's the problem?" he asked, shifting the rifle to the other shoulder.

"No problem. I have a message to relay to Cowboy. And I promised to deliver it personally. That's all."

He nodded, a derisive grin flickering across his face. "Sheriff Thompson gone so chicken-shit he's sending out female gofers to do his work? Is that the story?"

"I never met this Sheriff Thompson. I'm a friend of Cowboy's. And I think he'd be real disappointed to learn I was being treated this way."

"Is that so? All right, lady. I'll take you up. But you'll have to be leaving your vehicle parked right where she is," he said, bringing a bunch of keys out of his back pocket and struggling with the locked gate. I went back to the car for my bag, locking all the doors, one by one, and steeling myself for whatever surprises were in store before I joined the man on the other side of the fence.

The farmhouse and several out-buildings sat at the top of a grassy knoll. It must have been a lovely place at one time. But the property had been allowed to go to seed, both the buildings and the land surrounding the buildings. The only acreage being put to any use was a large vegetable garden to one side of the house.

"You haven't told me your name, have you now?" the man noted, stopping halfway up the porch steps.

"Just tell the Reverend I'm a friend of Cowboy's from San Rodino. Just tell him that."

"The Mystery Lady, is that it?" he said, shaking his head and disappearing into the house. A moment later, he stepped back out again. "All right, Mystery Lady. Just follow the hallway straight on through. The Reverend and the Mrs. are expecting you."

The long corridor led into a large sunny kitchen. A woman in her mid-sixties stood by the stove, rubbing her hands on her apron and giving me an anxious smile. "Ralph," she murmured to her husband, an iron-haired gentleman seated at the kitchen table, his head bent over a pile of nuts and bolts. He looked up.

"Reverend Kelsey?" I said, stepping forward and offering my hand.

He scooted back his chair and got to his feet, a scrawny man of medium height. He needed a shave. He also needed a bath. "Howdy," he said, leaning across the table and pumping my hand. "This here's my wife, Phoebe. Mother, how about fixing us up one of your pots of tea?" he suggested, rubbing his hands together and gesturing at me to take a seat. I sat down and took a quick look around. This was no ordinary kitchen. For one thing, there were all the guns. And for another, the assorted stickers and handbills plastered up and down the walls. Such whimsical catch phrases as 'Kill a Commie for Mommie.' 'Nuke Iran.' 'This farm is insured by Smith & Wesson.' 'Nuke Nicaragua.' 'Sickle cell: the Great White Hope.' 'Nuke Washington D.C.'

"You acquainted with our boy?" the woman asked, setting the teapot over the flame and turning back my way.

"That's right, yes. We worked together at DeSoto cabs."

"That so?" the man said, scratching his chin and leaning back in his chair. "Howie never mentioned working with a pretty girl like you, did he Mother?"

She shook her head and smiled. "Have you talked with him recently?" she asked, rubbing at her apron again.

"Not recently, no. Have you?"

"Well, no. We . . ." She paused, looking to her husband for direction.

"Why don't you just state your business, Miss. Nice and simple like," he suggested. "Jimmy tells me you have a message from our boy?"

"Not from Howie. *For* him. But I'm under obligation to deliver it to him personally, if at all possible," I added, looking back to the woman.

"But Howie isn't here."

"Could you tell me where I could find him?"

"What's your point, young lady?" Reverend Kelsey wanted to know.

"You're acquainted with Diana Stevens?" I asked, still addressing the woman.

"Well, yes of course. She lived right here under our roof for—"

"What's your point?" the man insisted again, scooting back his chair and jumping to his feet.

"I don't know how to say this," I said, looking from one to the other. "But I'm afraid I have some terrible news for you," I added, digging into my bag.

"What is it?" the woman murmured, sinking down in a chair.

I handed the clipping to the woman and turned back to the man. "Diana was robbed at gunpoint last Friday morning. Back in San Rodino. Then shot four times."

"She's dead?" the man muttered incomprehendingly. "Is that what you're saying? Someone *killed* her?"

There followed a long silence, the woman slumped against the back of the chair, her hands covering her face. And the man standing very still in one corner of the room. A silence which was suddenly broken off by the shrill whistle of the kettle. As if in a dream, the woman readied the teapot and cups and brought them to the table. She sank into her chair again, as did her husband, the man sending anxious looks her way.

"She was staying with her Ma, I suppose?" the woman finally murmured, her eyes and nose red from unwept tears.

"Excuse me?"

"Was that what she was doing in San Rodino? Staying with her Ma?"

"Wasn't that where you expected her to be?"

"Well—no. She left last month to join Howie in—to join our boy."

"Where is Howie?"

"What's your part in all this?" the man interjected.

"Like I said—I'm a friend of Cowboy's. And Diana's, of course," I added, looking back to the woman. "I attended the funeral last Sunday morning, fully expecting to see Cowboy there. But he never showed. I imagine he never showed because he doesn't even know that Diana is dead. Which is why I see it as my responsibility to let him know. Diana would have wanted that. And to pass on a few of her—well, some things she left behind that I and her mother think Cowboy would want to have."

"What kind of things?" he asked.

"Some letters. Photographs. That's why I stopped by here today. To find out where Howie is so I can pass on whatever—"

"I don't figure that's any of your business, young lady," the man said, sweeping some of his nuts and bolts across the table and to the floor.

"Ralph," the woman said softly, touching his arm. He shook her off and got to his feet, stomping out of the room. The woman got down on her hands and knees and gathered together the scattered pickings, giving me a fleeting, sad smile as she poured the contents from her apron onto the kitchen table. She turned back to the refrigerator, taking a couple of postcards off the door and bringing them to the table.

"We got this from Howie just a few days back," she murmured, handing me one of the cards. "First time we've heard from him in weeks."

The picture on the front was a large boxy tourist hotel, one of its balconies circled in red ink. I turned it over. Hotel Paradisio, Panama City, was printed in the upper left-hand corner. It was postmarked the 15th of December. 'Howdy!' was the only word written on the card save for the Kelseys' address.

"May I?" I asked, showing interest in the other two postcards she held in her hand. She passed them to me. The first card, showing beachfront property on one side, had been sent from Norfolk, Virginia, dated November 10. The second card had been sent from Mexico City, dated November 21. "Howie moves around a lot, doesn't he?" I said, handing her back the two postcards.

"What d'you think you're doing, woman!" Kelsey bellowed, tearing back into the room and snatching the cards out of his wife's hands and flipping them onto the counter.

"I can't see what harm it will do," the woman said, rubbing at her apron. "She only means to help."

"It's none of this gal's business where our boy is or isn't. You hear that? You hear that?" he repeated, turning back to me. "Now we're real sorry to hear about Diana. She was a good girl. She didn't deserve an end like that. Nobody does. We'll be passing the news on to our boy just as soon as we get the chance. You rest assured. And that is all there is to say."

"What's he doing in Panama?" I asked the woman, getting to my feet.

"Can't you understand plain English!" Kelsey demanded, slamming his open hand down on the table. "You done what you come here to do. Now get!"

"Where are you going, Ralph?" the woman asked.

"First, I'm going to escort this little gal off the premises. Then

I'm going to have me some target practice, that's what," he said, grabbing a couple of semi-automatics off the rack.

"Why all the guns?" I asked, in the vague hope of distracting the man enough to get my hands on one of those postcards, still lying face-up on the counter.

"This gal's really something, ain't she, Mother?" he said, yanking open a drawer by the sink and bringing out a box of cartridges. "They're for protection, that's what they're for. Protection and defense."

"Against what?" I asked, taking another sideways step.

"Against invaders, what do you think. Times have changed, case you haven't noticed. And we got to change with them."

"What kind of invaders?"

He shook his head again, rolling his eyes at his wife as he flipped the postcards into the drawer and shut it again. "Could be most anyone, couldn't it now, Miss-Snoop-and-Pry? Considering the times we're living through. And if you're so dang interested, allow me to inform you that there's widespread and coordinated chaos in the making. And either you're ready for it or you ain't. Understand? Playing ostrich and keeping your head in the sand don't hurt nobody but yourself. You hear?"

That said, 'Reverend' Kelsey escorted me back to his camouflaged friend, who escorted me back to the gate. On my return trip through Weatherby, Carrot-top popped out of Sparky's Luncheonette and flagged me down.

"Any luck?" he asked, leaning through the window.

"Not much."

"Yeah, well I've been thinking," he said, looking over his shoulder. "If it's all that fired-up important that you track down Cowboy, I know somebody who can probably help you out. My brother, see? He and Cowboy been buddies since way back. Comrades-in-arms you might say. If anyone's going to know Cowboy's whereabouts, it's Danny. He don't have no address," he added, eyeing the notebook I had pulled out of my bag. "No address. No telephone. No roads. Not even running water. Built himself a cabin up in the hills. Been living up there since—jeez, I don't know—since coming back from 'Nam, I guess. What you'd call your basic hermit."

"And you could take me to this cabin of his? Today?"

He shook his head, looking over his shoulder again. "You got to understand something about Danny. Nobody just drops in on him like that, see? He don't appreciate surprises. So we go through the proper channels, see? Leave him a message in his dead letter drop. If he's interested, he'll call me. And then me, I'll call you. Something like that."

"What's your name?"

"Me? Oliver."

"All right, Oliver," I said, circling the telephone number on the matchbook and handing it over. "Tell your brother I'm a friend of Cowboy's with an important message for him, all right? If he agrees to see me, there'll be fifty in it for you. That a deal?"

"Sure thing. Think you could toss a bottle of J&B in there?" he added, stuffing the matchbook into his jacket pocket.

"I suppose so, yes."

"A deal!" he said, grinning at me as he slapped the fender of the car and stepped back on the curb, back-pedaling his way into the diner as I drove out of town.

Back in San Rodino, I stopped off at the shopping mall and picked up the blowup of the cop's face. It didn't come to much. His cap threw a shadow over most of his features. The only detail I could pick up was a long, thin birthmark curling up the side of the man's neck. I dropped the photo into my bag and headed back to the motel. Mrs. Stevens was waiting for me there. A whiff of mouthwash and whiskey preceded her into the room.

"Tell me, Mrs. Stevens," I said, settling her back in her rocker. "Did your daughter ever mention a man named Cowboy?"

"Cowboy?"

"Howie Kelsey was his name, actually. He was a driver for DeSoto cabs?"

"Why no, I—why do you ask?"

"It seems this man and your daughter were on intimate terms before she disappeared. In fact, it's possible he was the father of her child."

"Is that what *those* people told you?"

"What people?"

"Over at the Salon?"

"Among others, yes."

She nodded, stared up at the ceiling, blinking back some tears. "Her first husband was a car salesman," she murmured, apropos of nothing.

"The one who died?"

"Of course, the one who died," she snapped, shifting in the chair. "And if you should locate this—this taxi driver. What then?"

"That's hard to say. I visited his aunt and uncle this afternoon. Your daughter stayed with them, on their farm in Weatherby, for a number of months. Before she and Howie went down to Panama."

"Panama?"

"Panama City, as a matter of fact. You wouldn't have any idea what they might have been doing down there, would you?"

"Certainly not. This is all just too—too preposterous for words," she said, darting me a hesitant, wary look, then turning away. With a certain note of ceremony, she set her purse aside and turned to face me directly again. "Miss Calloway. I think it would be best if you stopped this investigation of yours, if you don't mind."

"Of *mine?*"

"You heard me. After giving it some thought, I have decided it is preferable for all concerned if you look into the matter no further. My mind is quite made up about this, so don't try to change it."

"You can't be serious?"

"Quite serious. And I fail to see anything at all amusing in this, my dear."

"But this is crazy! I'm just beginning to get somewhere on this thing. And now you're asking me to drop everything? When you were the one to first ask me to get involved?"

"But you yourself remarked on the viciousness of these people, did you not?"

"Well yes. Of course. But—Mrs. Stevens, has someone been threatening you? Is that it? Has someone asked you to get me off the case?"

"Whatever put such nonsense into your head? I simply feel—well, that there really is no point to all this. The poor girl is dead. And nothing you or I can do will bring her back again."

"But Mrs. Stevens. There's a question of justice here, isn't there? Beside the fact that I'm beginning to suspect there's something very big going on here."

"I would like my daughter's letter back, if you please," she said, getting to her feet.

"The coded sheet?"

"That is correct."

"Mrs. Stevens, why are you doing this?!"

"The letter, if you *please*," she repeated, wiggling her stubby fingers in my face.

I brought the original coded sheet from out of safe-keeping in my suitcase. She shook it loose of baby-powder and folded it into her purse. Then started for the door.

"Mrs. Stevens," I said, blocking her path. "*What happened* between yesterday and today to change your mind like this? Has someone been threatening you?"

"You don't seem to understand. My daughter is gone. Forever. I do not see what purpose it will serve her or anyone else if we begin digging up nasty stories here and there. It won't bring her back, will it?"

"What nasty stories?"

"Miss Calloway! I am trying to be civil about this! I simply wish to guard my daughter's memory in peace. Is that too much to ask?" she added, dodging around me and to the door.

"Then take back your money," I said, going back into the suitcase.

"Keep the money," she said, ducking out the door before I could reach her again. I watched as she scurried down the walk, looking over her shoulder and hastening on her way.

Why this sudden change of heart? I asked myself, sinking back on the bed. The line about guarding her daughter's memory in peace didn't ring true. Unless I was to think that those 'nasty stories' she had alluded to involved her daughter and not herself. Or *had* she been threatened? And if so, by whom?

I brought the working copies of the code back out of the drawer—it was a compulsion by now—and took another crack. More than an hour passed before a second intriguing consistency came to light. There was one comma, and only one comma, in every line. I had made the assumption that the comma, like every other punctuation mark on this page, was standing in for a letter of the alphabet. But wasn't it possible that the comma, rather than being intrinsic to the code itself, was simply serving its usual purpose as punctuation between one piece of information and another? Say, for instance, as punctuation between the name of a person and the name of the city where this person could be found?

This last piece of guess work was a fairly obvious one, the tip-off coming in the very first line:

9ARIm98*Dm$A,CHICA3m

If those six symbols after the comma were indeed spelling out the city of Chicago, then I would have broken through two more of Diana's symbols, the 3 and the m. I went ahead and superimposed the letter *G* over every 3 on the page, and the *O* over every m:

9ARIO98*DO$A,CHICAGO

28**:CO*¢A:,)A*%O)8

R8&%A98)9C*A:,RI&8R)ID8

DR18I.8%?AR8$,9A*HA;;A*

R?28*)G?8RRA,9IA9I

DR1RA8I)RO98RO,)A*DI8GO

9IG?8)A*;O),%8R)8:CI;:

%811R8:;AoI*,9IA9I

DRRICHARD2RAGO,1OR;oA?D8RDAo8

DRO)CARoO.8$,.A)AD8*A

G8ORG89O)),9IA9I

RO*Aot¢I!I*)O*,)A*DI8GO

CARoO)9ORAo8),oO)A*G8o8)

Another break. The first six symbols at the beginning of line eleven could well be the coded script for the forename George. And if this were true, then the number 8 would be standing in for the letter *e*. After superimposing the *e* over every 8 on the page, it was the domino theory in motion, every new decoding generating another decoding, until I had a list of thirteen names and cities on the page:

1.	Mario Mendoza,	Chicago
2.	Benny Conway,	San Jose
3.	Rev. James McNally,	Riverside
4.	Dr. Felipe Juarez,	Manhattan
5.	Rubens Guerra,	Miami
6.	Dr. Francis Romero,	San Diego
7.	Miguel Santos,	Jersey City
8.	Jeffrey Talin,	Miami
9.	Dr. Richard Brago,	Fort Lauderdale
10.	Dr. Oscar Lopez,	Pasadena
11.	George Moss,	Miami
12.	Ronald Wilkinson,	San Diego
13.	Carlos Morales,	Los Angeles

I stared at the list for some time, as the chill factor slipped back into place. Who the hell *were* all these people? Moving over to the bed, I proceeded to call information for every individual and city listed here. These were real people, all right. Six out of the thirteen names showed up in the operator's directory, including all four of the doctors and the Reverend McNally. And what about the other seven names? Perhaps they were unlisted numbers? Or aliases? Or no longer living in the city so indicated on the list?

But why were so many latino names represented here? And why the geographical slant towards southern Florida and southern California?

I headed back over to the public library, in the hope of digging up some additional information on these people before making my next move. But the library was closed. I returned to the motel, parked the car, and headed into the tavern across the street. I had earned myself a good stiff drink today. Maybe two of them. Settling at the bar, I ordered myself a Manhattan on the rocks.

The more I thought about that damn list, the spookier it got. There couldn't be any doubt about it, anymore. I *was* onto something. Something big and messy, with a lot of merciless, hard-driving power behind it. The drink arrived. I popped the cherry in my mouth and almost choked on it.

"What the hell are you working on, Calloway?" I turned slowly on the stool to find the stranger from Diana's funeral standing behind me, a vague smile on his face and a bottle of beer in his hand. The man was taller than I remembered. And his eyes weren't grey, they were a light brown. And friendly enough to put me off my guard.

"Had yourself quite a day, didn't you?"

"No different than any other," I said, turning back to the bar.

"That so?" He settled down on the stool to my right, still smiling, ordering us another round of drinks.

"Not for me," I told the bartender. But he brought me a second Manhattan, anyway. "Who are you?" I asked. "What do you want?"

"Detective Ray," he answered, bringing a wallet out of his hip pocket and flashing a Detroit driver's license in my face. For whatever it was worth, the name and picture matched—Mr. Mark

Ray. Behind the license came the real credentials: a brass badge from the United States Drug Enforcement Agency. Was that what all this came down to? Drugs?

"So what's some Fed out of Detroit doing out here?" I asked.

He shook his head, shoving the wallet back in his pocket and picking up the beer. "I'm asking the questions, Calloway."

I looked behind me and back at him. "Says who?"

"Says me. And we're going to start with the lady's funeral. What was your business there? Let's start with that."

"I'm a reporter," I said with a shrug. "Murder interests me."

"Why so much interest in this one?"

"Maybe because I happen to be a friend of the family."

"Maude Stevens had a different opinion about that."

"So you've spoken to Mrs. Stevens?"

He nodded, bringing the bottle of beer to his lips for a long swallow and setting it down again. "I got a hunch, Calloway. You care to hear it?"

"Do I have any choice?"

"You're getting inside information. I want to know from who. I also want to know about those pictures you picked up today."

"Look, Mr. Mark—Ray—whatever. There's no way I'm answering any of your questions until you answer a few of mine. Until I understand what you're doing here in the first place."

The man looked away again, rapping out a jumpy syncopated beat on the top of the bar. "I think you're pushing it, kid," he finally said.

"I'm pushing it? Look, Mister. I don't owe you any answers. That's number one. And number two—there's that .45 under your jacket. And your black belt, or whatever other crap they train you guys in, to back you up. I've got nothing but my discretion, understand? I can't afford any wrong moves . . . Whereabouts in Detroit do you live, Mr. Ray?"

"Jesus, lady," he said, choking on his beer. "Don't do this."

"But Detroit's my home town," I pointed out. "Small world, right? The place as shitty as ever?"

"Is this what we're going to do now? Talk background? Family? Mutual friends? Get acquainted time?"

"We have to start somewhere don't we? Look, I just need a picture I can feel halfway comfortable with. You know—wife, dog, kids, white picket fence. The whole bit."

He looked at me, then away. "Yeah, well the wife and kids aren't in the picture any longer. Neither is the white picket fence."

"Been replaced by—what? Some burned-out bachelor's pad on Jefferson Ave?"

The man actually laughed. "Close, Calloway. Very close."

"Okay. So tell me, Detective Ray. What brings you here to sunny California? Did Diana get herself mixed up with a mean gang of poppy growers? Is that what this is all about?"

"What's your opinion on that, Calloway?" He seemed to like the sound of my name. He sure was using it enough.

"I don't have an opinion. At this point, I have no idea what's going on. You better believe me when I say that."

"Then what the hell have you been plugging at? You have a lot of explaining to do, my friend," he added, bringing out a cigarette and lighting up.

"You don't seem to understand. There's no way I'm going to talk until—"

"Yeah, I know. My black belt versus your discretion, right?" The guy looked over his right shoulder, then back at me. "Suppose—suppose I told you I was tracing a shipment of arms," he said quietly, watching me react.

"But I thought your department was drugs?"

"I got another hunch, Calloway," he said.

"Yeah?"

"I figure you and I are working the same hornet's nest, see? Only from different directions. And if we were to put these two angles together, we might come up with some fairly interesting results. What do you say?"

"Yeah, well . . ."

"You care to tell me what you're on to, *Ms.* Calloway?"

"I think we better stop right here," I said, slipping off the stool.

"And why's that?"

"Because I need some time. A day or two," I added, digging a five dollar bill out of my bag and flinging it onto the bar. As I turned to go, he grabbed my wrist, twisting it just enough for it to hurt.

"I wouldn't want things to get rough," he said, tightening his hold.

"Is that a threat?" I asked, glancing over at the bartender, who was doing his best to ignore us from the other end of the bar. "Are you threatening me?"

"Let's just say I'm giving you a little advice. And it's a .38, kid."

"What?"

"It's not a .45," he added. "It's a .38. If you're going to stay in this game, Calloway, you better learn how to play it. Otherwise, I'd advise you to clear out. You follow?"

I nodded, trying to pull away.

"You follow?" he asked again, twisting my arm a little further.

"I *got* it, okay? Jesus Christ," I muttered, when he finally let go, rubbing at my wrist. With a last look at the bartender, I headed out the door.

Back in the motel room, I checked the place for hidden bodies. It didn't look as if anything had been touched. But the man had been following me. That much was obvious. And would probably continue to follow me, just as soon as I walked back out that door. For the first time in days, I felt the need for a cigarette. Bad. But I sure as hell wasn't going to walk back across that lot to get it. I picked up the phone and placed a call to the San Francisco Police Department, finding my friend and contact—Sergeant Susan Welsh—where I knew I would find her come the holiday season, stuck up on Bryant street's seventh floor. I asked her to do me a couple of favors. To dig up any inside dope on the San Rodino Police Department. And to put a trace on one Detective Mark Ray, D.E.A. agent out of Detroit. After hanging up, I flipped on the TV and waited for her return call.

Before the hour was out, I had fallen asleep. I woke up around 3 a.m. with the image of Mr. Mark Ray floating between my eyes. I had just had an incredibly erotic dream about the man.

Stabilize, Calloway. I lay there, pondering the man's alleged slant on the case, some shipment of arms out of Detroit. And then it hit me—the memory of those Flash-Gordon-like rifles the two hitmen had been toting. Was *that* what had led the man to Diana's funeral? A ballistics check conducted after Diana's death? And if so, how would the arms shipment tie in with Diana's list of names? With these and other less savory thoughts to occupy me, I tossed and turned until dawn.

December 30, 1987

The phone woke me up at 9 a.m. It was Cory, the woman from the Interlude Salon.

"You can talk?" she asked, coming across somewhat breathless on the phone. I found myself checking around the room before I answered.

"Sure I can talk. What's up?"

"There was this detective hanging around our place last night, asking a lot of questions. Figured you may want to know."

"This detective—is his name Mark Ray, by any chance?" I asked, moving over to the window to check out the lot.

"Yeah, right. So you've met the guy? Easy on the eyes, isn't he," she added with a laugh.

I didn't answer her, as I sized up the aging Volvo parked some ten yards from my door. Hadn't I seen that car before? And unless my eyes were playing tricks on me, wasn't there someone sitting behind the wheel?

"Sarah?"

"Right. So what kind of questions was he asking?"

"That's what he wanted to know. What kind of questions *you* were asking. Sylvie told him everything. About your visit, I mean."

"Sylvie?"

"You know—Blondie. I get the feeling the guy is keeping tabs on you. What's going on, anyway? I mean, that guy's from the D.E.A. right? No way Diana was into drugs or nothing. That's what I told him, too. She didn't even touch booze."

"Did he ask anything about Cowboy?"

"I don't—I can't say for sure. It was mostly Sylvie he was talking to, see?"

"Well, I appreciate you for calling, Cory. And for keeping quiet about our conversation. If anything else comes up, don't hesitate to—"

"Well, actually, there is something else. Not that it amounts to much probably. But I thought of it yesterday, when I heard the detective using his not-so-hot Spanish on Tina, one of our girls. It's like, Cowboy was real good with the languages, see? I mean, it didn't seem to fit. He seemed kind of dumb to me. Well, maybe not dumb. But not smart, either. Know what I mean? But more than once I heard him speaking Spanish with Tina like he was a native or something. Even heard him speaking Vietnamese a couple of times! With Maryanne. It didn't—you know—fit. A cab driver speaking all those languages."

"Interesting," I conceded.

After a few more exchanges, and my repeated thanks, we said our good-byes. I returned the phone to the end table and checked out the window again. There *was* someone sitting behind the wheel of the Volvo. It was difficult to believe the man had nothing better to do than follow me around. Should I just go out there and confront the guy? Make some kind of deal? Exchange a little information? Before I could make up my mind one way or the other, the Volvo started up its engine and backed on out of the lot.

I ducked into a quick shower, picked up a black coffee to go, and headed over to the public library once again. With the help of a 1987 AMA membership index and a 1988 biographical index, I was able to zero in on three out of the four doctors. Interestingly enough, all three men were émigrés, Drs. Brago and Lopez from Cuba, and Dr. Romero from Mexico. More interesting still was the fact that Dr. Romero and Dr. Lopez had apparently crossed paths in the late sixties at the University of Guadalajara, in the city of the same name.

Over the next few hours, I canvassed every other professional index the library had on hand. Of the remaining nine candidates, two more came to light. Dr. Felipe Juarez, a published writer, was listed in *Who's Who in American Journalism* as a visiting professor at Columbia University in Manhattan. The Reverend James McNally was listed in the *Official Catholic Directory* as a Reverend-in-Residence at St. Teresa's Church, Riverside, California. No additional information was given on either of the two men.

I took a good look at my Southern California road map. Riverside was some forty miles east of San Rodino. I decided to pay the Reverend McNally a call.

St. Teresa's was a small church, as churches go, its white dome burning crystalline under a noonday sun. I walked around to a side entrance and rang the bell. An elderly woman answered the door, smiled, and before I could even state my business, had seated me on a wooden bench outside her office and rejoined a conversation on the phone.

I waited there as sounds from a conversational English class drifted down the hall.

I like to eat fish.

Chicken.

I like to eat chicken.

Eggs.

I like to eat eggs.

Getting back to my feet, I took a closer look at the series of photographs lining the corridor walls. What these photos amounted to was a grisly pictorial record of the civil war being waged in El Salvador. Dead or wounded civilians. Villages bombed out or burned to the ground. A young child, with what looked to be a terrible napalm burn on her chest, staring into the camera. Peasants being herded into the back of a truck. And the same incredibly young soldier in uniform, his semi-automatic carbine in hand, reigning over every scene.

It seemed most likely that St. Teresa's was a Sanctuary parish, one of the many so-called 'Sanctuary' parishes which had sprung up around America in recent years, opening their doors to the thousands of Salvadoran refugees who had been fleeing over our borders since the civil war had first begun some eight years ago.

A feasible approach to my conversation with Reverend McNally began taking shape.

A nun breezed in the side door, wished me a good afternoon, and disappeared further down the hall. Moments later a young priest popped out of one of the back rooms, his attention on the slice of pizza he was cramming down his throat as he strode right past me and into the office beyond.

Seconds later he side-stepped somewhat comically back into the hall to ask me if he could be of any help.

"Reverend McNally?" I asked, getting to my feet.

He gave me a sideways glance, swiping at his chin with the paper towel and balling it into his hands. "You are looking for Father McNally?" he confirmed, slipping a finger along the inside of his collar.

"Yes. I believe we have an appointment?"

"I am afraid that is quite impossible."

"Oh?"

"Yes. You see—" He paused again, tugging at his collar and clearing his throat. "You see, Father McNally is dead."

"Dead?"

"Yes. He had a heart attack two weeks ago and—and died," he added, with an apologetic lift of his shoulders.

"But that's terrible. I mean, well I'm sorry to hear that."

"Yes. Well, we were all sorry." The two of us stood there, blinking awkwardly at one another. "I'm Father Cardez. Perhaps I can help you with this—this appointment?" he finally suggested, rubbing his hands together and looking behind him. Then back at me.

"Perhaps, yes. I'm Sarah Calloway, a journalist from San Francisco," I said, offering my hand. "You're a Sanctuary parish, is that correct?" He nodded, waiting. "Yes. Well, you see, I had hoped to question Father McNally about—well, about the Sanctuary Movement in general, and this latest immigration bill in particular. It's probable effect on illegal immigrants from Central America."

"I see. You are referring to the so-called Amnesty bill, I assume?"

"That's right, yes."

"Father Cardez," the elderly woman whispered, waving the phone over her head and stepping into the hall.

"Just a moment, Frannie." He turned back to me. "Well, Miss—?"

"Calloway. Sarah Calloway."

"Well, Sarah. I would be most interested in discussing this immigration bill with you some time. It is shifty business. This evening, perhaps?"

"This evening?"

"If you like, we could meet for dinner and—What time is that baptism this afternoon, Frannie?"

"4 o'clock."

"Well then shall we say six o'clock?" he said, nodding his head. Without waiting for confirmation on my part, he took the phone from Frannie and turned back through the office door.

So Father McNally was dead? Of a heart attack, the young priest had said. I vacillated in place a moment longer, then slipped out of the church, heading into a restaurant across the street for a quick grilled cheese and another look at Diana's list. The ophthalmologist, Dr. Oscar Lopez, was my next closest candidate, 70 miles due west in Pasadena. I decided to give him a try.

Due to heavy traffic, it was a two-hour drive to Pasadena and another twenty minutes locating Lopez's office in a shopping mall at the center of town. There were two women in his waiting room ahead of me, but no receptionist in sight. I took a seat and began thumbing through a five-month-old *Ladies Home Journal* lying open on the chair next to mine. A woman came out of the inner office, nodded to us all, and continued on her way. A short, squirrely gentleman in a white coat now stepped into the room. "Mrs. Boleras?" he said, gazing up from his clipboard. The three of us looked at each other and then back to him. Would the real Mrs. Boleras please stand up?

"Yes?" I murmured, shifting the magazine off my lap and getting to my feet.

"Mrs. Boleras? Follow me."

Wasn't that easy, I congratulated myself, trailing the man into his inner sanctum. It smelled like cherry Kool-Aid in here. He settled me into a leather chair near his desk and proceeded to take down a few of my—or Mrs. Boleras'—essential statistics, including my form of payment, which I said would be cash.

"Are you here for a general checkup, Mrs. Boleras?" he asked, glancing back down at his papers. "Or do you have a particular complaint?"

"Bright lights," I said, scooting the chair closer to his desk. "I'm having this definite problem with bright lights. I suppose it's what—age? My eyes, they just start tearing uncontrollably the minute I wake up in the morning. Or whenever I first step outdoors. Is that normal?"

"It happens," he murmured, drumming his pencil against the palm of his hand. The man seemed very distracted. Or maybe he treated all his patients this way. "Why don't I put you through a few tests and we'll see what we can come up with."

The doctor wasn't kidding about his tests, as he moored me into a six-dimensional pair of binoculars and began trying out an inexhaustible combination of lenses on my eyes.

"Your expertise came highly recommended," I said, as he slipped off one lens and slipped on another. He didn't appear to have heard me. "Dr. Francis Romero recommended you to me," I added, pulling back my head and looking up at the man.

"Dr. Francis Romero? I don't believe I have met the man," he said, continuing to fiddle with a couple of lenses in front of my eyes.

"No? Well, he's working out of San Diego at the moment. But he told me you met back in Mexico." The hands stopped. "I believe he mentioned the Autonomous University of Guadalajara? That the two of you were fellow students down there in the late sixties?"

He shoved the machine away from my body and stared down at me, not looking so distracted anymore.

"So you remember the doctor?" I said, slipping out of the chair.

His eyes remained on me as he moved behind his desk. "Who sent you?" he asked brusquely, one hand going into a desk drawer. "Who the hell is this Dr. Romero? What do you want from me?"

"Want? Wait a minute. I don't understand. I happened to have been in L.A. last weekend and met the man at a party. That's all there is to it. And when he heard about the trouble I was having—with my eyes I mean—he brought up your name. That's all there is to it!" I insisted, my voice moving up an octave or two.

He continued to stare at me. I could hear my watch ticking. Or maybe it was his. He slammed shut the drawer, pressing the palm of one hand against his forehead. "Let's wrap up these tests," he muttered, pulling back my chair. Just like that? As if nothing had happened here? I slipped gingerly back into my seat, letting him push the ocular contraption up against my face.

"Dr. Lopez," the woman spoke up breathlessly, opening the door and taking a step or two into the room. "I am so sorry to be late. My daughter, she had a—a—" And she broke into a stream of Spanish.

"*Señora* Boleras?" I heard the doctor say, looking from her to me. The game was up.

Unwisely perhaps, I bolted, out of the chair, through the waiting room, and out the front exit. As I was grappling with the key in the car door, Doc caught up with me, grabbing me by the arm and poking a small revolver in my ribs. He wasn't going to shoot me, I told myself. Not here. Not now. Not with a hundred and one witnesses milling all over the goddamn place.

"This is all a crazy mistake," I stammered, backing away from the barrel. "I don't know who you think I am, but you've got things all mixed up. I love in—Jesus, I *live* in San Francisco. I was down in L.A. on assignment last week and ran into this Dr. Romero. At a party, like I said. He gave me your name. Told me something about the two of you having attended the same—the same university in Mexico. And that's all there is to it."

"Keep talking," he said, expropriating my shoulder bag.

"That's it," I muttered, cursing myself inside and out for having left the goddamn list in my bag.

"With all the eye doctors in San Francisco, you want me to swallow some line about you driving up here for an exam? On the advice of some man you met at a party?" He flipped through my wallet, then dropped it back into my bag. "So what's the story you're investigating, Sarah Calloway?" he asked, shoving the purse hard into my stomach. A woman was watching us from some ten yards away.

"Arson, at the moment," I said, watching her watch us and edging back to the car door.

"Yeah?"

"Yeah. Why? There's something else I should be investigating?"

"Look, smart-ass. You tell those friends of yours to lay off. Got that? Or there's going to be a price to pay. Hear me? You hear me?" he repeated, his fingernails digging into my elbow.

"I have no idea what you're talking about," I said, twisting free of his grip. To my surprise, the man put up no resistance as I jumped behind the wheel and locked the door behind me. I had one last good look at the doctor—squint-eyed and tight-fisted—as I backed the car out of the lot.

The drive back to Riverside and St. Teresa's Church was not a comfortable one. I could still feel the cold barrel of that gun sticking in my guts. "Tell your friends to keep their distance or they'll pay a price." What friends? What price? He didn't seem to be acquainted with this Dr. Romero. But he sure as hell was acquainted with the Autonomous University of Guadalajara. Why would the simple mention of some Mexican university set him off the way it did?

I had more than a few second thoughts about keeping this dinner appointment with Father Cardez. But then again, I reminded myself, he wasn't even one of the candidates on Diana's list. I parked the car in front of the church and crossed the street to buy myself a package of cigarettes, knowing damn well that I would live to regret this backsliding after so many weeks. But what the hell.

"So! You have arrived," Father Cardez observed gaily, slipping into a black sport coat as he strode toward me down the hall. "A cocktail before dinner, perhaps?" He slapped the bannister and bounded up the stairs. I hesitated a moment on the bottom step, then followed him up and into a largish sitting room on the second floor. As he shuffled a few bottles around on the makeshift bar in back, I took in the room itself. Cozy and warm. Cardez shoved two glasses into my hands, grabbed up his pitcher of Bloody Marys, and steered us into the library across the hall, settling me into one of the two frayed chairs placed in front of the hearth.

"To '88," he said, lifting his glass high in the air. "May it be an improvement over '87. God knows, it better be." He took a hearty sip of his drink. I did likewise. A mistake. There was enough Tabasco sauce in this glass to bring tears to my eyes. Cardez didn't seem to notice. He was already down on one knee preparing a fire, packing kindling and wads of newspaper under a log set on the grating, and slapping at his pockets for a light.

"Here, Father," I said, tossing him one of the many motel matchbooks still lying at the bottom of my bag; my calling card as it were, these last couple of days.

"Enrique," he corrected me, studying the matchbook a moment before setting a match to the kindling and dropping the matchbook into his pocket. He sank into his chair again and picked up his drink. "The only way to end a day, yes?" he submitted, waving his glass at the fire.

"Hmmn. Yes. Very atavistic, no doubt."

"Ata—what?"

"Goes back millions of years, right? Sitting in front of fires at the end of the day."

"Well now, for that matter what doesn't go back millions of years?" he pointed out. "Eating. Drinking. Talking. Making love," he added, smiling behind his glass. "Smoking," he added again, as I brought the cigarettes out of my bag.

"You don't mind?"

"Go right ahead," he said, jumping to his feet all the same and yanking open the window at our back. "I have a theory about women. Who smoke," he added, settling back in the chair, smiling again.

"Oh? Well, I'd just as soon not hear this, if it's all the same to you."

"Ah. Too bad. It was a most interesting theory."

"No doubt. Actually, I have my own theory. About Catholic priests. Who drink," I added, as he went for his glass.

"And what is this theory?" he asked, resting his glass on his knee, smiling.

"That it is a product of being—shall we say—of the world, but not in it?"

"*Of* but not *in?* What does this mean, of but not in? As a journalist are you in but not of?"

"I would say I am both in and of," I said, returning his smile.

"Ah. And what exactly does one miss by not being *in* the world?"

I shrugged. "Regular life?"

"Regular life? And what is this thing—this regular life?"

"Family. Marriage. Kids. The regular cycle of things."

"I see. And you, Sarah. You have many children, I suppose?"

"None, as a matter of fact."

"And are *you* married?"

"As a matter of fact, no, I'm not."

"I see. So tell me, Sarah. What makes you any more *in* the world than someone such as myself?"

"Maybe because I have fewer rules to live by?" I suggested, wondering just what the hell I was getting at here.

"Rules?"

"Well, yes. As a priest, you must admit there are certain parameters in your life that—"

"But every life has its parameters, no? Even yours, I am sure," he added, bouncing his fingertips off each other and pursing his lips. "Sex? Is this the parameter you are referring to here? The fact that you can have sex and I—so you assume—cannot? Is this what keeps you *in* the world and me out?"

"Not at all. That wasn't at all what I was saying," I lied.

"Then just what are you saying?"

"Frankly, I'm not so sure any more."

"I see." He laughed. "Well then, are you ready to hear *my* theory?"

"On why women smoke? I think I'll pass."

"You surprise me, Sarah. As a journalist, I would think you would welcome new thoughts. New ideas."

"Yes, well. Live and learn."

"Sublimation," he announced, settling back in his chair.

"Sublimation—what?"

"That is why women smoke. It is a form of sublimation."

"And just what are we sublimating?"

He smiled, shrugged. Apparently, he was referring to sex.

"I'm afraid you have it all wrong, Father."

"Enrique."

"Enrique. If we sublimate anything when we smoke, we sublimate eating. Eating, on the other hand . . ."

"Then there you have it!" he said triumphantly, jabbing a finger in the air. "Smoking—via eating—is your way of sublimating!" His hand circled vaguely in the air.

"And what is your way?" I asked.

"Ah," he said, and laughed. So did I.

"Listen, Father—ah, Enrique—do you think we could get down to the business at hand here?"

He laughed again, looking entirely too young and mischievous to fit the role of a Catholic priest. "So, tell me Sarah," he said, leaning forward, resting his elbows on the arms of the chair. "You are writing this immigration piece for a San Francisco paper, or—?"

"*Probe Magazine*."

"Ah, very good. *Probe*." Another smile. The man was incorrigible. "Well then, let us be frank with one another and admit from the start that this so-called Immigration Bill is a deportation bill in disguise. Yes? No different than this administration's attempt to label Iranian terrorists 'moderates.' Or the contras 'freedom fighters.' Or calling the MX missile a Peacekeeper. With these people, black has become white, and white has become black. They stand truth on its head before our very eyes, and get away with it! It amazes me to witness such a thing. Truly it does."

"But a substantial number of aliens *are* qualifying for amnesty?"

"Yes, of course. But unfortunately, it is not the people who are most in need of our compassion who will be reaping the benefits of this amnesty. We have created a vicious circle here. We refuse to call Salvadoran and Guatemalan exiles 'political' refugees. We insist they have been pouring over our borders for these last five or six years purely out of economic want. And then we turn around and continue to furnish the militaries of these two countries with the very weapons and training which creates this tide of so-called 'economic' refugees. If we wish to stem the tide, let us start at the source, and refrain from supporting these military juntas. The solution could well be as simple as that.

"Are you aware," he added, jabbing a finger at my notebook, "that we support the Salvadoran government to the tune of one million in military aid per day? One million a day into the military effort down there, into the helicopters and bombs and computerized spy networks which only add to the chaos and mayhem, and creates the very refugees we then choose to ignore. It is like setting a house on fire and then locking the doors and windows! That is what we are doing in Central America. Setting it on fire, then doing our best to slam shut the windows and doors. I ask you—and you ask your readers—what are we to do—as Christians, as feeling human beings—about the needy ones which our government has chosen to ignore? Truly," he added, shaking his head and staring into his glass. "It is a time to try men's souls . . . What are you smiling at?" he added, looking up at me. "Am I making a fool of myself here?"

"Not at all. It's just that I wouldn't have taken you for such an impassioned orator. You don't seem the—well—the type."

He settled back again, nodding, gazing into the fire. Then back at me. "Shall I tell you something, Sarah? Off the record, of course," he added, waiting for me to stop taking notes. "A very strange phenomenon has been occurring here in the weeks since Jim died." He set down his drink, folded his hands. "Do you believe in possession?"

"In possession?"

"In the possibility of a spirit or ghost taking over another person's soul?"

"Why do you ask?"

"Because I often feel as if Jim has taken me over."

"You mean Reverend McNally?"

"Yes, of course."

"Are you serious?"

"I'm afraid I am," he said, looking back at the fire. I shifted in place.

"There must be some kind of natural transference that takes place," I finally suggested. "I mean, when two people are so close like that, and one of them dies."

He smiled, shaking his head.

"You don't understand. It's not only that I catch myself saying his words. Or taking his side of a question. I actually feel him inside me doing it for me. Do you see?"

There came a knock at the door. It was Frannie with a message for Cardez.

"You will excuse me?" he said, jumping up from his chair and following Frannie out of the room.

I sipped my drink, mulling over the strange turn the conversation had taken. Then I lit a cigarette and crossed the room, checking out their library shelves. Someone here liked mysteries. And political thrillers. And conspiracies. Very big on conspiracies. There were at least five books on the Kennedy assassination. Another batch on the death of Martin Luther King. One about the Jonestown massacre. And another on the suspected assassination of the previous Pope.

I was more than a little surprised to find a book by Reverend McNally himself on the bottom shelf. Two copies, as a matter of fact. Entitled *Revolution and Faith*. I removed a copy and returned to the chair. The photo on the back cover was of a lean, tan, and extremely healthy-looking individual in his early forties, baling hay in the middle of some field, in Honduras I assumed, the country mentioned on the flap.

I opened the book and read the inscription written on the title page, the translation of a poem—or rather, an excerpt from the poem—written by a Guatemalan poet named Otto René Castillo. A man who—according to McNally's introduction—had been tortured and killed by Guatemalan death squads shortly after the poem had been written.

OPTIMISTIC HOLOCAUST

How terrible my age!

Nevertheless, it was my age.
Men of the future
when you think about our age,
don't think about the men:
think about the beasts
we were, biting
with homicidal fangs
the bits of soul
we had;
think as well
that in this battle
between animals,
the beasts died

forever

and humanity was born . . .

I reread the poem, then closed the book, studying McNally's picture again, wondering what kind of man he had been. Cardez returned to the room, twisted the book in my hand for a look, nodded, and settled back in his chair. Whatever had transpired out there across the hall had changed his mood for the worse.

"What was he like?" I asked, putting McNally's book aside.

"Jim?" He shrugged, waved at the book. As if to say that the answer was self-evident, or within the pages of the book.

"So he worked down in Honduras?" I confirmed.

"For almost twenty years."

"Ever in Mexico?"

"Why Mexico?"

"Ever at the University of Guadalajara?"

He raised his eyebrows at that one.

"I'm afraid those people would hardly be Jim's style."

"What people?"

"Why the interest, Sarah?"

"It's nothing, really. Just that the University of Guadalajara came into a conversation this afternoon. I was wondering what significance it might have."

"It's controlled top to bottom by the Tecos. Mexico's own brand of Nazis. You have your brands up here. They have their brands down there."

"And what do these Tecos actually do?"

"Do?" he repeated, shrugging as he leaned forward to refill my glass. Then his own. "What Nazis do everywhere. Spread bigotry and hate."

The conversation lagged momentarily, the two of us sipping our drinks.

"So who's the conspiracy freak?" I asked, glancing back at the library shelves.

"That's Jim," Cardez said, smiling for the first time since returning to the room. "You might say that assassinations were Jim's area of expertise."

"Oh?"

"He had theories on everyone. The Kennedys. King. John Lennon. Olaf Palme. Thomas Merton. You name it. Anyone and everyone."

"John Lennon?"

"That's right. Had him figured as the victim of some CIA/right-wing evangelist plot."

"What?"

"Figured the man who pulled the trigger—what was his name?"

"Mark Chapman?"

"Right. That he was one of those brain-washed assassins. A Manchurian Candidate," he added, shrugging, his smile getting wider.

"I wonder," I began, then stopped.

'What's that?"

"Well, I was just thinking, considering Father McNally's obsession with assassination plots and all, what he might have thought about his own death. I mean, if he could look back on it now, do you suppose he might be building conspiracies around his own demise?"

Cardez set his glass down most carefully on the table and stared at me.

"What do you think?" I finally asked. "How old was he, anyway? To judge from the book cover, not much more than forty? Forty-five . . .? Hey look, I didn't mean anything by it. It just kind of popped out."

"Popped out?"

"That's right. Yes. What is it, Enrique?"

He stared at me in silence a moment longer. Then looked up, nodded. Not at me, but at the attractive young woman standing behind me at the door. She addressed him in Spanish, appearing to be quite nervous and upset.

"I'm afraid we will have to postpone this dinner of ours," he said, springing to his feet. "A bit of an emergency has come up."

"Yes, of course."

He said something to the woman in Spanish.

"I'll show you to the door," he added, turning back to me, ushering me into the hall and down the stairs.

"Why have you come here?" he asked, when we reached the bottom step.

"Why have I—? The story on amnesty. As I've already explained."

"You have asked many questions today. Most of them having nothing to do with the amnesty question . . . We haven't finished this conversation of ours, have we Sarah?"

"No, we haven't. Shall I return tomorrow evening?"

"Fine. No—wait," he added, as I started out the door. "Tomorrow's New Year's Eve. We had better make it Friday. Friday afternoon."

"Friday then," I said, nodding a good-bye and heading down the walk, aware of his gaze on my back. I opened the car door and glanced back over my shoulder just in time to see him disappearing into the church.

By the time I got back to San Rodino, I had made up my mind to pay Mrs. Stevens a call. I needed to speak with the woman again, whether or not the feeling was mutual. The address in the phone book traced down to a woodframe at the south end of town. A stencilled wrought-iron sign over the porch informed all comers that 'The Stevens Live Here.' I rang the bell.

"Well, well," Mrs. Stevens drawled, peeking out, then propping herself up against the half-door. "If it isn't my little roving reporter."

"Good evening, Mrs. Stevens . . . Are you going to invite me in?"

Under the hall light, the woman had to be seen to be believed, from the Kewpie doll makeup and purple ostrich feathers in her hair, to the star-spangled tap shoes on her feet. The secret life of Maude Stevens, I thought, following the woman through a series of beaded curtains into the parlor beyond.

The first thing I noticed was the cats. Everywhere. And the

nativity scene in miniature laid out on her leopard skin rug. Mrs. Stevens plucked a fat Siamese number off the mantel and cradled it to her breasts.

"Might we turn down the music?" I suggested.

"Why? Don't you approve of Puccini?"

"A little on the deafening side, wouldn't you say?"

She whispered something nasty about me in the cat's ear, then deposited the cat in my arms and, with a peevish toss of her head, wandered unsteadily back through the layer of beads. I started counting. Nine cats in all, in a parlor that resembled someone's hokey idea of an opium den, with incense, erotic statuary, candalabra, and dark plum drapery covering three of the four walls.

I returned the cat to its post on the mantel and settled on the sofa, taking note of the open bottle of champagne, the single glass, the small tray of hors d'oeuvres set out on the table. A party for one? Her purse, open, was sitting on the arm of the sofa. I was about to check out its contents when Mrs. Stevens returned to the room.

"I know why you've come here, Miss Calloway," she said, standing before me, twisting the handkerchief in her hands. "And it's no use. I simply refuse to cooperate with you any further. I believe I made that *quite* clear the other afternoon."

"Mrs. Stevens, isn't it true that your daughter gave her very *life* in an attempt to alert you to something? Don't you owe it to her to find out just what that warning *was?*"

She looked away, at the wall, biting her lower lip. Then sank down at the far end of the sofa, her eyes on her lap.

"I—" she began, then stopped.

"Yes?"

"I don't deserve this. I don't! Not any of this."

"Of course you don't," I said quietly. "Neither did your daughter . . . Tell me, Mrs. Stevens. When did Detective Ray last speak with you?"

She looked at me and blinked.

"Monday. Monday afternoon. And I told him nothing, if that's what you're getting at. I refuse to deal with that sort. Always have."

"Was he the one to scare you off the case?"

"How many times must I tell you, Miss Calloway! No one has scared me off of anything. I simply wish to let my daughter rest in peace."

"In peace from what?"

"From despicable people like you, that's what," she said, beating her fists in her lap. "Who go around meddling in everybody's business but your own."

"Need I remind you, that it was *you* who asked me to investigate your daughter's death?"

"Very well. That is true. And now I am asking you to desist. Can I make it any clearer than that?"

"But why . . .? Mrs. Stevens, you are the only person I can turn to. The only person who seems to care what happened to Diana. If you won't help me, who will?"

The woman feigned deaf and dumbness, staring at the opposite wall.

"Okay, look. Could you at least lend me a recent snapshot of your daughter?"

She turned, blinking.

"Here I am," I went on. "Trying to trace down your daughter's past. And I don't even know what the woman looks like."

"But you were there. You saw . . ."

"Not well enough, Mrs. Stevens."

She sighed and pushed up to her feet, heading out of the room. When she returned, one or two nips of whiskey to the wiser, a large photo album was under her arm.

"This may—well, this may surprise you, Miss Calloway," she said, opening the album across our laps. "But we were quite a celebrated dance team in our day."

"Diana and you?"

"Well, no. Diana was only a youngster back then. My husband

and myself. We toured most every corner of Latin America, at one time or another. Brazil. Argentina. Peru."

Slowly, silently, she began to turn the pages of the album, her hand lightly caressing certain photos which held their own special memory cues for the woman. They made a curious couple, Mr. and Mrs. Stevens. She in her assortment of brightly-colored plumages and he in his cummerbunds and bandelero pants, and oily, slicked-down, Rudolph Valentino hair. The man was barely any taller than his wife.

"Where is Mr. Stevens now?" I asked.

"Harold?" She sniffed, shutting the album and pushing it off her lap. "My husband ran off with an Argentinian apache dancer in 1968."

"I see."

"A *male* Argentinian apache dancer," she added, her eyes darting at my face and back to her lap, as she picked at the sequins on her dress. "He wanted to take Diana with him, if you can imagine such a thing. I wouldn't hear of it, of course," she added, darting me another look. "And I must say, that when all is said and done, we made a rather fine life for ourselves, Diana and I. We were quite . . . quite . . ." Her lips began to quiver, her head bowed.

"Were you dancing when I arrived here tonight?" I interjected, in the interest of staving off the tears.

She blinked, then squinted suspiciously at me. "Why? Do you think it foolish of a woman my age to be indulging in such—"

"Not at all. I think it's great. Keeps you in shape. Keeps you young. Why not show me one of your routines?"

"You mean dance for you? Here? Now? But I haven't danced before an audience in years."

"One little turn can't hurt any, can it? I always wanted to be a dancer myself," I added, taking note of her feet, which were already tapping out their own autonomous two-step on her leopard skin rug.

"Well, now, I suppose I could—I mean, if you really—" She got to her feet again, hesitating in place a moment before disappearing back through the braided beads. In seconds, the opening strains of the Spanish concerto "Aranquez" came pouring into the room. When Mrs. Stevens returned, the taps had been traded in for a pair of well-worn pink ballet slippers. With a quick nervous nod in my direction, she positioned herself in front of the fireplace, solemn and poised, an ostrich feather in either hand. At a downbeat of the lead guitar, her fan dance commenced.

I had the simultaneous urge to laugh and cry as I watched this short, plump, lonely middle-aged woman soar away on her two feathers: bending, dipping, swaying, arching her way into another time zone as she swept around the room. Suddenly, the cats scattered en masse. And Mrs. Stevens, in the middle of a grand arabesque, groaned and crumbled to the floor.

"Mrs. Stevens?"

I knelt over her body, letting out a muted scream at the sight of the blood oozing from her chest. Gunfire cut across the front yard. The woman had been shot?! In panicky confusion, I scuttled behind the sofa as someone broke through the front door and started moving around the room.

"You all right, Calloway?"

I jerked around to find Detective Ray standing behind me, a revolver in his hand.

"Jesus," I murmured, edging toward the wall.

"You okay?" he repeated, his eyes darting around the room.

"She . . . Mrs . . ."

"She's dead," he said tonelessly, shoving the gun under his jacket and peering through the drapes.

"Who did this?!"

He turned back to face me. "You tell me. Now I would suggest we get the hell out of here," he added, moving toward the door. "You coming, or aren't you?"

His right hand, the one holding up his left shoulder, was covered in blood. I wavered in place a moment. Then grabbed up Mrs. Stevens' purse, took one last look at the woman, and followed him out the door, in the process stumbling feet first over a second body sprawled across the lawn. It was a young man attired entirely in black, in a sickening replay of the two men who had gunned down Diana one week ago.

Detective Ray grabbed up the rifle that lay just beyond the man's outstretched hand and tossed it into the back seat of my car.

"Hey!"

"I'm going to need your help," he muttered, moving around to the passenger side and getting in.

"The hospital?"

"No hospitals, Calloway. Your place will be good enough."

"My place? Are you crazy? You're bleeding bad, Mister. You need a doctor."

"Please, lady," he said, taking in a sharp breath.

The guy was in real pain. Dying for all I knew. What the hell had I gotten myself into here? I asked myself frantically, starting up the car and veering down the hill.

By the time I got us back to the motel, the man had lost so much blood that the left side of his shirt was soaked in it. I helped him out of the car and up the walk. He stopped me midway, shoving some keys in my hand and asking me to dig a bottle of vodka from under the front seat of his car, which happened to be parked a few spaces down from mine. Not a Volvo, but a Dodge Dart. In the state I was in, it was no easy matter locating the vodka under the shitload of discarded pizza boxes, Pepsi cans, and various other assorted crap littering up the floor of the auto.

"Some clean towels?" he mumbled as we pitched through the motel room door. I headed straight for the bathroom, plugging up the sink and turning on the water full tilt.

"Calm down, Calloway," he said, following me in there and settling down on the edge of the tub.

"Calm down! People getting murdered before my very eyes! Poor Mrs. Stevens—why would anyone—And who the *hell* was that guy on the front lawn?! Who the hell are you?! Bleeding to death all over my bathroom floor! And you're asking me to calm down?"

Having no other choice in the matter, I helped him out of his shirt and what I took to be a bullet-proof vest. He proceeded to pour some of the vodka directly onto his wound, wincing sharply, then took a couple of quick swigs from the bottle himself before passing it my way. I pushed it back at him.

"Let's go," he said, shoving the bottle back in my hand.

"You expect me to dig that thing out, don't you?" I said, eyeing the knife he had dropped on the sink.

"You got any better ideas?"

"A doctor, for one."

He shook his head, bringing a book of matches out of his back pocket.

"Look. I got to tell you. I've never done anything remotely like this before," I said, eyeing his wound. The bullet was just visible, lodged in the tissue under his collarbone.

"There's always a first time, isn't there, Calloway," he said, weighing the matches in his hand, something in his voice evoking a jolting sense of déjà vu.

I forced back a wave of nausea, washing it down with a good swallow of the vodka, then proceeded to burn the blade of the knife in the flame of one match. Then another. While rehearsing a neat, clean twist of the blade that would carve out the bullet in a single stroke.

"Just do it," he muttered through clenched teeth . . . "God-damn," he gasped moments later, when I finally had the bloody thing in my hand. His face had gone sheet-white.

"You okay? Look, Mister. I warned you I—Hey!" I murmured, as he slumped forward and slipped to the tile floor. "Damn. I knew I shouldn't—shit!" I turned him over on his back. The man was out cold. Between additional swigs of the vodka, I dressed and taped the wound. Everything seemed slightly unreal. More than slightly.

The phone rang. I staggered into the other room and picked it up.

"Sarah?"

It was Sergeant Welsh—Susan—with the information I had requested concerning the San Rodino Police.

"No proof. But a lot of rumors making the rounds. All right . . .?

You there, Sarah?"

"Yeah."

"Seems to be some kind of drug ring working from inside the force—in connection with the California Rangers; a paramilitary group down there that quite a few of the police apparently belong to. The drug operation stretches from Mexico clear up here to San Francisco. This all came out when a couple members of the force were indicted, put on trial a few years back. Of course, everyone's denying it, down the line. So, take it for what it's worth."

"And Detective Ray?" I whispered, moving across the room, checking things out. The man was still out cold.

"I was just getting to that. According to all the computer checks I could get into, there is no D. E. A. agent named Ray working out of Detroit. Which doesn't mean there isn't. Just means I couldn't pick him up. That will do it for you?"

"Yeah, thanks."

I put the receiver quietly back in its cradle and moved around to the other bed. Rifling through the man's shirt and jacket, I came up with nothing more than a half-empty pack of Pall Malls. I stepped up to the bathroom door.

"Mark? Ray?"

Very gently, I rolled the man over on his side and extricated his wallet from a back pocket of his pants. He gave signs of coming to. I moved back into the room and checked things out. Behind the D. E. A. credentials was a credit card for some bank in Stockholm, made out to a Peter Nystrom. And behind the credit card, a Swedish driver's license made out to the same name.

What was going on? So the guy was Swedish? But he sure as hell didn't sound Swedish. And why would some Swede be passing himself off as an agent for the United States Drug Enforcement Agency? Pacing the room, I tripped over my feet and nearly fell flat on my face. I was feeling damn woozy myself. Whether from the booze, or from the overdose of blood, guts, and double-dealing, I couldn't say. I slipped a cigarette out of his pack and lit up, stretching out on the bed in an effort to recoup whatever wits I had left. Then I let out a nervous shriek at the man's sudden reappearance in the room.

"You always like this, Calloway?" he asked, a vague smile on his face as he settled at the foot of the bed. Fresh blood was seeping through the towelling.

"Feeling any better?" I asked, getting to my feet.

"Just dandy."

"Well, you don't look so dandy . . . Isn't it about time you tell me who you're really working for, Mister? Who you really are?"

He stared at me, one hand pressing into his shoulder. "Haven't we already been through this?"

I hesitated a moment. Then went under the pillow for his wallet and tossed it to him. He flipped it open and shut, then nodded slowly, making a prime-time show out of studying me, the motel room, and me again.

"How do you say 'Good evening' in Swedish, Mr. Nystrom?"

In answer, he did indeed mutter something in Swedish. But I had a strong suspicion it had nothing to do with 'good evenings.'

"Are you some kind of double-agent or what?" I asked.

"Jesus," he muttered, shaking his head at some invisible commiserator on the other side of the room.

"Well? What am I suppose to think, for God's sake?"

He started to rise, then seemed to think better of it, sinking back down on the bed.

"The way I see it, Calloway, you know a fair piece of my story," he said quietly, looking at me through tired, lowered eyes. "Now you damn well owe me a piece of yours. What's your connection with these two Stevens women? What do you know about them that you're not saying? Why have both these women been killed?"

"I have no idea"

"Don't give me that crap. When are you going to stop your goddamn stonewalling and become a team player? That's what I want to know."

"A *team* player? Next thing I know, you'll be talking game plans and hardball tactics, am I right? Maybe a full-court press? And the joke of all this is, I don't even know what team you're on. Do I, Mr. Nystrom?"

He studied the opposite wall, then me again. "ISI. Swedish Intelligence."

"You have some kind of I.D.?"

That got me a wince. Or a smile. "You'll just have to take my word for it, won't you?"

"Why?"

"Because you have no other choice. Now how about explaining your interest in the young Stevens woman's death?"

I returned his studied gaze with one of my own as conflicting spiels whirled in and out of my head.

"You explain your interest," I said. "Then I'll explain mine."

He closed his eyes, inhaled, and opened them again. "I'm over here tracking down a political assassin."

"A political assassin?"

"I have good reason to believe that the man I'm tracking is mixed up with the men who murdered the young Stevens woman."

"Why? What's the connecting link?"

He shook his head, leaned back, one hand pressing into his shoulder. "Your turn, Calloway. Why don't you tell me just how the hell you got hooked into this circus." Another extended pause.

"I saw the whole thing happen," I finally muttered, recrossing the room.

"You what?"

"I saw Diana murdered. I was sitting in my car, staking out this family clinic for a story I'm working on. She was standing at the bus stop down the street. Suddenly, these two men stepped out of a side alley and gunned the woman down. She didn't have a prayer. The paper wrote it up as a robbery, but it sure as hell was no robbery. It was an execution, plain and simple. And the woman was seven months pregnant. It didn't make any sense! What harm was the woman going to do anyone? That's why I went to the funeral. To speak with her mother. To tell her what I knew. What I had seen."

"How good a look did you get of these two characters?"

"Good enough. Neither of them match up with the guy you left on the Stevens' lawn, if that's what you're getting at. They were older. Fatter."

"Why haven't you gone to the police with this story?"

"Why haven't you?"

"Goddamn it, lady. You have no idea what you're mixed up in here."

"Okay, so tell me. What am I mixed up in? Who's behind all these executions? And how does Swedish Intelligence fit into the picture?"

He exchanged sour looks with the wall again. Then pressed his fingers into his forehead as a wave of pain passed across his face. Several seconds passed before he looked up again.

"You need a doctor," I said.

"I need some goddamn sleep. Got any ideas why that bozo back in Pasadena pulled a gun on you today?"

"You keep tailing me around like this and we're going to have to work out some kind of deal."

"Do you have *any* idea who that Lopez character is?"

"Not really."

"So why the hell were you paying the man a call?"

"I was trying to connect up with Diana's past. Hoping for a lead. Her co-workers at the Salon. Her priest. Her eye doctor."

"You were checking out her *eye doctor* for a lead? Give me a break, Calloway," he said, shaking his head and getting to his feet. He took two or three steps toward the bathroom before his knees gave out. "Jesus," he muttered, stumbling back to the bed. He sat there, head lowered, for a good minute or two.

"Mind if I sack out here a while?" he said, nodding at the other bed.

"Here? But where are you staying?"

"Where do you think I'm staying?"

"The car?"

"What's the matter, Calloway. Afraid I'll bite?"

"Yeah, well . . ."

"Okay, kid. We'll do it your way," he said, rising slowly to his feet. He picked up his bloodied shirt and jacket off the back of the chair and headed for the door.

"Wait," I said.

He turned, the wry smile back on his face.

"What are you smiling at?" I asked.

"You going to offer me a little of your hospitality, Calloway?"

"A little, yeah." I went over to the closet for the extra pillow and tossed it onto the other bed.

"I do appreciate this," he said, settling down on the bed, using his good arm to pull off his shoes. First one, then the other, dropping to the floor. He sank back on the mattress without even bothering to pull down the spread. I started rummaging through Mrs. Stevens' purse. Mascara. Lipstick. A vial of perfume. Handkerchiefs. A small flask of whiskey. The matchbook I had given her the morning of the funeral. But no wallet.

"There's a slight problem here," I suggested, rummaging some more. "I left Mrs. Stevens with one of my business cards. With my San Francisco address on it, my telephone number, the works."

"You keep a low profile, don't you kid?"

"Yeah—well, the point is, sooner or later the San Rodino police are going to be following a trail to my door, aren't they?"

"And if they do? You saw her once or twice. Nothing to tie you back into tonight."

"Yeah—well, the point is, I'd rather not get involved."

"You—*what?* Should have thought of that a little earlier, Calloway."

"Yeah?"

"If it makes you fell any better, I have someone watching this room, around the clock."

". . . Why?"

"Until you tell me what you're on to, I have no other choice. Do I? Besides, I'm working on a hunch."

"Oh?"

"Yep. That you're going to lead me to my triggermen."

"Me?"

"It worked tonight, didn't it?" he said, reaching up, switching off the light.

Yeah. It *had* worked tonight. Why?

"Who are those guys, anyway?" I asked, referring to the gunmen. He didn't answer. To believe the evenness of his breathing, the man was already asleep.

Sleep came less easy for me that night. At one point, I vaguely considered the idea of heading back to San Francisco in the morning. But it was the San Francisco address 'they' had in their hands. So who the hell *were* these assassins, with their black garb and sophisticated rifles? And why would some Swedish agent—if in fact he *was* a Swedish agent—be over here tracing them down? I reviewed what Susan had told me over the phone. The affiliation or crossover between the San Rodino Police Force and the California Rangers. A crossover which had apparently given support to some kind of drug ring between Mexico and San Francisco?

So—were these assassins Rangers? Was it as simple as that? But how would the list fit into that? Someone like McNally? Mexico? Panama?

The questions kept coming, one after the other. Obscured by the reality that Mrs. Stevens—beaded, feathered, bespangled Maude Stevens—was dead.

December 31, 1987

When I opened my eyes next morning, it was already light outside and the room was strangely quiet. Propping myself up on one elbow, I stared at the bed opposite. It was empty. For one crazy second, I convinced myself that I had dreamed up last night's whole bloody affair. But no—there was the bottle of vodka staring me in the face. "Mark . . .? Peter?" I stumbled out of bed and up to the window. His car was gone, as well. After double-locking the door, I sank back on the bed, the image of Mrs. Stevens collapsing to the carpet, flashing across the screen.

Why had he abandoned ship like this, without getting out of me what he had wanted to know? Not to mention the information I had hoped to get out of him. As uncomfortable as I had felt sparring with the man last night, this didn't feel any better. It felt worse. Mrs. Stevens was dead. Diana was dead. Reverend McNally was dead. How soon until I too would be joining their ranks?

Enough, I told myself, dragging the suitcase from under the bed. ENOUGH. I've had it.

I sprung open the latch and stared at the contents. My suitcase had been ransacked. Not a doubt about it. The bastard must have done it early this morning, while I slept. I dug out the bottle of Johnson's Baby Powder and unscrewed the top. Miraculously enough, the coded sheets and list of names were still intact. Round one for my side, I told myself, tossing all and sundry into the case. It wasn't until I tried slipping into my running shoes that I found one of my matchbooks tucked into the toe of one shoe. 'Later/ M. R.' was scribbled on the inside cover.

The phone rang. I let it ring two more times, then answered it.

"It's all set," the voice said on the other end of the line. It was Oliver, my carrot-topped friend from the lunch counter. "Danny just called me a few minutes ago. Set up a meeting for twelve o'clock."

"Today?"

"You can make it, can't you?" he whined. "I sure as heck can't be calling him back. He don't have no phone."

"Just let me *think*, Oliver," I said, sinking back down on the bed and staring at my reflection in the mirror.

"Lady?"

"All right, Oliver," I finally murmured. "We'll give it a try." We arranged to meet at a truck stop outside Weatherby at 10 a.m. I finished dressing, kicked the suitcase back under the bed, and headed out the door, well aware of the Volvo, back in position, to one side of the lot.

When I arrived at the truck stop some fifty minutes later, Oliver was waiting for me, a wind parka tucked under one arm and a box of donuts under the other.

"The bottle of scotch is under the seat," I told him, when he got into the car. "The fifty will be coming when the mission's accomplished, if that's okay with you."

"Sure thing," he said, slapping the bottle and wrapping it into his parka.

"How old are you, anyway?"

"Twenty-six. But this ain't for me. It's for my Pa. He can't afford much in the line of luxuries these days. Figure he'll appreciate it."

"How much do you know about this so-called Brotherhood organization?" I asked him, a few minutes down the road.

He shrugged, popping half a donut into his mouth. "Not much. A bunch of kooks, is all."

"A bunch of well-armed kooks. How can they afford all that stuff, anyway? They sure can't be earning any money off that farm."

"Robbing banks."

"What?"

"That's what some folks say, anyway. That they've gone and robbed themselves a couple of banks. Also been rumors about them taking off with other folks' farm equipment. Things like that."

"And what does your sheriff think about all these rumors?"

"Not much. Hell, he's as scared of them as anybody. Can hardly blame him, neither. They'd just as soon blow his head off as to let him come in with warrants on those guys. Things are getting out of hand. No doubt about it," he said, scooping up another donut.

"I should say so."

"You got to remember, though," he went on. "Them folks got their share of sympathizers in these parts. Like my Pa, for instance. People who can't help kind of respecting Old Man Kelsey and the rest of them. You know, for sticking it to the government like they are, see? Instead of laying down and taking it like dogs. Like dogs," he repeated, staring out the window. "I'll tell you this much. I wouldn't want to be no sheriff in these parts, that's for sure. Not now, not no-how. And no banker, neither. And no judge. Cause there's no telling what's going to happen in the days ahead. Danny wasn't sounding so hot," he added, picking at still another donut.

"What do you mean?"

"I don't know. Jumpy. Wired. More than wired. Weird. Kept asking all these questions about you. What could I tell him?" he added with a shrug, spitting a bit of his donut my way.

"How does he make a living up there, anyway?"

"Danny? Lives off the land. No fooling. Hunts. Fishes. He can even make his own clothes. Out of animal skins, if you can dig that. Knows how to tan 'em, the works. He's what I'd call a real nature boy, my brother. And I'm not saying that just cause he's my brother. Ask anyone. What's this message? You know—this message for Cowboy?"

"It concerns Diana Stevens. Does Danny know her?"

"The pregnant lady? I suppose he does, yeah. Actually, I know he does. She used to make stuff for him. Cakes and cookies. Things like that. Even knit him a couple of sweaters. Suppose she didn't have all that much to do on that farm, day after day, right? 'Sides, I think she kind of felt sorry for Danny, all alone up there and all . . . So this message, it's about her, is it? Cowboy's ah—girl?"

"That's right, yes."

"What about her?"

I hesitated a moment, then went on. "She's dead, Oliver."

"Huh?"

"Some guy robbed and shot her last Friday morning. Christmas."

"Oh shit," he moaned, shifting in his seat. "Maybe—maybe this isn't such a good idea," he said, taking off his baseball cap and scratching furiously at the back of his neck. "I mean, I don't see

Danny taking this so well. He kind of—well, no harm meant or nothing, but I think he was kind of stuck on her. In a way. You know what I'm saying? She was so nice to him and all. Always thinking of him . . . Oh shit," he moaned again, slouching lower in the seat.

"I had no idea they were such good friends."

"Yeah. Well." He shrugged, muttering under his breath and shaking his head.

"Was your brother in love with Diana? Is that what you're saying?"

"Shit, I don't know. You got to understand something about Danny; which is that he's been having a lot of trouble connecting up with people these last few years, see? You'd think it'd be getting better, but it's not. It's getting worse. Which is why he spends so much time in that damn cabin of his. But with her—with her it was different. She could get to him in a way no one else could. Know what I'm saying? Hard to figure, too. 'Cause she's a real shy lady, far as I could tell. Could never get 'boo' out of her. Man-oh-man," he added, punching at his baseball cap and shaking his head. "Danny is *not* going to like this."

"Where does Cowboy fit into all this?"

"Hey, don't get me wrong. There was nothing underhanded going on there. She being pregnant and all. Besides, Dan isn't like that. It's just that Howie was hardly ever here, see? More than likely, he asked Dan to watch over her. Something like that."

"So where was Howie?"

"Huh?"

"If he's hardly ever home, then where is he?"

"Shit, I don't know. Maybe Africa or something. Central America. If it's not one war he's fighting, it's another."

"So Cowboy's a mercenary?"

"Yeah."

"A California Ranger?"

"Yeah. Guess that's what they call themselves. Kind of a looney bunch, if you ask me."

The first piece, or two, fell into place.

"Do the Rangers have any connection with the Brotherhood?" I asked.

"Nah. Well, yeah. Maybe in a way. Reverend Kelsey being his uncle and all. They're gun freaks, the whole bunch of them. But the difference is, the Brotherhood is mostly ex-farmers, see? The California Rangers is mostly ex-soldiers. It's not land they're hungering after. It's war. Least, that's the way they talk. A lot of it's horseshit, that goes without saying. Turn here," he added, as we passed a sign for the San Rodino National Forest. We followed a dirt road some three miles further, then parked the car.

"Just how far away is this cabin of his?" I asked, locking our belongings inside.

"We ain't going to his cabin. We're meeting him at a waterfall here in the park."

"And how far away is this waterfall?"

"Jeez, I don't know. Something in the neighborhood of a mile as the crow flies?"

Unfortunately, neither of us was a crow. And the trail was one long and tedious series of ascents and descents. No switchbacks. No flats. Just up. And down. Before long, I was reduced to scooting down every damn rise on my butt. And as if the chutes and ladders terrain wasn't bad enough, along came the manzanita bushes, with these sticky, prickly little leaves that tore into anything in their path.

"It's me, pal!" I heard Oliver cry out. Coming to the top of the next rise, I saw him at the bottom, his hands held high in the air.

"Come on, man! It's me! Put down the stupid gun!"

In slow, mincing, sideways steps, I managed to join Oliver at the bottom of the rise, my hands held as high as his. Maybe higher. It wasn't until I reached his side that I caught sight of Danny—or whom I assumed to be Danny—crouched behind a boulder to the right of the trail, a rifle in his hands.

"Come *on*, man!" Oliver whined again, dancing back and forth in my peripheral vision. "She's clean."

He stood up and tossed the rifle behind him, then made his wary approach. The man was of medium height, stocky, with wire-rim glasses and a ski cap on his head. He nodded at his brother, then turned to face me, his fists rolled tight at his side.

"Who are you?" he asked.

"I'm a friend of Diana's. From San Rodino. I need to find Cowboy and bring him a message. Your brother seemed to think you would know where Cowboy is."

He didn't open his mouth. He didn't even blink behind those glasses.

"Do you know a way I might contact him?" I tried again.

"What's the goddamn message?" he asked through gritted teeth.

I looked over at Oliver, who was shaking his head at me, and then back at Danny. There seemed to be only one way to break this thing. I brought the newsclipping on Diana's death out of my pocket and handed it to him. He scanned it, taking in a couple of sharp inhalations, as if having trouble catching his breath. Then balled up the paper in his fist and tossed it at my feet.

"Jesus fuck," he gasped, pressing his hands into his temples as he sank down on his haunches. "Jesus fuck almighty. What—what's going on?"

"I don't know, Danny," I murmured, exchanging glances with Oliver. "I just don't know."

His head jerked up, a look of unadulterated loathing in those eyes. "Get her out of here," he snarled at his brother, snatching the rifle off the ground and getting to his feet. "Get her fucking out of here."

Oliver grabbed my arm and started pulling me up the trail.

"Danny!" I called out, breaking loose of Oliver's hold. He stopped in place but didn't turn around. "Danny, please. For Diana's sake. To give justice its due. I need your help!"

He gave a fierce shake of his head, then stepped over the next ridge and disappeared from view.

"I told you, didn't I?" Oliver yammered in my ear as he continued to drag me along the trail. "Didn't I try to tell you it wasn't such a good idea just telling him straight out like that? Didn't I?"

"And how would you have suggested I tell him? Besides, that guy looked like he was ready to blow my head off before I even opened my mouth. One hell of a nature boy, I must say."

"But that just ain't—Danny isn't like that. I've never seen him pull a gun on nobody before. Not ever."

"Well, there's a first time for everything. Isn't there, Oliver?"

Oliver scrambled on ahead, leaving me to pick my own way back to the car.

I got back to San Rodino at four o'clock, parked the car in front of the room, and headed across the street, settling at one end of the bar and ordering myself a cold beer. The next time I looked up, Detective Ray AKA Nystrom was standing behind me, picking a manzanita leaf out of my hair.

"Where the hell have you been?" he asked, tossing the leaf on the counter and joining me at the bar.

"I could ask you the same question, couldn't I?" I said, my glance taking in his fresh shirt and jacket. Even the bandages seemed to have disappeared.

He fingered the bartender for another beer, then brought a snapshot out of his jacket.

"Friends of yours?" he asked, waving it in my face. It was a fairly recent photo of Maude Stevens standing next to a tall, slender gentleman dressed entirely in white.

"Mrs. Stevens," I said, surprised at the emotion in my voice. "The man—I have no idea. You got this out of her purse?"

"Happens to be one Roberto Carlotti," Nystrom said, watching my reaction to the news.

"If that's supposed to mean something to me, it doesn't."

"Colombian. Been living in Calfornia for the last five or six years. One of the biggest cocaine dealers in or out of the country."

"And that's him?" I asked incredulously.

"This little friendship comes as a surprise to you?"

"Damn right. The only thing she ever told me about was the

dancing. The tours she and her husband used to take around—around South America. But that was years ago."

He nodded, looking around the bar and then back at me. "Have any plans for the evening?"

"Tonight?"

"We have a little New Year's party to attend, if you're interested," he said, nodding down at the photograph.

"At Carlotti's? And you've been invited? Mind telling me how you managed that?" I asked.

"Friends in high places, Calloway," he said, slipping the photo back in his jacket and settling down on the stool next to mine, acknowledging the arrival of his beer.

"So what happened between last night and tonight, that suddenly you should have so many friends?"

He ignored my question, picking up the bottle, taking a sip, putting it down again.

"I need your eyes, Calloway."

"My eyes?"

"There's a good chance that one or both of the two characters who showed up Christmas morning will be there tonight."

"At this party? But I'm not even sure I'd recognize these guys. I mean, I saw them for what? Three seconds from fifteen yards away?"

"You saw them clear enough to know that last night's casualty wasn't one of them. You might surprise yourself, kid."

"To tell the truth," I said, swiveling around on the stool, "I'd feel a lot more comfortable about all this if you would just play it straight with me. Tell me exactly what you're doing over here and why."

"Hey look, Calloway. I'm ready for that talk whenever you are."

"But I've already told you everything I know."

"No, you haven't."

We sat there staring each other down. He won.

"So how about it?" he asked.

"About what?"

"Accompanying me to this little shindig tonight?"

"But who is this Carlotti going to think we are? A couple of cops?"

"I've been introduced around town as a private arms broker, tracking a certain deal. Why don't we leave it at that."

"I see. And are you?"

"Am I what?"

"A private arms broker tracking a certain deal?"

"What do you think, Calloway?"

"That's just the problem here. I don't know what to think."

He shook his head at the wall, and got to his feet. "What do you have to wear?" he asked, tossing a couple of bills on the bar.

I looked down at what I had on.

"Uh-uh. You go in that getup and our cover will be blown the minute we step through the door."

"And just what *is* my cover, if you don't mind my asking? The Swedish arms broker's American assistant? Your secretary? What?"

"How about traveling companion," he said, a trace of the smile back on his face. "I'll be back around eight. No jeans, Calloway. No running shoes. You'll be with grown-ups tonight. Dress like one."

"And what the hell is that supposed to mean?" I asked his retreating figure. He raised his hand in a vague salute and headed out the door.

I finished my beer and considered my options. What options? Either I cooperated with this guy—on the assumption that he would turn around and cooperate with me—or I didn't cooperate.

But where would that get me? Obviously, the man knew something that I didn't know. Something I needed to know. So obviously, there was something to be gained by playing along. Maybe something to lose, as well. Only time would tell . . . The tug-of-war continued unabated, as I headed back to the room. A part of me wanted nothing to do with this little 'shindig' this evening. On the other hand, I wouldn't have missed it for the world. Still, scrounging up a decent dress between now and eight p.m. was going to be no easy task.

Cory came to mind. We had similar builds, of that I was fairly certain. But would she be at home at 4 p.m. on New Year's Eve? I put through a call. She was home. And generous soul that she was, sounded more than happy to help me out.

"I've made it easy for you," Cory said, ushering me into the bedroom. Three dresses were laid out on her bed: a cherry-red wraparound with a fancy slit that went well up my thigh, a white knit that left nothing to the imagination, and a purple silk number which, in spite of a regrettably low-slung back, seemed to be the lesser of three evils.

"You're sure you don't have anything a little more . . . subtle?" I asked, eyeing myself in her closet mirror.

"Subtle? Who wants subtle, girl? In that getup, you're going to knock the socks off that cutie-pie detective of yours. Count on it."

"This isn't a *date*, Cory. Jesus. I'm in the middle of an investigation, remember?"

"Yeah, right," she said drily, pursing her lips. "So? Whoever said you can't kill two birds with one dress, right? Try these on for size," she added, tossing me a pair of black high-heeled sandals she had pulled out of a wardrobe drawer. I put them on and looked again. It was getting worse. I looked like a goddamn street-walker, that's what I looked like. A fact I was reluctant to share with my friend, under the circumstances.

"What about your hair?" she asked.

"What about it?"

"Come on, girl. You're not going to let it just hang there, are you? You look like Raggedy Ann. Get out of that dress and come over here," she said, yanking out her dressing-table chair. "I'm going to do you up right."

"Really, Cory. I—"

"Trust me. No one can do up a head of hair like old Cory can. Isn't that right, sugar?" she asked her daughter, who was watching the proceedings quietly from a corner of the room. "I'm always doing up the girls' hair at the Interlude. Fact is, I even did Diana's a couple of times, now that I think of it," she said, pulling the hair off my face. Then piling it on top of my head. "First, girl. We're going to wash this mop."

Later, as Cory was just beginning to devise an elaborate hair-do, the phone rang. Tammy scampered off to answer it. It was for Cory. She was gone for some time. When she returned to the room, she looked different. Scared.

"What is it?" I asked.

"She's dead!" she murmured, looking from her daughter back to me. "Diana's Mother. Mrs. Stevens. She's dead."

I reacted with as much shock as I could muster under the circumstances. Cory hustled her daughter out of the room and closed the door.

"Brandy just heard it over the radio," she added, settling on the edge of her bed.

"Brandy?"

"She—you know—works over at the Interlude. Mrs. Stevens was found shot. In her house! And some man was found dead on her front lawn! Something very weird is going on here, right? First Di. Then her mother? The police are looking for some 'Mystery Guest,'" she added, looking around the room, then back at me. "Guess someone was visiting Mrs. Stevens last night before—you know—before she was shot. You know something I don't know?" she added, eyeing me carefully as she shifted on the bed.

"Me? Cory, I'm as much in the dark about all this as anyone."

"That so? Sylvie thinks you're a cop."

"Do I *look* like a cop?"

She blinked, smiled vaguely. "No. But that don't mean much."

"I'm a reporter, Cory," I said, going into my purse for my card. "Looking for a story. That's all there is to it."

She read over my card. "So why didn't you just say so in the first place?" she asked, handing it back.

"Because some people don't like reporters. I had a feeling Blondie was one of those people."

"She don't like you, anyway," Cory said, smiling. "Doesn't matter what you are. So, what kinds of things do you investigate?"

"Anything. Everything."

"What are you investigating now?"

"I'm not sure. All I really know about this case is what Detective Ray has told me. Which is that Mrs. Stevens apparently had some very unusual friends," I said, going on to tell her about this Colombian cocaine dealer Stevens had been associating with.

"Well, it don't surprise me much," Cory said with a shrug, unplugging the hair dryer and tossing it onto the bed. "She really was something, Diana's Ma."

"You don't think Diana could have been mixed up with this Carlotti character in any way?" I asked.

"Di? No way. Like I said, that girl was as straight as they come."

Cory started working on my hair again, teasing it, swirling it on top of my head in such a way that I came out looking like a hybrid of Annette Funicello and Tammy Wynette. Your basic Barbie-Doll-Goes-Western look. Which is to say, about as subtle as the purple dress.

"Funny," Cory murmured, backing off, squinting at my profile in the mirror.

"What's that?"

"You kind of look like her."

"Like who?"

"Diana. No kidding. Same kind of—I don't know—bone structure. Yeah . . . Okay, so now for the makeup," she added, pulling out various tubes and pancakes from the dresser drawer.

"No makeup, Cory."

"Come on, girl! This is my speciality. One night, I turned Sylvie into Marilyn Monroe. Now if I can turn that old bag into Marilyn, just think what I can do with the likes of you."

That was precisely what I was afraid of. Over Cory's protests, I forewent the cosmetic make-over, heading back to the motel with the dress, the sandals, and a white fake-fur she had insisted I take along. Once in the room, I flipped on the TV. But the local newscasts had come and gone. I drew myself a hot bath, poured out a bit of Nystrom's vodka, and settled in for a half hour soak. It worked wonders, both on my state of mind and on the Funicello hairdo, taming the curls down to more human proportions. I dressed, helped myself to more of the vodka, and waited. 8 p.m. 8:15. 8:30. And an impatient rap at the door.

"I could use some of that," Nystrom said, looking neither left nor right as he headed straight for the vodka on the end table and poured himself a hefty glass. He took a swallow, then grabbed up the phone and placed a call.

"Kelly. Yeah, Mark here. Get me Sanders. Not bad, Calloway," he acknowledged in an aside, raising his glass. He actually *liked* the way I looked? "Sanders, it's not . . . yeah, that's it. So we'll drop it until . . . right. Got it." And he hung up.

"You've heard the news?" I asked, settling at the end of the bed. "The police are looking for Mrs. Stevens' so-called Mystery Guest. The visitor she had last night, before she was killed. That would be me, wouldn't it."

"Your secret's safe with me, kid," he said, peering through the blinds.

"But it does put me in a bit of an awkward situation, doesn't it?"

"No more awkward than mine," he suggested, a grim smile crossing his face as he turned back around, picked up his drink.

"But what I'm saying is—they have my name, remember? Which sooner or later they might decide to match up with their Mystery Guest. Which sooner or later might lead them to this motel. Which means, the sooner I check out of this place the better. Like tonight."

He took another sip of his drink, settled into the chair.

"I checked you out, Calloway."

"Oh . . .? And when was this?"

"This morning."

"I see. And checked yourself in?"

"That's right."

"You might have told me."

"I just did."

"Yeah . . . Thanks."

"What's wrong, Calloway? It's still your room, all right? The way you were talking last night, just thought we'd be better off with your name off the register."

"Yeah. Well, I can't argue with that one . . . Anything more you can tell me about this Carlotti fellow before we go crashing his party?"

He stared into his glass, then back to me. "The guy's swung some kind of a deal. Doesn't get indicted for his drug smuggling activities as long as he keeps up an arms smuggling network down to the contras. He supplies the aircraft and pilots to get the arms down there, and everybody looks the other way when he ships the coke back up. Everybody's happy."

"Are you saying the contras are involved in all this?"

"Hard to call."

The phone rang. Before I had taken a step, Nystrom had answered it, muttering a few words into the receiver and hanging up.

"All set?" he asked, downing the last of his vodka and scooping Cory's fur off the chair.

"But couldn't this guy Carlotti be connected to these assassins?"

"He could," Nystrom said, slipping the fur over my shoulders, his hands moving down my arms as I turned to face him. "But he isn't."

"You're quite sure about that?"

"Quite."

The drive out to Long Beach was a silent one. Small talk was impossible. As were the weightier topics. And so we sat there, adrift in our respective mind games, as the radio filled in the spaces with the past year's 'Greatest Hits,' none of which I could remember having heard before tonight.

Carlotti's home was more like a fortress, with an honest-to-God moat running around the property. Once we had crossed the draw-bridge, an armed chauffeur in green and gold uniform directed our way into a parking space, his white gloves glowing neon against the midnight sky. With a slight bow, he opened the passenger side door. I stepped out, then waited while Nystrom worked out a transaction of keys and tips with the man. To judge from the assortment of silver-blue BMW's and Mercedes already parked in the lot, this was going to be no ordinary party.

"This place gives me the creeps," I murmured, as we made our way past two savage-looking Dobermans chained up to posts on the front lawn. A second armed guard awaited us at the door.

"Mr. Nystrom and guest," Nystrom told the man. The doorman relayed the message through the intercom, then waited, eyeing us in impassive silence as we eyed him right back.

"Welcome, Mr. Nystrom," came the sultry response from the other side of the box. A buzzer rang and the door opened. The doorman ushered us in.

The place was rocking: a huge ballroom-full of gyrating humanity, set loose in a sea of loud music, swirling disco-lights, and heavy perfume. Nystrom grabbed my arm and we made our way along the edge of the crowd into another enormous room, outfitted with an equally enormous buffet. The variety of food offered here, like everything else in this place, was on the staggering side. Everything from caviars, patés, and oysters on the half shell, to chafing dishes full of sirloin tips and curried lamb. Assorted French pastries and cakes filled up a second smaller table. On a third table at the end of the room, sat a large gold bowl filled with white powder and surrounded by a neat circle of silver spoons. Another of these gold bowls rested on the bar.

"Champagne for the lady?" the bartender suggested, holding up a bottle of Dom Perignon. I opted for an iced vodka—I was actually getting used to the stuff—and Nystrom ordered the same.

"What do you think?" he asked out of the corner of his mouth, as we stood on the sidelines watching the passing parade. What I thought was that I had never even been close to this kind of money before. Nystrom, on the other hand, appeared to be perfectly at home.

"Hey, partner!" A plump, pleasant-looking red-cheeked gentleman in his early forties came up behind Nystrom, clapping him on the back. They shook hands, and we were introduced. 'Butch' gave me an openly appraising look which I returned in kind. He seemed to know exactly who I was. For my part, I assumed he was the 'Sanders' Nystrom had spoken to just an hour ago.

"You can take care of yourself for a while?" Nystrom said, his look taking in the entire setup.

"Of course." That said, I watched the two men disappear into a room behind the bar. Vodka in hand, I took myself on a tour of the premises. The first floor was mausoleum-like, one large cold room after another, with extravagant chandeliers dripping from the ceiling and gold-gilded dull landscape paintings decorating the walls. The Beautiful People were everywhere. Especially, it must be said, the beautiful women. I had never seen so many gorgeous-looking females under one roof at one time. In fact, it took something of an effort to find a woman who wasn't a looker in this crowd. Wine, women, and song, updated for the eighties into coke, beautiful young women, and raucous rock. Let me out of here, a voice squeaked inside my chest. I returned to the bar for another vodka on ice.

Feeling somewhat revived, I retraced my steps through the rooms, searching the crowd for familiar faces. Would I even recognize my Christmas morning assassins—either gunmen or cops—should I come upon them face to face? I wasn't at all sure that I would. Following a trail of people down a spiral staircase, I wound up where the living quarters appeared to be: a lovely sunken living room, a library, a small screening room, and a kitchen—and more food—beyond that. Just past a set of double doors the smells and atmosphere changed. There was a glassed-in swimming pool down here, a sauna, and a racquetball court, all of which were in full use.

I wandered into a room just off the sauna, lured in there by the sound of an old Beatles album piped in through the ceiling. It took a moment of adjusting to the dark to realize that the woman humping so energetically across the way was stark naked. I moved on. Into a rec room of sorts, fitted out with video games, pool and backgammon tables. A variety of African tribal masks decorated the walls. There was a second bar down here. And another of those golden bowls.

"You lost, darling?" asked a skinny gentleman with a droopy moustache, grinning down at me as his beer bottle rubbed up against my bare back. I informed him I was not lost and headed for the bar. But I never got there. The sight of my Swedish 'arms broker' huddled in cozy conversation in a near corner, stopped me in my tracks. I took a couple of steps back, settling against the wall to observe the scene. Was it the blonde he was talking to? No, it was the fat man. I watched as the fat man handed over an envelope, which Nystrom tucked into his coat.

A second young woman tripped up to the group, smiling brightly as she offered up her silver spoonful of cocaine. First to Nystrom. But he shook his head, smiling down at the woman and murmuring something which made all of them laugh.

I turned on my heel and headed back out of the room, suddenly in the need of some fresh air. The living room opened through sliding glass doors into a garden terrace and still another heated pool. I stood on the tiled patio, taking in swallows of the cool night air while ghostly swimmers rose and fell in the steam suspended over the water's edge.

"Extra suits in the cabana, if you're interested."

I turned to find a bear-like gentleman in black tie and tails bouncing on his heels beside me, his hands clasped behind his back. Even in the dim light of the terrace, the coco-burn shone brightly in his eyes.

"I'm allergic to chlorine," I said with a smile, digging a cigarette out of my bag.

"Yeah? Well now, that's a real shame. Me—I'm allergic to strawberries."

"You don't say?"

"Yep. Hell, any kind of berries will do the trick. Blueberries. Raspberries. Blackberries. Any kind of berries you can think of. Pop one of those babies down my throat and I start breaking out in little spots."

"You don't say?"

"The goddamn truth. Yep. Nice dress," he added, giving me thumbs-up approval.

"You think so?"

"Has a nice—what do you call it? Line?"

"Why, thank you."

"Yeah, well. I say it like it is. The name's Ronnie," he added, extending his hand. "Ronnie Wilkinson."

"Sarah."

"You ah—a good friend of Roberto's?" he asked.

"A friend of a friend. And you?"

"Same here," he said, bouncing on his heels and giving me quick, sidelong glances. "Allergic to chlorine, are you? That's—well, I never heard of that one before. My brother, now. He's got one of the screwiest allergies going. I mean, really off the wall, right?"

"Money?"

"Huh?"

"Is he allergic to money?"

"Ha! Ha! Nope. If there's one thing Calvin isn't allergic to, it's money. I'll tell you that right now."

"Sex?" I suggested.

"Sex?" he repeated, a leerish grin spreading across his face. "Nope. It isn't sex, neither. You're some funny lady, Sarah. You know that?"

"Yeah?"

"Yeah."

"Would you happen to have a light?" I asked.

"Jeez. Real dumb, right. You standing there waving a cigarette in my face, and me just—" he muttered, searching his pockets and bringing out a silver lighter which he flashed in my face. His name was engraved on its surface: R. W. Wilkinson . . . Ronnie Wilkinson . . . Ronald Wilkinson. Was my imagination working overtime? Or was that one of the names on Diana's list?

"So what *is* your brother allergic to?" I asked, exhaling smoke above our heads.

"Lead."

"Lead?"

"Yeah. The doctors figure he caught it by eating paint when he was a kid or something. You'd be surprised what a pain in the neck it gives the guy."

"A real problem for him?"

"Hell, yes. I mean, there's lead in everything, right? Glue. Paint. Gasoline. Walking into a freshly-painted room can practically kill the guy. So can—" He stopped talking, turned. So did I. A commotion had started up on the other side of the patio. On first impressions, it looked like two drunks were trying to drag a young lady into the pool. She was protesting, but whether as part of the game or for real was difficult to say. Until she got closer to the pool's edge, whereupon her pleas for help took on a distinctly desperate edge.

"Isn't anyone going to stop them?" I asked of Ronnie.

He shrugged, smiling sheepishly. "They're only having a little fun."

"*Who?* Let go of her!" I yelled futilely from our end of the patio.

Into the pool the woman went, bouffant hairdo, three-inch heels and all, resurfacing a moment later looking and sounding like a drowned puppy dog. No one, including myself, stepped forward to help the lady out. She whimpered her way up the ladder, then buried her face in her hands and rushed into the house.

"You—ah, live around here?" Ronnie asked, as if nothing had interrupted our conversation.

"Just visiting, actually."

"Yeah? So, where're you from?"

"San Francisco."

"No kidding?" He grinned. "Looneysville U.S.A.—right?"

"No more looney than right here. Where are you from, Ronnie?"

"Can't say I have a home to speak of. I'm what you'd call a traveling man."

"Is that so?"

"Yep. Course, I got my sailboat down in San Diego. But that don't exactly count for home, does it."

"Why not? You enjoy sailing, Ronnie?"

"You kidding? Does a bird fly?"

"Does a cow moo?"

"You got the picture," he said, grinning and socking a fist into his open palm. "Goldie's my first love, you might say. When nothing else is going for me, I always got her."

"Hey, Wilkie!" a man called out, standing at the glass doors. "Step on it, man!"

Ronnie waved off his friend and turned back to me. "Well look, Sarah," he said, jamming his fist. "It's been—you know—real nice talking with you. So ah, I guess until next time—right?"

"Right. Maybe you can take me sailing on that boat of yours, sometime?" I suggested, jabbing at his arm.

"No kidding? You like sailing, do you Sarah? Well, listen here," he said, looking over his shoulder and back to me. "You just give me some way of getting in touch and we'll call it a date."

"It's a little difficult reaching me these days," I said, nodding vaguely toward the house. "But if there's some way I can reach you . . .?"

"Sure thing," he said, bringing his wallet out of a back pocket and handing me one of his cards. Adventures Unlimited was written across the middle of the card in dark block letters. His name and telephone number was printed in one corner. "It's only an answering service, see?" he said, tapping the card. "But I check it real regular like, so it shouldn't be a problem. You just pick the day,

Sarah," he added, grinning at me as he back-pedaled toward the house, his hands stuffed in the pockets of his pants. With a last nod, he turned and headed through the door.

Ronald Wilkinson. San Diego. I was a good 80% sure that that name was on the list. Dropping the card into my bag, I dug out another cigarette, deciding on one last smoke before hunting down my Swedish friend. No sooner had I lit up, then I noticed one of the two asshole-drunks, the skinny one with the greasy hair, making his approach, a lopsided leer sliding off his face. Was I to be his next victim? Was that the plan?

"Excuse me," I mumbled, trying to dodge around the man and into the house.

"What's your hurry, baby?" he asked, grabbing hold of my wrist. The man looked like a Latin Sammy Davis Jr. Right down to the seven pounds of metal hanging off his scrawny neck.

"I don't want any trouble, okay?" I said, trying to wrench loose of his grip. His nails were longer than mine.

"Trouble? Who's talking trouble? Johnny don't want no trouble. I just want to be friends. See?" he said, his free hand slithering up my back.

"Get away from me," I hissed, twisting loose of his hold. He grabbed at me again.

"You heard the lady." It was Nystrom, appearing out of nowhere, his hands on the sleazeball's shoulders. The man did as he was told, letting go of me but now leering in Nystrom's direction. What happened over the next few seconds happened much too quickly to register in any detail. Sleazeball drew a knife, the knife went flying in one direction and he went flying in another, tumbling backwards over a patio chair and landing flat on his back on the flagstone cement.

"Let's get out of here," Nystrom said, grabbing my arm, and making me suddenly feel as if I'd been grabbed at just a little too often in my recent past. We didn't go back through the house, but around it this time, and out to the parking lot in front. The chauffeur must have been apprised of our imminent departure, since Nystrom's Dodge Dart was waiting for us when we got out there. The guard helped me into the car, the same impassive look on his face.

"Friendly people around here," I mumbled, slipping into the front seat. Nystrom motioned me silent and we rode back to the motel without exchanging another word.

"The car is bugged or what?" I asked, the minute we got through the door.

"I've been told it's within the realm of possibility," he said, pulling off his sport coat. It was obvious the shoulder was bothering him again.

"You mean to say this guy goes around wiring his guests' cars?"

He nodded, pouring himself some vodka and settling into the stuffed chair, his legs stretched out in front of him.

"Enjoy yourself tonight, Calloway?"

"Yeah, right. Next time you get invited to one of those little bashes, just leave me out. Okay?"

"I'll remember that . . . Any luck?"

"No familiar faces, if that's what you mean. Neither gunmen or cops. I never even got a glimpse of the host."

"What cops?" Nystrom asked, leaning forward in the chair. I hesitated, having momentarily forgotten just what I had told the man and what I had not. "*What* cops, Calloway?"

"Guess that's one part of the story I never got to, isn't it? That morning—the morning Diana was killed—and just minutes after she was gunned down—a police van popped around the corner, and these two San Rodino police officers got out and whisked the body away. There was no question of normal police procedure. All they were interested in was getting the body out of sight as fast as they possibly could. Which is why I never—"

"Why you never contacted the police," Nystrom finished off for me.

"That's right. And as long as we're on the subject—why is it that you seem to be avoiding the police?"

He settled back in the chair, taking a good look at the glass in his hand. "Let's just say that I'm here on very unofficial business, and leave it at that."

"Unofficial, meaning what?"

"Meaning that your Intelligence Service doesn't want me over here butting my nose into what they consider to be their affair."

"This assassin you're tracing? They consider him to be their affair?"

"Not exactly."

"Then *what*, exactly?"

He shook his head, smiled grimly.

"Tell me, Mr. Nystrom. How the hell can you expect me to cooperate with you, when you keep holding out on me like this?"

"You're a journalist, Calloway."

"So? What's the point?"

"My investigation concerns a very sensitive matter. My interest is in keeping things under wraps. Your instincts run counter to mine."

"Says who?"

"Don't give me that crap. If it's news, you'll print it. Just like anybody else."

"Give me a little credit, okay? I'm not after some short-lived scoop here. I'm after a story. I don't need to blow your cover for that. Besides, it's *not* only a story I'm after. I want to get to the bottom of that young woman's murder. Period."

He shook his head again, stretched, got to his feet.

"*Damn* you," I said, getting to my feet, as well. "The way I see it, I took considerable risk going to that party tonight. Putting my trust in you. How about returning the favor?" He turned, gave me a long look.

"Come over here," he said.

"What?"

"Just come over here." Reaching out, he drew me closer, one hand moving behind my neck as he bent over to kiss me. It felt very strange, this kiss. And very good.

"What was that all about?" I asked, when we finally broke off, unable to keep the smile off my face.

"Just testing the waters," he said, smiling back at me. Then turning sober again. "Sit down, Calloway," he added, pacing across the room. "I'm going to take your word for it, all right?" He paused, considering his words. "Let's say that it all started with a cache of arms found in a deserted apartment. A cache which we are presuming links up with our assassin."

"And this deserted apartment is here in California?"

"In Stockholm. Our Intelligence channels sent out the alarm. Some weeks later, your D. E. A. linked the cache up to a cluster of arms stolen out of Camp Pendleton. By a paramilitary clique out here calling themselves the California Rangers."

"I see," I murmured, as another piece or two fell into place. "So it was this tie-in with the California Rangers that has brought you out here?"

"Let's say it was a first step."

"And Diana Stevens' murder was the second step?"

He nodded, heading across the room, cracking his knuckles one by one. A habit I hadn't noticed before tonight.

"So a ballistics check done on the bullets that killed Diana linked her assassins and your assassins together? The fact that they all seem to be using weapons from this same cluster of stolen arms?"

"That's right."

"And both set of assassins are members of the California Rangers—right?"

"Wrong. According to our sources, the Rangers themselves rarely use the arms they steal. The question we're dealing with is: who did they turn around and sell the weapons *to?* Get our hands on a list of buyers and we have our hands on a list of suspects."

"People who might have bought the arms off the Rangers and then slipped them into Sweden?"

"More or less."

"And according to your sources, who are the Rangers' usual customers?"

"We're having a tougher time with that one. The contra network had a long-standing arrangement with the Rangers. A drugs-for-arms swap. But this particular cache was stolen in '82. Before the contra deal had gotten off the ground."

Nystrom stopped in front of the dresser, picked up the vodka bottle, then put it down again, grabbing up the ice bucket instead and heading out of the room. I sat there a moment, shuffling information. Then went into my suitcase for Diana's list. Before I could get my hands on it, Nystrom was back in the room. I brought out the peanut butter and crackers instead.

"You're eating?" he suggested, stating the obvious.

"I'm starved."

"After the spread they served back there?"

"Couldn't touch it. To be perfectly frank, there was something about that whole scene that turned my stomach. Disco lights should have been outlawed years ago."

"Not your bag, Calloway?" he suggested passing me an iced vodka.

"That's right. Not my bag."

He nodded, smiled vaguely as he settled on the other bed, a low moan escaping when he tried propping himself up against the wall.

"Shoulder bothering you again?"

"Damn right."

"What did you do today? Get it shot through with novocaine or what?"

"Close enough."

I put aside the peanut butter and shifted on the bed.

"Peter—why don't our Intelligence agencies want you over here?"

He shook his head, staring back in his glass. "Obviously, we stumbled onto a cover-up. Maybe the arsenals, which in themselves would be worth a cover-up. As far as I can figure it, security regulations are so out of whack in this country, anyone and their mother can walk into those military warehouses and walk right out again with a shitload of hardware, no questions asked. And we're not just talking rifles here, getting lost in the shuffle. We're talking hand grenades, anti-tank rockets, plastic explosives. You know anything about C-4? A chunk of that stuff no bigger than your fist can split open a six-room house. And those kooks are out there selling that garbage to anyone who will come up with the bucks. Think about it. If we can link our assassins back to arms stolen out of a U.S. arsenal, how many other terrorist investigations could do the same thing . . .? But then again," he added, tossing back some of his vodka, wiping his mouth with the back of his hand. "There might be something else in here we haven't tapped into yet."

I studied him studying his drink, considering the pros and cons of showing him Diana's list.

"What's on your mind, Calloway?"

"Hmmn? Just thinking, actually. About all those explosives and rot being passed on to anyone who can afford them. Kind of spooky. And obviously an angle I should be covering in my clinic-bombing story, right? Where in hell are all these terrorists getting their explosive devices in the first place?"

"Is that it?"

"Is that what?"

"That all that's on your mind?"

"What are you getting at?"

He shook his head and took another sip of his drink, then set the glass aside and got to his feet, heading into the bathroom.

"What do you say we start this conversation up again in the morning?" he suggested, upon returning to the room.

"Okay. Sure," I said, his suggestion taking me totally by surprise. I had my own turn in the bathroom and re-emerged, expecting to find Nystrom fast asleep. But he wasn't asleep. He was sitting up in bed, the blanket drawn to his waist, his clothes hanging over the dresser chair.

"Get your drink and come over here," he said, patting the mattress.

"What's up?" I asked, standing somewhere between his bed and mine, my hands stuffed into the pockets of my robe. The bandages on his wound were definitely of a different order than the ones I had slapped on him the night before.

"Have a seat," he said.

"I'm quite comfortable where I am, thank you."

"You still scared of me, Calloway?" he asked, smiling as his hand reached out and took my arm, moving up the sleeve of my robe.

"Not really," I said, flinching all the same.

"That's good to hear. Because as I see it, it's about time that you and I break the ice here. What do you say?"

"Just like that?"

"Just like that."

"And this—this breaking the ice, as you put it. Is this to give us some of that 'team spirit' you were talking about the other night?"

"Maybe," he said, smiling again. Looking almost playful and awfully damn sure of himself.

"And what about your shoulder?"

"Why don't you let me worry about that?"

"I have a question," I said, settling down on the edge of the bed.

"So, what else is new?"

"Is that your honest-to-God real name—Peter Nystrom? Or am I in for another surprise?"

His hands went behind his head as he leaned back against the bedboard, staring at the opposite wall, then back to me.

"I was afraid of that," I said, getting to my feet.

"Mikhail," he said, pulling me back down.

"*Mikhail?* As in Gorbachev . . .? How did you get a name like that?"

"Inherited it from a Russian grandfather."

" A Russian grandfather? And have you ever lived in Detroit? Or was that all bullshit, too?"

He crossed his heart, down and across. "Lived there till I was fifteen. My father worked for the Ford Motor Company up there."

"And what happened at fifteen?"

"My parents got a divorce. My mother and I moved back to Stockholm . . . There you have it, Calloway. My life story."

"Yeah, right. What did they think of a name like Mikhail back in Detroit?"

"They knew me as Mick."

"Mick?"

"How about you, Calloway? Who were you named after?"

"My German grandma."

"That's a nice name—Sarah."

"Think so? Then why not try using it once in awhile?"

"You would prefer this?" he said, smiling. "All right then, Sarah. Now what do you say about getting out of that robe of yours and joining me in here," he said, tugging gently at my belt.

I didn't move, one way or the other. Immobilized by an uncomfortable mix of heightened desire and emotional ambivalence. Stanley was still very much in my thoughts, in spite of his stubborn silence from the other side of the world. Nystrom didn't say a word, just continued tugging at the belt until my robe fell open. With one hand, he slipped it off my shoulders, letting it fall to my waist.

"You think we should stop right here?" he teased, his hands moving up my arms and over my shoulders, one finger tracing and retracing the curve of my lips and slipping into my mouth.

"You bastard," I murmured, all shyness and reservation temporarily out the window as I stretched out beside him, luxuriating at last in the feel of his body against mine. His hands were everywhere—no shyness there either—engulfing us in a white-hot undertow that was over much too quickly, much too fast. Love with the proper stranger. And that was definitely how the man still felt to me, inspite of the shared intimacy. A stranger in my bed. Or rather, I the stranger in his.

He reached across me to the end table for the proverbial cigarette, lit it, then fell back on the mattress. Oddly enough, his shoulder didn't seem to be bothering him at all.

"Asleep?" he asked.

"Nope."
"That's good."
As matters developed, we were to 'test the waters' two more times that night, I won't deny with a little encouragement from yours truly from time to time. Each occasion was slower, sweeter, and more venturesome than the one that came before it.

The next time I looked at my watch—his, actually—it was 4:30 a.m. In slight, wary movements, I shifted his weight and slipped from under him, settling onto the other bed for a moment or two, until I was persuaded the man was still asleep, then stepped quietly around the bed and up to the chair where he had hung his clothes. I found what I was looking for in the inner pocket of his sport coat—the envelope which the 'Fat Man' had passed to Nystrom earlier tonight.

I headed into the bathroom and had a look. What I found inside was a one page FBI printout on a man named Virgilio Corvo Suarez. WANTED BY FBI topped the page. And under that, three pictures of the man. The first taken in 1976. The second in 1977. And the third a 'touch-up,' to give an idea what the man would look like with neither moustache nor beard. Under the set of pictures was a set of ten fingerprints and a written description of the man:

Aliases: Alejandro Bontempi, Virgil Paz, Jose Suarez, Janvier Suarez, 'Romeo'

HEIGHT:	5′7″ to 5′9″	EYES:	brown
WEIGHT:	150 to 185	COMPLEXION:	light
BUILD:	medium	RACE:	white
HAIR:	brown	NATIONALITY:	Cuban

OCCUPATIONS: clerk, truck driver, used car salesman
REMARKS: may be wearing beard and/or moustache or be clean-shaven
SOCIAL SECURITY NUMBERS USED: 142-82-9611; 053-43-5472

Cuban?

I studied the pictures again, convinced this was the man we had left for dead on Maude Stevens' front lawn. I read on:

CAUTION:

Virgilio Corvo Suarez and Jose Esquivel Espinoza, identification order no. 3522, members of a terrorist group reportedly responsible for several acts of violence in which deaths and injury have occurred. Are known to have been armed in the past and are being sought in connection with the bombing deaths of a former Chilean ambassador and female business colleague. Considered both armed and dangerous.

A federal warrant was issued April 16, 1978, at Newark, New Jersey charging Suarez with unlawful making of destructive devices, unlawful storage of explosives and conspiracy (Title 26, U.S. Code Sections 5231 (f) and Title 18, U.S. Code Section 371 and 842.) A Federal warrant was also issued on May 6, 1978, at Washington, D.C., charging Suarez with conspiracy to murder a foreign official. (Title 18, U.S. Code, Section 1117.)

IF YOU HAVE INFORMATION CONCERNING THIS PERSON, PLEASE CONTACT YOUR LOCAL FBI OFFICE. TELEPHONE NUMBERS AND ADDRESSES OF ALL FBI OFFICES LISTED ON BACK.

I slipped the paper back into the envelope and the envelope back into his jacket. Then I dug out the peanut butter again, settling on the other bed for a post-midnight snack while I tried reprocessing the bits and pieces of information now at my disposal. A circular diagram began taking form in my mind's eye:

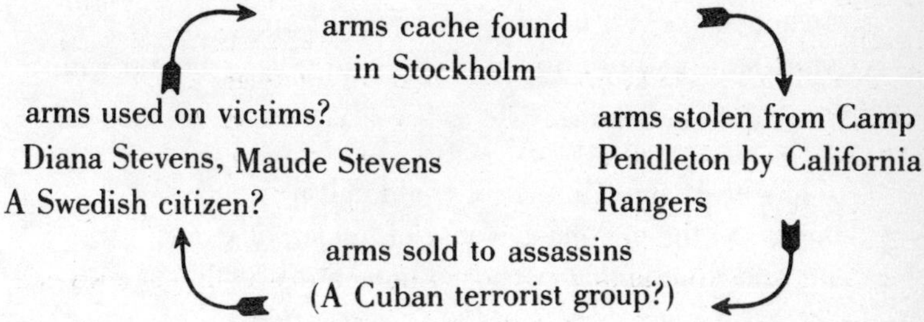

But where did Diana's list fit into the picture? Reverend McNally's presence ruled out the possibility of the thirteen men being members of the California Rangers. It also ruled out the possibility of their being affiliated with the Cuban terrorist group alluded to on the FBI flyer. But then again, Dr. Lopez *was* Cuban. As was Dr. Brago. Or rather, they *had been* Cuban. Now they both lived and worked in the United States. Another possibility came to mind. That these thirteen men were intended victims of the supposed assassins? But if the assassins did in fact come from Cuba, why the hell would Cuba be interested in killing off a man like Reverend McNally? The guy believed in revolution. Seemed to have dedicated his life to it. You'd think he'd be right up their alley.

I went into my suitcase for the bottle of Johnson's Baby Powder and headed back into the bathroom . . . Ronnie was here, all right. Ronald Wilkinson—San Diego. The twelfth person on the list. If I played my cards right, I had my hands on a legitimate and cooperative source, I told myself, dropping the bottle into the suitcase and settling back on the bed. I helped myself to more crackers, more peanut butter, while working over a feasible approach to take with the man tomorrow. It was going to be a tricky affair. At some point, Nystrom rolled over and propped himself up on one elbow, eyeing me through the semi-darkness.

"Did I wake you?" I asked.

"What the hell are you doing, Calloway?"

"We're back to Calloway, are we?"

"Sarah. Don't you ever get sick of that stuff?"

"Nope."

He reached over for his cigarettes and lit up.

"Could be a painting in that," he said, sizing me up with the match.

"Oh?"

"Nude with Peanut Butter, we could call it."

"Hmmn. So the man has a sense of humor, after all?"

". . . And what is that supposed to mean?"

"Nothing. Except that you are pretty damn serious most of the time."

"I happen to be involved in some pretty damn serious business."

"Yes, I know. So am I . . . Peter—since this cache of arms was found in Stockholm, I can assume that the assassination took place in Stockholm?"

He didn't answer me, which in itself was answer enough.

"Who in Stockholm was killed?"

He puffed on his cigarette, staring straight ahead. I popped another cracker in my mouth and waited.

"Sleep on it, Calloway," he finally said, snuffing out the cigarette and sliding down in the bed.

"Peter."

"Sleep-on-it."

Damn. I put the peanut butter aside again and crawled under the covers, as bits and pieces of a childhood poem started running through my head. How did that go? Something about a bat's cave? Getting deeper and darker . . .?

> Deeper and darker the bat's cave went—
> More deeper, more darker, than God ever meant . . .

January 1, 1988

When I opened my eyes next morning, Nystrom was already dressed and pacing the floor.

"What time is it?" I asked, blinking into the light. Too bright.

"Time for some talk, Calloway," he said, cracking his knuckles and pacing back across the room.

I checked my watch. It was 11 a.m. I felt like shit. My friend, on the other hand, looked remarkably bright-eyed. I ducked into a cold shower, dressed, and re-emerged to bum a cigarette from his pack on the dresser.

"Funny," I mused, settling down at the end of the bed.

"What's that?"

"Me. With your cigarettes. This guy I—well, that I was seeing the last year or so. He was always cadging my cigarettes, right? Now here I am, turning around and doing the same thing to you," I added, reminded of my conversation with Cardez. "You know, Peter," I added, getting back to my feet. "I'm going to need some coffee in me before we do any serious talking. And some food."

"Don't you ever stop thinking about food, Calloway?"

"What?"

"Come over here."

"Are you aware how often you say that? You enjoy giving orders, don't you?"

"I don't need your flack this early in the day. Just come here."

I compromised, making it halfway across the room.

"Sleep okay?" I asked, still marveling at how good the bastard looked.

"Best in months."

"I make a good sleeping pill. Is that what you're saying?"

"Hardly that," he said drily, tossing me some matches. "This tight-fisted friend of yours. Is he ah—still in the picture?"

"A very good question."

"Not that it matters, of course."

"Of course."

"We're bound to go our separate ways, you and I."

"Two ships passing in the night."

"Damn it, Calloway. What is it about you?" he said, pulling me closer. "At that blowout last night, there were any number of dames as good-looking as you are."

"Don't remind me."

"Any number," he repeated, his lips coming dangerously close to mine.

"You've made your point."

"So why do you look so much better than any of them?" he said, holding my face in his hands.

"Maybe you're stuck on me," I said, smiling up at him.

"Think so?"

"It's been known to happen."

"And you?" he said. "Where do you stand in all this?"

"I should think I've made that perfectly clear."

"How can I be sure you're not one of those American sharpies I've heard about who take advantage of any innocent hick who comes along?"

"Innocent hicks such as yourself, I assume?"

"That's right."

"Yeah, right. Let's eat."

Nystrom settled at a table in the motel's coffee shop. I went in search of a cigarette machine, came up empty-handed, and returned to the table. Nystrom's attention was buried somewhere in the middle pages of the newspaper. When he looked back up at me, there was a touch of murderous speculation in those eyes.

"What are you onto here, Calloway?" he asked, pushing the paper across the table. I expected to see screaming headlines on Mrs. Stevens. But what Nystrom was pointing out to me had nothing to do with Mrs. Stevens. But rather, Dr. Oscar Lopez.

Car-Passing Outrage—Pasadena Man Shot in the Head

> County sheriff's detectives were seeking clues yesterday in the highway shooting death of a Pasadena man off Highway 210. Authorities say the victim, identified as 42-year-old Dr. Oscar Lopez, was killed when six shots were fired from a passing car on the highway near Todd Road, just south of Pasadena, shortly before 6 p.m. Wednesday.

> Two of the shots struck Lopez. He was driving with his wife, Estella, 40, and their 13-year-old son, Francisco. The wife was unhurt, but the son suffered internal injuries in the crash that followed the shooting and underwent surgery at Memorial Hospital in Pasadena. He is listed in stable condition.
>
> Sheriff's investigators have discovered no motives for the shooting, which is the 45th incident of roadway violence in the state since June. The shots were believed to have been fired from a dark brown 1977 or 1978 Monte Carlo or Buick with an orange vinyl top.

"As I see it from here, you have a hell of a lot of explaining to do," Nystrom muttered, shoving back from the table and getting to his feet. Waiting for me to do the same. "And don't give me any more crap about the guy being Miss Stevens' eye doctor. I did enough of a background check on the man to know there's a hell of a lot more to him than that."

"Who is he?" I asked, once we were back inside the room.

"Stop playing dumb with me, Calloway!"

"Honest to God, Peter. I have no idea who the man really is. Was."

"Then why the *hell* were you paying the man a social call?"

I pulled my suitcase from under the bed, dug out the baby powder, and presented him with the list of names.

"You going to tell me what this is all about?" he asked, scanning down the paper.

"Diana mailed that list to her mother the morning she was killed. No message came with it. No explanation. Just that list of names."

"Mailed from where?"

"San Rodino. I saw her mail it. But she didn't send it in the form you see it in now. She sent it in code," I added, passing him one of my working copies. "That isn't the original, either. Mrs. Stevens took back the original. Maybe talked to someone about it. Showed it to someone. Maybe that's why she was killed . . ."

"Who the hell decoded this thing for you?"

"I did."

"You?"

"That's right. You find that so difficult to believe? All it really came down to was finding a pattern or two."

"This damn piece of paper goes a long way towards explaining your fixation on the entire case, doesn't it?"

"And the fact that I saw it happen. That poor woman's death."

"And just how much longer were you planning on keeping this from me?"

"If we had talked any longer last night, I probably would have brought it up right then and there. Because you see, at last night's party, I—"

"You are fucking incredible, you know that! I lay my ass on the line confiding in you. And what do I get in return? Nothing but your bloody questions. Do you know how many days, how much precious time was possibly lost because you couldn't see your way to a little square-dealing here?"

"Hey look, buddy. Mind taking my side for a minute? I mean, think about it. 'What's in a name?' people say. Well I, for one, am learning there's a hell of a lot in a name."

"What are you talking about?" he muttered angrily, getting to his feet.

"Your incessant name-games, that's what I'm talking about. When we first meet, you introduce yourself as Detective Mark Ray. And that is how I begin to see you—how I begin to *relate* to you, to use a favorite California expression—as Detective Ray. And then along comes Peter Nystrom. Okay—I can deal with that. So you're not really Mark Ray, American drug enforcement agent. You're a Swedish Intelligence agent named Nystrom, pretending to be an American agent named Ray. Or maybe—maybe you really *are* an American agent, pretending to be a Swedish agent pretending to be an American agent. Follow? But wait—that's not it, either. Now it turns out that you're a Swedish Intelligence agent pretending to be a Swedish arms broker. Unless of course, you really *are* a Swedish arms broker pretending to be a Swedish Intelligence agent pretending to be a Swedish arms broker. A possibility which must be considered. At any rate, when I finally begin to accept you as Peter Nystrom, see you as Peter Nystrom, *relate* to you as Peter Nystrom, along comes Mikhail. Mikhail? And people call you Mick? Under all these aliases is there anything but more aliases? Where is the real man? *Is* there a real man?" I added for good measure, sinking down on the bed.

"You finished, Calloway?"

"For now."

"Good," he said, grabbing my notebook off the dresser, settling at the desk and starting to scribble out another copy of the list.

"What are you going to do with that?" I asked.

"Punch a few of these names into a computer, for one."

"Whose computer?"

"Friends, Calloway."

"What friends . . .? *Peter.*"

He looked up, then back to the list. "Let's call them the disillusioned, and leave it at that. All right?"

"Disillusioned *what?* Look, Peter. You're the first person I've showed that list to. Even Mrs. Stevens didn't see it. Now I damn well have the right to know just who you intend on sharing it with."

He sat back in the chair, tapping the pen against his open palm. "Ever hear of DeWinkey?" he asked, the slightest of smiles on his face.

"De—what?"

"DeWinkey. Defectors from the White Male Killer Establishment. A couple of their members are helping us out."

"Come on, Peter. I'm serious."

"So am I."

"Defectors from the—? You're going to tell me some group like that actually exists?"

"Yep."

Nystrom started up his scribbling again while I paced about the room.

"What do you now about this Lopez guy, anyway?" I asked.

"Cuban."

"I know. A Cuban exile. What else?"

"Owned a gun shop down in Miami. Possibly a CIA proprietary. Fronted and run by his wife. The two of them were also FBI informants. Had their fingers in a lot of pies. Including the Cuban legion, a right-wing group down there busy collecting money for the contras. Early in '86 something soured. Lopez and his wife split for California."

"The contras again?"

"This explains your visits to Riverside, doesn't it?" Nystrom said, looking from me back to his scribbling.

"That's right."

"And what did you learn from this Reverend McNally?"

"Not too much. He's dead too."

Carefully, Nystrom set his pen down on the table and waited.

"Of a heart attack. Or so the story goes," I added, going on to give him a sketchy wrap-up of my conversation with Cardez.

"You'll have another talk with this priest?" Nystrom confirmed, ripping the page out of the notebook, tucking it into the pocket of his coat. "Find out the particulars around McNally's death. Be sure to ask about the autopsy," he added, getting to his feet.

"Mind telling me how Diana's boyfriend Cowboy fits into all this?"

"Howard Townley? We're still trying to get a handle on that."

"Townley? I thought his name was Kelsey?"

"I'm not the only one who can use aliases, Calloway," he said, picking up his cigarettes and moving toward the door.

"Have you talked to him yet?"

"He's holed up in Central America."

"In Panama City—right?"

"How the hell do you know that?"

"I visited the Kelseys—remember?"

"And they told you where he was?"

"Not exactly. Mrs. Kelsey showed me a postcard."

"Incredible," he murmured, yanking open the door. "I have to pull every Intelligence string in the book to locate the guy, and you get it off some postcard."

"Peter."

He turned, waited.

"What can you tell me about the man who killed Mrs. Stevens? The one we left for dead on her front lawn?"

"Don't have anything yet."

"You're *quite sure* about that?"

He gave me another of those long looks—I was getting used to them by now—then went into his jacket, bringing out the envelope and weighing it in his hand.

"What do I have to do, Calloway? Tie you up whenever I want some sleep?"

"You talk about me holding out on you?" I pointed out, shutting the door again. "It's getting goddamn tedious the way I have to pull information out of you! Weren't you the one talking about 'team spirit' the other night? So how about it. . . .? You lied to me, didn't you? You *do* know who bought up that cache of arms. You do know who your assassins are? This Cuban terrorist group, right? Right?" I repeated, waiting for some—any—confirmation on his part.

"The more you know, kid. The more dangerous it's going to be for you. For the both of us."

"As I see it, I'm a hell of a lot better off knowing just what I'm dealing with here. Wouldn't you agree? *What is going on?* Is there some kind of drug-arms ring reaching between Sweden and California? With Cuba in between?" I was far enough off track to bring a trace of a smile to his face. "Who got assassinated in Stockholm?" I asked, almost whispering by now. "A Cuban? An American? A drug dealer? A contra supporter? Who?"

Nystrom continued to stare at me as he carried on some inner dialogue with himself.

"The assassination I'm working on is Swedish Prime Minister Olaf Palme's."

"Palme? Swedish Prime Minister Olaf *Palme?* My God . . ."

"I can assume this is going no further than this room?"

"Of course. But why the secrecy, Peter? His assassination has been in all the papers. So has the investigation."

"Let's put it this way," he began, then paused.

"Yes?"

"Let's say it's not only your Intelligence service that opposes my investigation over here. So does my own."

". . . But why?"

"I'm not sure. Now why don't we get back to this tonight, Calloway. All right?"

"But why would some guys from Cuba be killing off Olaf Palme?" I asked, following him into the hall.

"They're not from Cuba. They're from Miami."

"Miami?"

"Members of the Cuban exile community."

"But why—"

"Later," he suggested, a finger lightly touching my lips, smiling vaguely again.

"Be careful," I murmured, as he headed down the stairs.

Why had I said that? I wondered, locking the door after him and settling down on the bed. Why, suddenly, did I sense the very real danger the man was putting himself in by following through on this investigation? Because he didn't seem to have the official sanction—and thus protection—of Swedish Intelligence? Because he was a lone wolf digging into messy, unexplored territory, whose death, and the end of his investigation, might serve the purpose of both our side and theirs?

But why on earth wouldn't Swedish Intelligence want him investigating the death of someone as important to Sweden as Prime Minister Palme? Unless, of course, Swedish Intelligence was somehow involved . . .?

I placed a call to St. Teresa's Church. Frannie answered. Father Cardez was not expected back from his rounds until after 5 p.m. Hanging up, I settled at the desk and sketched out an approximate replication of the blueprint I had conjured in my mind's eye the night before, feeding into it the information which Nystrom had given me today.

Arms cache found in Stockholm

Stolen out of Camp Pendleton by California Rangers

Sold to assassins: Cuban-American terrorist group

Used on victims
Olaf Palme
Diana Stevens
Maude Stevens
Dr. Lopez
Other names
on the coded list?

Digging out Ronnie Wilkinson's card—Adventures Unlimited—I gave the man a call. As expected, I got his answering service. I told the young woman I would be trying again, a little later in the day. My third and last call was to my editor at *Probe*.

"You're off the story, Sarah," Eddie said, the moment he came on the line. "As of yesterday afternoon."

"Listen, Eddie. Could you track down a Howard Townley for me in the dirty tricks file? Townley," I repeated, spelling out the name for him.

"Maybe you didn't hear me right, Sarah. You're off the story. You're on your own from here on out. Paying your own way."

"You're going to live to regret this, Eddie. I'm fucking onto something down here."

"Care to give me any of the details?"

"I tell you what I'm *going* to do, which is to send you along some of the relevant details in this morning's mail. I might be in a much safer position, knowing that someone else knows what I know. All right? Now how about tracking down this Howard Townley for me? Kelsey's an alias."

With exaggerated reluctance, Eddie agreed to help me out and get back with me later in the day. I passed the next hour memorizing the list of names, and the cities each was linked with. Then folded the list and the coded sheet into an envelope, along with the blowup of the one cop's face. And headed over to the post office, a couple of blocks from the motel.

Recrossing the parking lot after mailing the letter, I passed near enough to the ever-present Volvo to get a good look at the man sitting inside, a slender, elderly gentleman, who actually smiled at me as I checked him out. I found myself smiling right back. So this was one of Nystrom's watchdogs? One of his sources? One of the 'disillusioned' who was giving him a helping hand? The man seemed nice enough. *Too* nice, considering the amoral viciousness of the 'other side'.

No sooner had I stepped into the room, then the phone rang. It was Oliver.

"Danny wants to see you again," he blurted out, the moment I said hello.

"About what?"

"He didn't say. Just that I should set up a meeting at one o'clock."

"Oliver, there's no way I can make it back to that park by—"

"Not in the park this time. He wants to meet you at this bar."

"A bar? And you're going to take me to this bar?"

"Nah. He don't want me along. Just you. He's still sounding kind of funny-like. Know what I'm saying? I don't mean to discourage you or nothing. You got to see him. He's counting on it."

He proceeded to give me directions to a country tavern, just a mile or so east of the Agua Caliente Indian Reservation. I thanked him for his trouble and hung up, asking myself if this couldn't be some kind of trap. But if Danny, for some screwed-up reason of his own, wanted to do me harm, he would hardly be using his brother to run interference for him. Or have set up our point of rendezvous in some public bar. I tried Eddie again up in San Francisco. The line was busy. Gathering together all the loose papers about the room and stuffing them into my purse, I headed on my way.

The Lantern, as this bar was called, was situated kitty-corner to an Exxon gas station in the middle of nowhere. I headed up front and ordered a black coffee, then settled at a table in back. No sooner had I done so then Danny himself showed up at the door. There was something in his stance, in the way he hesitated in the halo of light around the door frame, that harkened back to a thousand and one old-time westerns of an age gone by. Here was the real Cowboy, I thought, as he stepped across the room.

Only he wasn't wearing a cowboy hat. He was wearing the same navy blue ski cap he had been wearing at our last meeting. The same red flannel shirt and heavy combat boots. And the same hostile stare.

"Who are you working for?" he asked curtly, standing over me, his hands tucked under his arms.

"No one. No one but myself."

"Horseshit."

"Why, Danny? Who would you be expecting me to be working for?"

His only answer was that cold, hostile stare.

"I'm a friend of Diana's, Danny. And it's as a friend of Diana's that I'm here today. In the hope that somehow you and I can do something about redressing the woman's death. Why don't you have a seat?" He refused to budge. "So what's on your mind, Danny? Why did you call me out here?"

"Come on, lady. Don't play dumb with me. It's not only Diana anymore. Now her Ma's been killed! What the fuck is going on!"

"This was in this morning's paper?"

"This morning's paper! Last night's news! You trying to tell me you didn't know she'd been killed?!"

"What I'm telling you is that I didn't have a chance to read any papers this morning. That's what I'm telling you. What did they say, Danny? About her death, I mean?"

"That she'd been shot in the back, that's what. And that some other poor sap had been found dead on her front lawn. No murder weapon or nothing. Even the paper was saying there's got to be some connection. I mean, hell. In the space of one week, first Diana, then her Ma! There's got to be a connection. And I'm not going to let you leave here, lady, until you tell me just what that connection is."

"Danny, you've got to believe me when I say that I know no more about all this than you do. What I *do* know is that Diana cared for you very much. That much I know. Which is why I came to you for help."

He blinked, looked away.

"Please sit down, Danny." At last, he sat. "Can I get you something? A beer?" He shook his head, pressing the palms of his hands into the table. I waited in silence, at a loss as to how to go about this thing. Diana had obviously meant more to him than even Oliver could have guessed.

"Maybe—maybe I could have saved her," he mumbled into his collar.

"What do you mean you could have saved her?"

"I got a message, see? In my letter drop. Just before Christmas. She said she couldn't make it up to the cabin, on account of her condition, and could I meet her in town? She was having these crazy thoughts, see? But I didn't get the message until too late. When I went down to meet her, she'd—she'd gone."

"She had asked you to meet her in San Rodino?"

"And if I'd gotten there. If I'd had the chance to speak with her—"

"Then chances are that you would have been killed as well, Danny. And that's the bare fact . . . What do you mean, she was having crazy thoughts?"

He shrugged, uneasy. "Like about putting the kid up for adoption. That Howie had turned bad on her and how as she didn't want him bringing up her kid. Things like that. Like I said, crazy thoughts."

"Did she say just how Cowboy was turning bad?"

He shook his head, taking in a deep breath and looking around the bar. "I couldn't make much sense out of it. But I've been thinking, and I don't guess she was serious about giving up the kid. I mean, I think she just needed some reassurance, see? Someone to tell her everything was going to be okay. Someone to—oh, damn to hell," he mumbled, shoving away from the table, staring down at the floor.

"Maybe Diana wasn't having such crazy thoughts, Danny. Maybe Howie *has* turned bad."

"How can you say something like that? You don't even know the guy."

"All right, Danny," I said, pushing aside my coffee cup. "If you want a connection between Diana and her mother's death, I'll give you one. I'm only telling you this because I think that Diana was going to tell you. In fact, this was probably the reason she needed your help."

"What are you talking about?"

"The morning Diana was killed, she mailed something off to her mother. It was a list, Danny. A list of names. Thirteen names. Nothing else came with it. No note, no explanation. Just that list of names. Now think about it. First Diana has her hands on this list, and she gets killed. Then her mother gets her hands on the list and *she* gets killed. And the only scenario that makes any sense is that Diana got that list from Cowboy. Where else could she have gotten it? She was down in Panama with Howie, wasn't she?"

"Who told you that?"

"Howie's folks. Are you aware, Danny, that a ballistics check done on the bullets that killed Diana was linked back to a cluster of arms, stolen *by* the California Rangers over five years ago? Now Howie must surely have *some* connection with those arms, isn't that right?" Danny's only answer was to stare harder, unspoken thoughts churning away behind that unflinching gaze. "Does Howie have a connection to the Cuban exile community?" I finally asked.

"How do you know all this?"

"I've been talking with people, that's all. People like you. So Howie *is* connected to the Miami Cubans?"

"Why you so interested?"

"I'm trying to get to the bottom of Diana's death. Isn't it as simple as that?"

"Nothing's simple. Not ever," he said, shoving back from the table and getting to his feet.

"Danny, why do you insist on protecting Howie like this?"

Danny glared down at me for what seemed like a very long time, tightening and untightening his fists. Then jabbed a finger in my face. "I'm protecting no one. Understand? And I've had about enough of you, lady. Me and Howie go back a long way. Howie has his ways, sure. But he'd never go so far as to kill off the mother of his own kid."

That said, he turned on his heel and marched toward the door, pausing a moment in the halo of light, his eyes on the floor, before letting the door drop shut again and heading back to the table, grinding up sawdust under his boots. "I'll tell you one thing, lady," he said, jabbing me with the finger again. "If I find out that Howie *is* mixed up in this shit, I'm going to personally exterminate the son-of-a-bitch." He made another about-face and headed out the door.

I shifted in my chair to find the barman eyeballing me from across the room. Then I got to my feet, and followed Danny out of the bar.

It was 1:25. Cardez wasn't due back for another three hours or more. Approaching the freeway, I made a last minute decision, swinging onto the ramp heading west rather than east. In little over an hour, I was in downtown Pasadena. Street signs just off the freeway directed me to the Memorial Hospital on the south side of town. I parked the car in a lot behind the hospital and made my way back around to the front, entering through the glass swinging door. The young nurse at the front desk informed me that Francisco Lopez was in room 528.

"But I'm afraid the boy is still in a coma. We aren't admitting any visitors save for his immediate family."

"Yes. Well, I'm not here to visit the boy. I'm here to visit his mother," I said, continuing down the hall before the woman could raise another objection. I stopped off at the hospital florist just opposite the elevators for a bouquet of irises. Then headed upstairs.

Two nurses were wheeling an empty bed out of Room 528. A woman—Mrs. Lopez, I assumed—was sitting in a straight-backed chair, her hands in her lap, her eyes fixed on the young man who was 'asleep' in the remaining bed, his head swathed in bandages and gauze. I stepped into the room and up to the bed without the woman taking the slightest notice. It was only after I had placed the flowers in a glass on the night table that she seemed to come out of her trance, looking at the flowers and then at me, an impassive indifference in her eyes.

"Might I speak to you a moment, Mrs. Lopez?"

She blinked, waited.

"I was so sorry to hear about—well, about everything," I said, gesturing vaguely at her son. "Might I speak with you in the hall?" I suggested again.

She got up and bent over her son, touching his forehead and murmuring something to him in Spanish. Then preceded me out of the room. In the hall, she went into her purse for her cigarettes and lit up, inhaling deeply, exhaling, looking down the hall. She was a woman in her early forties, of medium height, slender, her face smothered in layers of makeup which in no way succeeded in camouflaging the swollen eyes. Quite the contrary, in fact. After another deep drag on her cigarette, she tucked her purse under her arm and looked back at me, her gaze surprisingly direct.

"Who are you?" she asked.

"I'm a journalist. I work out of San Francisco," I added, flashing one of my cards. "At the moment, I'm doing a story on the contras. I know all about you and your husband's work for the cause. And now—now your husband winds up dead. Why? Was this a random act of violence, as the newspapers are saying? Or was it something more?"

"Why do you come to me about this?" she asked quietly, her eyes searching my face.

"Let's put it this way, Mrs. Lopez. If your husband was killed because of his involvement with the contras, he wouldn't have been the first. Nor will he be the last. Your husband—"

"My husband was an honest man."

"Yes?"

"A man not afraid to speak out. To tell what he saw with his own eyes."

"Yes?"

"Why do you come to me now? Are you from one of the committees?"

"I'm a journalist, Mrs. Lopez. As I just told you . . . And what was it that your husband saw with his own eyes?"

"Mostly, very young, very poor soldiers who had little more than rotten beans and rice to eat. And in place of real medicine, aspirin and rags. So where is all the money going? All the millions America's been throwing at the freedom fighters all these years? Where has it been going, if not into the camps? This was the question my husband was asking over and over. The question that no one wanted to hear. My husband disassociated himself from the contra cause over a year ago," she added, dropping her cigarette to the floor, crushing it under foot.

"You mentioned committees? What committee?" Her eyes darted from my face into the hospital room. "Was Dr. Lopez talking to one Congressional committee or another?"

"I tell my husband over and over again, to what purpose telling the truth? No one wishes to hear the truth these days. No one."

"Tell me, Mrs. Lopez. What do you know about an individual named Virgilio Corvo Suarez?"

She turned again, eyes flashing. "If you are so hungry for such dangerous information, I suggest you bring your questions to a man named Benny Conway. Unlike myself, Mr. Conway has nothing to lose by talking to a reporter. Perhaps even something to gain."

Benny Conway? The second person on Diana's list.

"In San Jose?" I said, ducking under the nurse's arm and following Mrs. Lopez into the room.

"In Santa Rita jail. Now, good *day,*" she added coldly, turning her back on me again and settling at her young son's side.

On the drive down to Riverside, I mulled over my conversation with Mrs. Lopez. In spite of the brevity of the interview, and the woman's apprehension, I had picked up a considerable amount of information. First off, and of primary importance, was the location of another name off the list: Benny Conway, apparently doing time at Santa Rita county jail. Then too, if Mrs. Lopez had known of Benny Conway, I must assume that her husband had been acquainted with the man, as well. Which implied at least a minimum mutuality, a crossover, some common link between the people on this list. The contras, perhaps? And thirdly was the possibility that Lopez had been scheduled to testify before a Congressional committee some time soon. Concerning what? And why hadn't I asked Mrs. Lopez that simple question? Because I knew she wouldn't have answered? But neither did she answer my question concerning Virgilio Corvo, the Cuban in Nystrom's FBI report. But in effect, she had answered the question. Obviously, she did know of the man. All too well.

My thoughts shifted back a week in time, to the visit I had paid her husband, Dr. Lopez. And to the fact that I might have saved the man's life, and the present agony of his wife and son, if only I had said something to him—given him some kind of warning—when I had had the chance.

I arrived at St. Teresa's Church at 5:20. Cardez was still out making his rounds. I decided to wait for his return. Ten minutes passed. Twenty. As the clock struck 5:45, the man came bursting through the front door, striding right past me without seeing me, and starting up the stairs.

"Father!" I cried out, jumping to my feet.

He turned, gazed down at me a moment in silence. Then made his way back down the stairs, an ironic smile on his face.

"So, you have returned?" he observed, picking a softball off the hall table and tossing it back and forth in his hands.

"Well, yes. Wasn't that the idea?"

“Was it?” he said, checking the hall. Then indicating with a nod that I follow him into his office. “All right, Sarah,” he said, closing the door after us and settling into the swivel chair behind the desk. “Why don’t you tell me exactly what you’re doing here?”

“What do you mean?”

“You’re not writing a story on immigration. You’re writing a story on abortion clinics. So why the ruse? I called your magazine,” he added. “They were kind enough to inform me of your assignment. So why the ruse?” he repeated, starting up his ball tossing again.

“It wasn’t a ruse, Enrique. I often do this kind of thing. Fit two projects into one expense account. I had finished one story, I saw no harm in starting another.”

He brushed off my explantion with a shake of his head, getting back to his feet and pacing across the room.

“Why are you having such trouble believing me? It’s the absolute truth,” I lied.

He turned his back on me, his arms stretched out along the mantel, for a minute or more. “I must admit to having been unsettled by your suggestion the other night,” he said, facing me again. “I myself have harbored such suspicions about Jim’s death.”

“Oh?”

“Yes. Circumstances, shall we say.”

“What kind of circumstances?”

“Circumstances,” he repeated, taking a look at his watch. “And now, I’m afraid I must prepare for the evening mass. If you wish to continue this conversation—and I trust that you do—I would suggest meeting up in the library at seven.”

He headed out of the room. I stewed in place, feeling roundly disgusted with myself, with the layers of deceit I had been using on everyone, from the Kelseys to Cardez, from Danny to DeSoto Cabs, in my efforts at getting closer to the truth. Bringing Ronnie’s card back out of my purse, I gave the man another call. This time around, the woman asked me to leave a number, assuring me that Ronnie would be getting back in touch at the soonest opportunity.

That taken care of, I took advantage of Sergeant Susan Welsh’s generous nature once again, prevailing on her, up in San Francisco, to give me whatever information she could dig up on one Benny Conway, doing time—according to Mrs. Lopez—in Santa Rita County jail.

"The guy's already out," Susan said, coming back on the line. "Got paroled the 2nd of December to Santa Clara County. Then to—hold on a minute, Sarah. Let me check this out." In the minutes she was gone, I could hear the mad tapping of computer keys. "The man's dead," she announced, coming back on.

"What?"

"Died of a cocaine overdose on the 14th of December. An accident, according to the report. Happened right outside his San Jose apartment . . . Sarah?"

"Yeah, I—*damn*. What can you tell me about him?"

"Strictly low-life, from the looks of it. Get this—had a flaming skull on his right bicep. 'Death before Dishonor' on his left. Some naked hula dancer eating grapes on his chest. Where do they come *up* with this tack?"

"It's his record, I'm interested in, Susan."

"Yeah. Let's see. There was a dishonorable discharge from the Air Force for alcohol abuse. That was in '76. Then in '78, a grand theft conviction for—will you get a load of this—ripping off his mother's engagement ring. Who *is* this guy? Then comes the drug-smuggling charge that got him into Santa Rita. He was booked down in Costa Rica in '85, then bonded up here. Put on trial right here in San Francisco. Given seven, with possible parole after—now, that's interesting. The guy wasn't even supposed to be considered for parole until March of this year. Must have pulled a few strings."

"I need to get a look at that trial transcript. I suppose they'd have it over at City Hall?"

"It was a criminal trial. The transcripts should be right here at Bryant."

"What do you say, Susan. Think you could take a look?"

"Just what is it I would be looking *for?*"

"I'm not sure. Names? Leads? The guy was assassinated. At least, that's my hunch. Take it from there."

Providing Susan could find the extra time this evening, she promised to give it a try.

I hung up and swiveled around in the chair, taking note of all the hand-drawn pictures decorating Cardez's office walls. Children's drawings, of flowers and animals and mountains and suns. Lots of suns. It was the big fat, red one over the desk that kept pulling back my attention. A blood-red sun with yellow flames bursting out of its rim. The longer I stared at it, the more sinister the drawing became. Until it didn't look like a sun any more, so much as an explosive. Maybe some of that C-4 Nystrom had been talking about last night. Or a time-bomb, ticking away somewhere, about to blow sky-high. I shook off the image and got to my feet, heading around to the back of the church.

Evening mass had just ended. A group of elderly women, many of them shrouded in black, were chatting in Spanish with Cardez at the top of the church steps. It was imposible to say who were enjoying themselves more, Cardez or his flock of admirers. One by one, the parishioners slowly took their leave. I waited them all out.

"Would you have time to hear a confession?" I asked, blocking Cardez's way down the steps. He stared at me, smoothing over an invisible moustache on his upper lip. "It won't take but a minute," I added, joining him on the top step.

"*Your* confession, we may assume?"

"That's right, yes."

He hesitated a moment longer. Then with a shake of his head, turned and ushered me up to one of the confessionals at the rear of the church. Crossing himself, he stepped into one side. I stepped into the other, took a seat, and waited as he mumbled some latin incantation into the grill.

"You may proceed."

"Yes. Well, you see Father," I began, then stopped, reconsidering exactly what I was going to say.

"Yes?"

"Well, you see, I *was* lying earlier today when I insisted I was doing a story on immigration. I'm not, of course. I came to St. Teresa's last week in order to speak with Father McNally. And my interest in speaking with the man stemmed from one thing, and one thing only. His name is on a list. In total, there are thirteen names on this list and his is one of them." I paused. Cardez remained silent. "This list was given to me by a woman who in turn had received it from her daughter. Through the mail. The very day her daughter sent off the list, she was gunned down in cold blood. One week later, the mother was gunned down, as well. Why? I have no idea. Nor do I understand the meaning behind the list of names. Except that at least two other people on the list have already died. So I come here today, in the hope that you can help me solve this puzzle . . . That is my confession," I finally added, shifting on the hard wooden seat.

"Why haven't you gone to the police with this story?" he asked, a jagged edge to his voice.

"Because—because there's a strong possibility that the police—at least the police out of San Rodino—might be involved."

More silence. Then Cardez stood up and stepped out of the booth. I followed suit, finding him leaning over a pew, his chin resting on his hands, his eyes following me up the aisle.

"You have this list with you?" he asked.

"I have the names. Assuming this stays between you and me."

"That was the point of the confessional, was it not?"

"More or less."

He nodded to himself, lifting the silk stole over his head and folding it. "Shall we go upstairs?"

Back in the library, Cardez stood by the hearth, pouring over the roll of names I had copied out from memory for him.

"Do you recognize any of those names?" I asked. He shook his head, his gaze still set on the paper.

"What more can you tell me about all this?" he asked.

"It's my assumption that a certain Howard Townley may have had original possession of the list. He's some kind of roving mercenary. A California Ranger. Ever hear of them?" He hadn't. "Whether Townley had any part in putting the list together, I have no idea. But it was his girlfriend who brought it up here. From Panama City, of all places. Apparently, they had been hanging out down there for a month or more. Doing what, I have no idea."

He nodded, put the list aside, walked over to the mantel, where he stood for some time, lost in thought.

"What exactly happened the night McNally died?" I finally asked.

He shrugged, looking distractedly about the room. "Frannie found him. But not until the following morning. According to the doctor who was called in, Jim had been dead several hours by then. Of myocardial infarction. A heart attack," he added, turning back in my direction.

"This was learned through the autopsy?"

"There was no autopsy."

"A man of his age dies of a heart attack, and no one considers an autopsy?"

"Sarah, Jim was forty-four years old. Heart attacks *do* happen to forty-four-year-old men. And you must understand, I was not at the church the night Jim died. Nor the following evening. Regrettable, but the case."

"Where were you?"

He seemed to find that a strange question to be asking. Which perhaps it was.

"Even priests have their days off," he muttered. "And I believe I need a drink," he added, heading out of the room. He returned with two glasses and a bottle of cognac.

"Enrique, did Father McNally have any contact with the Cuban exile community?"

"I suppose via the contras he might well have."

"He had contact with the contras?"

"Of course. His parishes were in Southern Honduras. In the very area where all the camps were being set up. In fact, he had been scheduled to testify for the Organization of American States next month about the contra presence down there. They're in the process of prosecuting the Honduran government for its escalating use of the death squads."

"And the death squads tie in with the contras?"

"Certainly, indirectly. Possibly directly, as well. The one brought on the other. The more bases and air strips the contras demanded, the more land had to be taken away from the campesinos, the more widespread the protests against the contra presence. Hence, the need for the death squads, to squelch the protests, out-of-hand. I don't think many people are aware how completely the American military machine has taken over that country. U.S.S. Honduras, they're calling it now. The place is swarming with military personnel. And not only contras. Thousands of American marines, mercenaries, Special Forces, CIA personnel. According to Jim, Tegucigalpa has become another Saigon, bars, brothels, and all. Yes, Frannie?" he added, turning to the woman, now standing at the open library door.

"Miss Calloway has a call on line one."

I took it across the hall.

"This damn transcript has been immunized," Susan informed me, hissing the word in my ear.

"What does that mean?"

"It means, it was a royal bitch getting my hands on it. That's what it means. So here's the setup. Your friend Conway was picked up by a couple of Costa Rican feds—this is back in '85—loading cocaine into his C-123. They confiscated the drugs and threw him in jail."

"This was down in Costa Rica?"

"Right. Now, a month goes by with nothing happening. The guy gets a little jumpy, figures he's being hung out to dry down there. So he starts talking to the local reporters, telling them his story. And his story is that he's been working for the CIA. That it was some CIA operator who had given Conway the assignment in the first place."

"What assignment?"

"To fly a shipment of arms out of El Toro Marine Corps Air Station down to a contra camp in Costa Rica. Then turn around and fly a shipment of dope up to some secret training camp in Southern Cal that goes unnamed. All under the auspices of the CIA. So he says. The longer he cools his heels in this Costa Rican jail, the more people he peddles his story to. Which does the trick. He gets bonded up to the States. And at his trial, uses the same CIA connection story for his defense. Only now, the elaborations set in. Now he's claiming that he got set up with this drug charge because he wouldn't go along with some crazy CIA plot to assassinate a U. S. Ambassador, blow up the American Embassy down there, and then blame the whole mess on the Sandinistas, providing us with an excuse to invade. The judge didn't buy his story. Neither would I. Too many gaps. Like the fact that he couldn't even identify this CIA operator who was supposed to have hired him on in the first place. Also it was kind of hard to swallow the idea of the CIA hiring on low-lifes like this guy, right?"

"I'm not so sure . . . Seems like some plot like that has already hit the papers."

"Well, I have a name for you. Carlos Morales. Under cross—"

"Wait a minute. Carlos *Morales?*" I repeated, spelling out the name. The thirteenth and last name on Diana's list.

"That's right. Under cross-examination, Conway kept insisting that if they would only subpoena this guy Morales, he would be able to corroborate his story. But since Morales happened to have been doing time in Soledad for his own set of drug charges, the judge wasn't too interested in hearing his corroboration."

"He's still there in Soledad?"

"Nope. Got paroled on the same day that Conway did. The 2nd of last month. Not so good, huh?" Not so good. I took down the L. A. address Susan gave me—Morales' official parole address—without holding out much hope of locating the man, alive or otherwise.

I rejoined Cardez in the library. "What if these people are all being killed off because of what they know? Not only because of what they know, but because of their willingness to talk about what they know. And even more specifically, their willingness to talk about what they know in connection with CIA/contra dirty tricks over the last couple of years? Benny Conway used to work in the contra supply network. Or so he said. After getting arrested, he started shooting off his mouth about the network's involvement in drugs. Drugs and assassinations. Now he's dead. Dr. Lopez was apparently scheduled to testify for some Senate committee. Now he's dead. Father McNally was about to testify in front of some O. A. S. committee about the contra connection to the death squads, and now *he's* dead."

Cardez shook his head, not buying my hypothesis.

"You've read his book," he said with a shrug.

"Actually, I haven't read his book."

"Well, he's ten times more indicting in that book then he would ever be at some O. A. S. symposium. You have to understand something about Jim. He's never been one to refrain from speaking out. All those years in Honduras—with the death squads breathing down his neck—he never hesitated in saying what he felt had to be said. If they didn't nab him down there, where it would have been a relatively simple matter—he certainly would not have been the first priest to be the victim of a Central American death squad—then why do it up here, with all the obvious risks involved?"

"But Enrique, you *do* accept the fact that this is a hit list? And it does stand to reason that some kind of death squad—Cuban or otherwise—is behind it? And we can't deny the uncanny coincidence that every man so far has had some involvement with—"

"Why are you insisting on this Cuban link?" Cardez interjected.

"Because we already know that at least one of the assassins *is* Cuban. Or rather, Cuban-American. Virgilio Corvo Suarez. A Cuban exile out of Miami."

"I see . . . Sarah, isn't it about time that you filled in some of the gaps for me?" he suggested, waving me back into the chair.

I settled down again and proceeded to give Cardez a blow-by-blow account of the last several days. Starting with Christmas morning, and moving on to the funeral, Mrs. Stevens, the coded sheet, and my successive visits to the massage parlor, DeSoto Cabs, the Kelsey farm, and Dr. Lopez.

"Then Mrs. Stevens was murdered two nights ago," I said, helping myself to more of the cognac and going on to give Cardez the barest account of that evening; one which introduced Mark Ray, Drug Enforcement agent, but passed over Peter Nystrom or any other suggestion of a Swedish link.

"The following day, Detective Ray tracked down Mrs. Stevens' assassin—through fingerprints left on the rifle, I assume—to a man named Virgilio Corvo. According to the FBI report I saw on Corvo, he and other members of this terrorist group—it goes unnamed—are responsible for several acts of violence. Assassinations are implied. Bombings. Sabotage . . . Then this morning, there was that piece in the paper about Dr. Lopez. And this afternoon, the news about Benny Conway's death. Boom, boom. One right on top of the other. God knows how many others among them are already dead . . . The question is, how does a man like McNally fit into this strange cast of characters? And if the contras aren't the connecting link, then what is?" I added, turning as Frannie once again poked her head through the library door.

"What is it, Frannie?" Cardez asked, sounding unusually brusque with the woman this time around.

I had another phone call. This time it was Ronnie Wilkinson. But he wasn't calling from San Diego, as I might have expected. He was calling from Ontario, a suburb east of L. A. We settled on dinner that night at a steak house located approximatedly midway between his neighborhood and mine.

When I returned to the library, Cardez was no longer alone. A young couple had joined him there, the woman holding a tiny infant in her arms.

"I have to be heading out," I said, grabbing up my purse and looking from the couple back to Cardez. Since he made no move to introduce us, I nodded and headed out of the room.

“We need to talk further, Sarah,” Cardez suggested, accompanying me into the hall.

“Yes, of course. Enrique, have you thought to check out McNally's recent mail? Letters he might have received before his death?”

“All of Jim's correspondence has disappeared. Perhaps he disposed of the letters himself. Perhaps not.”

“I see . . . Well then, what about recent phone bills. Any unexplained calls, long distance or otherwise? Or have you already checked into that?”

No, he had not. But he planned to do so, at the first opportunity. We made arrangements to get back in touch on the following day.

“How're you doing?” Ronnie greeted me, clapping me on the shoulder the minute I stepped through the restaurant door.

“Pretty good. And yourself?”

“Couldn't be better. Some joint huh?” he said, guiding us through the crowd to a booth he had reserved in back. “This place is always jumping. Weekends, forget it. So—what'll it be?” he added, settling across the table from me and giving the waiter the high sign. “A little taste before dinner?”

I ordered a Manhattan on the rocks. Ronnie ordered a draft.

“You look different,” he said, squinting at me, cocking his head.

“My hair?”

“Yeah, right, It's not all—puffed.”

“And you, Ronnie, look exactly the same.”

“Yeah? Well, like my sister-in-law calls me. Mr. Predictable Joe.”

“Hmm. A lot to be said for predictability.”

“Think so?”

“Absolutely.”

We smiled at each other as the waiter served up our drinks.

“You spend a lot of time in Ontario?” I asked, when we were alone once again.

“My brother and his wife live out there. Gives me a place to go.

Sort of a substitute family, you might say. They got great kids," he added, flicking some foam off the top of his draft.

"Have any kids of your own?"

"Me? Nah. Hell, I never even been married."

"A bachelor? Seems like an awful waste of all that predictability, if you ask me."

"Yeah?" He settled back in the booth, grinning at me over his glass. "You're not what I'd call a shy lady, Sarah. Not that I'm complaining. Course, I don't pretend to know you or anything. After all, we only talked for five minutes or something, right. But all the same . . ."

"Do you know me enough to trust me?" I asked.

"Huh? What kind of a question is that? I wouldn't be here if—" He paused, giving me a sidelong glance. "Hey, wait a minute. What's the—"

"Listen, Ronnie," I said, reaching across the table, taking his arm. "I like you. Which is why I wanted to see you tonight. Because I think you might be in some kind of trouble. *Are* you in some kind of trouble?"

"What the hell are you talking about?"

I sat there a moment, staring at him. Aware that he really didn't know what I *was* talking about.

"I better begin with the beginning, Ronnie. When I met you the other night—"

"Last night," he corrected me.

"Right. Last night. I told you I was from San Francisco. But that's not exactly true. I'm from San Jose. Have you ever heard of a man named Benny Conway?" I asked.

He gave me another side-long glance, shifting in his seat.

"Maybe."

"You have? Did you know Benny?"

"What's the point, Sarah?"

"He was my brother, Ronnie."

"Jesus, I—I'm real sorry to hear that."

"So you know about his death? The overdose?"

"Heard something about it—yeah," he said, looking around the restaurant, shifting again.

"It was written up in the papers as an accident. But it was no accident, Ronnie. Benny was murdered. Plain and simple."

"You got proof or what?" Ronnie asked, shifting again.

"Proof enough. One afternoon he leaves the apartment to pick something up at the corner Safeway, and the next thing I know, I'm getting a call from the local police station telling me Benny is dead."

"But you never know, Sarah. I mean, you never know what might have happened between—maybe he was meeting somebody or something."

"That's not all, Ronnie. Just a few days before Benny died he received something in the mail. A list of names. Thirteen names. And his name was one of them. He figured somebody was trying to tell him something, right? 'Cause of all the talking he's been doing. You know about that, right? The talking he did at his trial? About the contra-drug connection. The assasination plots. All the rest. He did it to save his skin. Figured he was being made the fall guy for something that had been going on for years. So anyway, he gets this list and he figures somebody's trying to tell him something. Like—shut your mouth or you're a dead man. Two days later, Benny's dead."

"Yeah, well—that don't look so good. No doubt."

"And Ronnie? Your name. It was also on this list."

"What?" he said, jerking back from the table.

"Ronald Wilkinson, San Diego. When you first introduced yourself last night, I wasn't sure. But given time to think about it, I was convinced I'd remembered it right. Which is why I felt it was my responsibility to warn you. Since obviously you may well be in danger yourself."

"You got this list with you?" he asked hoarsely.

"I'm afraid I don't. But I had occasion to look at it any number of times. And Ronnie. Benny isn't the only person on that list who's been killed. A Cuban-American named Oscar Lopez was killed two nights ago. And a Reverend McNally some three weeks back. Do you know either of these two men?"

"What the shit are you telling me?" he said, grabbing up his jacket and glancing back around the room.

"I wanted to warn you, Ronnie."

"Well, thanks anyway, lady. But this kind of news I can—"

"Ronnie," I said, grabbing at his arm as he moved to his feet. "Don't you have any idea why you might be on such a list?"

"The hell I don't. Did your brother?"

"Like I said. He assumed that having informed on some of his fellow contra supporters—the ones dealing the drugs—might have had something to do with it."

"Yeah, well I've never done any informing. And I don't plan on starting now."

"Please, Ronnie," I murmured, following him back through the restaurant. "I need a few questions answered."

"Why?" he demanded, letting the door slam behind us and striding across the lot.

"They killed my brother! I want to get to the bottom of this. Surely you can understand that, can't you?"

"Yeah," he said, stopping at what I assumed was his car, a covered jeep. "But I don't see how that has anything to do with me."

"You're on the list. Benny was on the list. There's got to be some connection there. But *what* . . .? You've been working for the contras, right?"

He shrugged, looking about the lot. "I'm splitting, Sarah. This place is giving me the spooks. *You're* giving me the spooks."

"Ronnie," I said, my hand on his arm as he went to unlock the jeep door. "I'll show it to you, all right? I'll show you the list."

"You're really something—you know that?" he muttered, eyeing me with disgust as he leaned up against the roof of the car.

"I *don't* have it with me. But I—well, I memorized it. Let's get in the car," I suggested.

He eyed me a moment longer, shaking his head. Then unlocked

the door and gestured me in. I maneuvered myself over the gear shift into the passenger side and waited until he had also settled in and closed the door after him.

"A deal?" I suggested. "I show you the list. You tell me what you know about any of the people you're familiar with?"

"No deals, Sarah. You've been fucking with me from the beginning, haven't you?"

"I'm trying to help you, that's what I'm trying to do. Is it unreasonable to expect that you might be able to help me in return?"

"You show me this list, and we'll take it from there. All right?"

For the second time tonight, I took out my notebook and scribbled out all thirteen names, leaving out the cities this time around. I handed it over and waited, as he stared at it, silent.

"Well?"

"Are you leveling with me, Sarah?"

"What do you mean?"

"I *mean*—are you really who you say you are? Benny's sister? You're not like Benny. Not one bit like Benny"

"So what? What can I say?"

He stared at me, trying to read something in my face.

"What kind of tattoo did your brother have on his arm?"

"Which arm? He had a flaming skull on his left. 'Death Before Dishonor' on his right. There. Does that satisfy you?"

He continued to stare at me, wary and unresolved.

"So if you're Benny's sister, why are you coming to me with questions? He must have told you plenty. He must have told you everything. If he's talking in court, he sure as hell is talking at home. With his own sister, for God's sake."

"He didn't tell me much of anything. He wanted to protect me."

"Then the way I see it, I should be thinking the same way. You don't want to be messing with these guys, Sarah. They'll wipe you right out. Like that."

"Are you talking about the Cubans?"

He gave a start, then squinted sideways at me again.

"If he didn't tell you anything, how come you seem to know so much?"

"Ronnie, all I want to know is who these people *are*. Who *you* are. Why they are killing you all off. And that is what they're doing, Ronnie. One by one. Getting to every single one of you. *Why?* And is there anything I can do to stop it from going forward? *Anything?*"

"Nothing but to shut your trap and forget it all. Everything," he added, handing me back my notebook. "Because there's no way you're going to come out on top. You understand? Now if you don't mind, I'm going to be heading out. I appreciate you showing that to me. If I come out of this in one piece, I appreciate that too. Might as well be thanking you now. Don't suppose we're going to be seeing each other after this."

"You're going into hiding?"

"Got any other ideas?"

"Yes, I do, as a matter of fact. Talk to the press, Ronnie. Tell them what you know. Everything. Then they'll have no more reason *to* kill you."

"No thanks," he muttered, leaning across me and opening the passenger side door. "That's not my style."

"Maybe you're going to have to change your style, if you want to get out of this thing alive."

"Talking didn't help your brother any, did it?"

"But is it *just* drugs, we're talking about here? How about a plot to kill a U.S. Ambassador? Or are we talking about something even more serious than that?"

"Maybe we are, Sarah. And I think I better be heading along."

"If I contact you at your answering service, get any more information, will you consider answering my call?" I said, getting out of the car.

"No promises."

"Yeah . . . Well, good luck Ronnie. I'll be thinking of you."

"Yeah." He tried a smile that didn't quite come off. I shut the door. He started up his jeep, and headed out of the lot without even a backward glance.

I had been on the freeway some twenty minutes before I first noticed the squad car in my rear view mirror. I stayed in the right lane, going a good ten miles under the speed limit. The squad car hung back with me. I speeded up and pulled into the center lane. It followed suit. Traffic slowed to a snail's pace around the scene of a jackknifed truck. Then quickened again. With the black and white cruiser staying right where it was, one to two cars in my wake.

The first San Rodino exit came and went. So did the second. I drove on for another thirty miles or so, praying to God that the squad car would fade into the night. It didn't. My gas tank was creeping too close to empty for me to keep up this game much longer. I took the exit for a town called Allston. So did the cruiser. Once on the dark service road, the cops started flashing their red light. I pulled onto the shoulder and shoved the purse under the seat, for whatever good it would do me. I was all too aware of the notebook. And in the notebook, the list of names I had scribbled out for Ronnie, just minutes before.

Big trouble, I told myself, as the cruiser pulled onto the shoulder some ten yards behind me. Big, big trouble.

Both officers got out of their car. I could feel my right hand, cold and clammy on the gear shift as the two men made their way towards me, cool and casual-like, silhouetted in their headlights. One of them held back, apparently checking out the numbers on my license plate. The other one came around to my window, flipping open the logbook in his hand. As he did so, I eased the gear into first and stepped on the gas. For one horrible split-second, the wheels spun in place. Then the car lurched down the shoulder, swinging wildly on and off the highway as I shifted into second and then drive. Pushing the accelerator to the floor, I managed to straighten out the wheels and shoot down the highway, with the two cops scrambling back to their cruiser in my rearview mirror.

I found myself sweet-talking the speedometer, coaxing it. 60. 65. 70. The police siren ripped into action at my back. 75. 80. I jammed on the brakes, swerved onto Route 28, and drove on another mile or two before swerving onto a second, narrower road. I started coaxing again, egging the needle back up to 85, only vaguely aware of the scenery flashing by. The billboards, the shrubbery, distant lights of farmhouses or bars. And the sound of the siren thinning out behind me. Then no shrubbery, no billboards, no lights. And no siren . . . Could I have lost them already?

I sped on for another five miles, slowed to a crawl, and listened. Then I pulled off the road, turned off the motor, and listened some more. The only sound was the crickets. I started up the car and moved slowly down the road, trying to get my bearings as I kept a lookout for the squad car. Eventually, I pulled off the road and went into the glove compartment for one of my maps.

My suspicions were confirmed. By accident, or subconscious design, I had driven myself back to the Agua Caliente Indian Reservation, where I had met Danny earlier today. Backtracking a couple of miles and hanging a left brought me face to face with the Lantern Saloon. It was a familiar and not entirely unwelcome sight. I parked the car in back, well out of range of the road, and made a concerted effort to slow down my heart beat and gather my wits about me.

Where the hell had that police car come from? Did it have anything to do with Ronnie? Or was it possible that they had traced the name off my business card to my rented car? I stepped out of the car, locked the doors behind me, took in a few deep breaths, and headed into the bar.

It was almost as empty in here tonight as it had been earlier in the day. I stepped up to the phone booth in back and tried the number back at the motel. No answer.

I settled at one end of the bar and ordered myself a cold beer.

"You okay, lady?" the bartender asked, giving me a funny look as he slid the bottle my way.

"Yeah. Thanks," I mumbled, avoiding his gaze as I took a long swallow on the beer. Then literally fell off my stool when a hand touched my shoulder.

"Jeez, I thought it was you," Oliver said, staring down at me, a can of Dad's Root Beer in his hand. "You seen a ghost or something?"

"A ghost?" I murmured, getting back to my feet and catching another of the bartender's funny looks.

"That's what you look like. Like you've seen a ghost. Is something up?"

"What are you doing here, Oliver?"

"I was hoping to run into Danny. Is that why you're here, too? You set up a meeting with my brother? Is that it?"

"How could I be setting up meetings with Danny, without you to set them up for me?"

"I don't know. I suppose you could manage it. So if you're not meeting my brother, what are you doing here?"

"Guess I lost my way," I muttered, heading back to the phone, trying the motel room one more time. Still no answer.

"Listen, Oliver," I said, rejoining him at the bar. "Think you could give me a lift down to San Rodino?"

"San Rodino, California?"

"Of course, San Rodino, California. My car is giving me some trouble. What do you say?"

"Yeah, okay," he said with a shrug, getting to his feet.

In a matter of minutes, I was riding shotgun in Oliver's pickup, my five senses back in reasonable working order again. Which had something to do with the cold beer in the bar. And something to do with Oliver here beside me, the can of root beer still in his hand.

"What do you know about the California Rangers?" I asked, a few miles down the road.

"Nothing much."

"But your brother's a member?"

"Nah. Howie tried to get him interested, but it just wouldn't take. Know what I mean?"

"You said something about Danny and Howie being comrades-in-arms? They fought together in Vietnam?"

"Yep."

"What has Danny said about that? About Vietnam?"

"Not much. Why're you asking?"

"Just curious."

"Well, I'll tell you one thing he said. Which is that it took only two or three days over there before you realized you weren't saving no Vietnamese from no Communism. That all you was doing was staying alive. That's it. Bottom line. Staying alive . . . Course, he wasn't only in 'Nam, you know. They moved his whole squadron over to Laos sometime in there. Had them bombing the hell out of the Ho Chi Minh trail. You know—trying to stop the movement of arms from north to south."

"Howie was with him in Laos?"

"Sure. Howie was Danny's squad leader. A lot of guys in their unit never made it back. They did. Kind of forged a blood-tie between them, know what I mean?"

"So, tell me, Oliver. If Danny and Howie are such comrades-in-arms, why isn't Danny down in Panama with him right now?"

"Howie's in Panama?"

"That's what I've been told. I suspect your brother knows a lot more than he's been saying. So, why isn't he down there with him now?" I tried again.

Oliver shrugged, re-adjusted the rearview mirror. "Like I said, one war was enough for Danny. More than enough. Know what I'm saying? I mean, look at the guy. He can't even stand being around people any longer. A place gets too crowded and he wants out. It's like—he's afraid of what he might do or something.

"One night when he was real tanked, he started talking to me about traffic lights. How as he couldn't stand the sight of them anymore. Like they was driving him crazy or something. And we're talking plain old traffic lights," he added, shaking his head. "Red lights, yellow lights, green lights. But the way I figure it, he wasn't really talking about traffic lights at all. He was talking about—you know—just plain old living. Life. Which is why," he started, then paused, scratching at the back of his neck.

"Why what, Oliver?"

"I don't know. Just like—it was kind of a double tragedy, that lady getting shot up like that. 'Cause like I said, she was beginning to change him. Bring him around to the way he used to be. Know what I'm saying? Now, he's worse than ever. What's up, anyway," he asked, looking over at me again. "You a fugitive from justice or something?"

"What are you talking about?"

"Come on, lady. I'm not blind, you know. I seen you scrunch down in that seat at least twice now, every time a police car comes cruising by. You in some kind of trouble?"

"Rattled nerves, Oliver."

"Yeah?"

"Yeah."

We rode the rest of the way out to San Rodino in silence.

"What are you doing tomorrow, Oliver?" I asked, as we took the turn in front of the Parkside Motel. There were no lights on in the room. But the Volvo was still parked in one corner of the lot.

"Me? What I do every day."

"And what's that?"

"After my morning chores, nothing much."

"How would you feel about giving me a hand? I have some people to see. And like I said—no car."

"You want me to chauffeur you around? Is that it?"

"That's right. I'll pay you for your services, of course."

He scratched at the back of his neck, then looked over at me.

"Think you could tell me what this is all about?"

"I've already told you, haven't I?"

"You're a friend of Diana's, is what you said. But it seems to me there's gotta be more to it than that. Which is what my brother's been thinking too, 'case you're interested."

"Why don't we talk about this in the morning?" I suggested, getting out of the truck.

"Okay," he said with a shrug, jamming his baseball cap back on his head.

"Mind waiting here a minute, Oliver?" I added, nodding toward the room. "While I check things out? Like I said—rattled nerves."

He shrugged again, scratching at his neck. I headed up to the room, unlocking the door and flicking on the switch.

"Peter?"

No one. Leaving the door ajar, I searched the place, including under the bed, and found my suitcase just where I had left it this morning. Nystrom had been in here today. That much was obvious from the newly-purchased bottle of Stoly sitting on the dresser.

I stepped back out on the balcony, giving Oliver the high sign. He answered with a couple of beeps of his horn and headed out of the lot. After double-locking the room door, I moved into the bathroom, peeling out of clothes thick with the grime and grit of ten thousand car exhausts. There were a lot of conflicting emotions churning around in my chest. Concern for Ronnie's safety. Concern for my own safety. Concern for Nystrom's safety. Disappointment mixed in with a bit of anger that the bastard wasn't here as a means of tangible support. I sure as hell could use some at the moment.

He has his own investigation to work on, I reminded myself, stepping under a hot shower. The shower helped. So did the vodka and peanut butter back in the room. Somewhere into my second glass, the haze of doom and gloom began to lift. Bottom line, I had my hands on one hell of a story. Assuming that I found out just what that story *was*. I dug out my notebook for another look at my notes . . . When I had suggested a deeper skeleton in the closet behind the contra-drug scandal, hadn't Ronnie implied I was on track? Or out of sheer desperation, was I conjuring up from scratch? For the fact was, Ronnie hadn't told me much of anything tonight. In fact, *nobody* so far had told me much of anything. Neither Danny, nor Dr. Lopez, nor his wife. Nor Mrs. Stevens. Not even Cardez. Not a particularly impressive track record, when you thought of it. The truth of the matter was, I had gotten my most valuable information from Benny Conway, and he was already dead.

I poured myself a little more vodka and settled back against the pillows, allowing visceral pieces of the day to float across the screen. The sound of Danny's combat boots scraping up the barroom floor. The musty vestiges of Mrs. Lopez's perfume. The nigh-claustrophobic feel to that confessional booth. The look on Ronnie's face when I told him his name was on the list. The sound of that police siren ripping up the landscape behind me. The feel of Oliver's hand grazing my shoulder, back at that bar. My thoughts moved on to Nystrom. To last night . . .

The phone rang, jolting me back to the here and now.

"Where have you been, babe?" It was Eddie. And it felt damn good hearing his voice.

"If I told you, Eddie, you wouldn't believe it. Tell me you have good news."

"Good news and bad news. Sergeant Shaw from the San Rodino Police Force called us today at the *Probe* office. Asked about your whereabouts. Seems they're placing you as a possible key witness to some woman's murder down there. . . ? Anything to that, Sarah?"

"Did you tell him where I was?"

"Told him I have no idea where you are. That you're on assignment in L.A."

"Thanks, Eddie."

"I don't particularly enjoy lying to the police, Sarah. I want you to understand that. Now just what the hell is going on?"

"Wait a minute. Was that the good news or the bad?"

"The good news concerns your Howard Townley. The guy's tied right into the so-called Secret team that was behind the whole Iran-contra scandal. General Bracord. Philip Stackley. William Pines. Townley's been hanging onto their coattails from Day One. Back with Operation 40, the covert anti-Castro scheme cooked up by Vice–President Nixon and his pals in '59. Lo and behold, we find your man Townley was one of the Marine Corps officers retained to train the Cuban expatriates taking part in the operation. Down in some secret camp in the Everglades. Sabotage, economic terrorism, assassination. The usual bag of tricks."

"Against Cuba?"

"Right. An operation which continued unabated until '63, with the Kennedy assassination. At which point our team is shipped out to Laos, where they set up another of these anti-Communist 'neutralization' operations. Are credited with bumping off some 100,000 non-combatant Asians over the next couple of years. No small potatoes, these guys. From Laos, they move to Chile. From Chile back to Vietnam. From Vietnam on to Iran, still under the Shah. And then on to Nicaragua, setting up these neutralization programs every step of the way."

"And Townley's linked up to this Secret team right to the end?"

"Not quite. In '79, he does a disappearing act. Can't pick up anymore trace of the guy. But we might assume . . ."

"And Howard Kelsey?"

"Nothing on Kelsey . . . All right, Sarah. What's the word? What are you onto down there?"

"What I'm onto—what I literally stumbled across—is a hit list. One that is being carried out at this very moment. And the assassins behind this list, I'm beginning to think maybe they're some of these Cuban expatriates—the ones Townley helped train back in Day One, as you put it. As far as the question of who is behind the Cubans, I don't have an answer to that. Nor do I have a finger on just *why* these men are being picked off. Possibly their connection to the contra network—or to this Secret team you're talking about—possibly something else. I sent you the list itself, Eddie. It should be in tomorrow's mail."

Eddie proceeded to throw a barrage of questions at me, only some of which I could answer, then agreed to run all thirteen names through the computer tomorrow, on the off-chance of picking up a common link. A few more words were exchanged. It amounted to Eddie's usual line of advice—secure my sources and cover my ass—and we hung up.

I opened my notebook again, turning to my diagram and feeding Eddie's information into the evermore expanding, evermore demoniac circuitous maze. Could this so-called Secret team be the monstrosity lurking behind the Cuban-American terrorists? Had these same Cuban-Americans taken part in any of the other 'neutralization' programs set up around the world by this Secret team?

That single statistic Eddie had thrown at me was staggering to the extreme. 100,000 *non-combatants* killed off in Laos, in the span of a couple of years? Not to mention the havoc the team must have wreaked in Vietnam, Chile, Nicaragua, or Iran. And all for what? We went on to 'lose' Southeast Asia. To 'lose' Iran. To 'lose' Nicaragua. In fact, with the exception of Chile, wherever the Secret team had gone, we had 'lost.'

What did the lives of thirteen men mean in comparison to all of this? But of course, every life meant something. Think of Ronnie, I told myself, crawling under the covers. Or a man like Reverend McNally. Who could say there wasn't another McNally on the list?

I turned off the light. Then turned it on again, finding the darkness too much to take. It was one a.m. Too late to be making phone calls, but I made one anyway. To Laurie Schoenberg in San Francisco, the friend and neighbor who was watching over my apartment and feeding my cat. It was obvious from the first words out of her mouth that I hadn't dragged her out of bed. And two—that the San Rodino Police had yet to try pounding down my door.

"There's a pile of letters waiting for you, kiddo."

"What?"

"From Israel."

"*Stanley?*"

"Who else? Four or five of them came on the same day, if you can figure that one out. Maybe they're holding them back, over there. Censoring them. Who knows?"

"Would you mind reading me his latest one, Laurie? I could sure use a shot in the arm right now." She very willingly complied.

> 'Dear sweetheart,' he began,
>
> It's Christmas Eve in the old town and where the hell are you? The typewriter break down? Run out of ink? Keep this up much longer and nice old agreeable Stanley might start to get surly on you. And we know what happens then—

"What happens then?" Laurie interjected.
"Just read."

Whatever you're hearing about this mess back home, I guarantee it's worse. The place is literally and figuratively blowing apart. Painful to watch. Although I'm not sure just how much more 'watching' I'm going to be doing over here. Journalists have become persona non grata, and with a vengeance. We're being seen as 'the enemy' as much or even more than the Palestinians themselves. I had a bit of a hairy experience today, which I will relate to you at a later and safer distance. What truly amazes me about a certain faction in this country, is how their high moral ground perseveres. Through hell and damnation.

Speaking of high moral ground, I picked you up this little number at a backstreet shop in Cairo, last weekend. Wild place, Cairo. The man informed me it was a nightgown. I had intended on sending it to you for Christmas. But on second thought, decided to keep it on hand for Paris. (We *are* still meeting in Paris this spring?) It gives me something to chew on. The thought of you inside this—ah—nightgown. It becomes you, Sarah. Take my word on that.

About this one-way correspondence I seem to be carrying on. It's beginning to feel as if I were dropping these notes into a river of no return. Is she reading them? Is she even opening them? Has she thrown me over for some punk rocker she met at a Madonna concert? Seriously, Sarah—you'll have the decency of telling me what is going on?

I end this dispatch on the same melancholy note it was meant to begin on. After all, it is Christmas Eve.

Stanley

"Sarah?"
"Yeah?"
"Miss him?"
"What do you think?"

"Yeah. Heck, I think *I* even miss him. So why *haven't* you written him?"

"No address!"

After hanging up, I sat down at the desk and tried my hand at writing Stanley a letter. It wasn't easy. Stanley, and everything connected with Stanley, in fact everything connected with San Francisco, seemed like another lifetime ago. Back when the world was a far simpler, more predictable, and less violent place then it seemed today. I wound up with a note that said nothing and everything, stamped and addressed it, and dropped it into my purse. Then crawled into bed again, trying to think Paris. Paris in springtime. But it wasn't working. I kept hearing noises, kept having to get up and check things out, kept having to assure myself that the Volvo was in place, which it was. I kept reviewing, over and over, the different and more effective tacks I could have taken with Ronnie this evening, or with Danny, or Mrs. Lopez. And wondering what my chances were of finding this Carlos Morales—Benny Conway's alleged collaborator—alive. It was some time after three a.m. when I finally dropped off to sleep.

January 2, 1988

I woke up in the morning feeling inexplicably refreshed. Almost optimistic. A state of mind which was impossible to square with anything out there in the real world. So I didn't try. No sooner had I emerged from a quick, cold shower, than I heard Oliver's horn beeping for me outside the motel room door.

"Had breakfast yet?" I asked Oliver, climbing into his pickup.

"A bowl of my Ma's oatmeal," he said, giving the steering wheel a couple of karate chops. "If that counts for breakfast."

Apparently it didn't, to judge from the stack of blueberry pancakes and double order of Canadian bacon Oliver helped himself to at the beachside cafe. I nursed consecutive refills of strong black coffee while deflecting the young man's growing curiosity.

"How much has your brother told you about all this?" I finally asked.

"Danny? Nothing. Which is nothing unusual. He's never told me much of anything for as long as I can remember."

"Can I count on your discretion, Oliver?"

"My discretion? I can keep my mouth shut, if that's what you're asking."

"I don't believe Diana's murder was a random one."

"Huh?"

"I think she was purposefully killed. That someone wanted her out of the way. Why—or who—I can't say. Although I have a strong suspicion that Cowboy fits into this somewhere."

"You saying that Howie had something to do with the lady getting shot?

"Diana and Howie go to Panama together. Next thing we know, Diana's up here on her own and gets herself killed. There's got to be some kind of cause and effect working here, wouldn't you say?"

"Beats me . . . So what are you looking for in L.A.?"

"Probably a wild goose chase," I admitted, getting up to pay the bill.

I had hoped that we would miss rush hour traffic by lingering over breakfast. But no such luck. 10 a.m. and the freeway was still a stop-and-go affair. We arrived in East Los Angeles just before noon. For an outsider, it was a sprawling and uninviting part of town. The address Susan had given me corresponded with a somewhat makeshift bungalow at the end of Ramona street, a street narrow enough to be called an alley. Several trashed automobiles were sitting in the driveway and on the front lawn.

Oliver waited in the truck while I took a look around. A man was working on a car parked at the top of the driveway. At least, I was assuming it was a man, though all I could see of him was a pair of well-worn Adidas sticking from under the rear bumper.

"Mr. Morales?"

The man scooted from under the chassis of the car on a surfboard with wheels.

"Yes, Miss?" he said, getting to his feet, wiping his hands on the top of his overalls. "What I can do for you?"

"Mr. Carlos Morales?"

"No. Carlos he is my brother."

"I see. May I speak with him? Is he home?"

"Not home."

"Where could I find him?"

"*Por que?*"

"Why?"

"Why you want my brother?"

"It is very important. I want to help him, do you understand?"

"*No se,*" he said, suddenly turning monosyllabic on me.

"*Señor,* your brother's life is in danger. *Su vida es . . .* in danger. Do you understand?" He continued to shake his head, at one point glancing quickly over his shoulder, causing me to suspect his brother might be right there in the house. "It is most important that I speak with Carlos. *Today.* I come as a friend. *Una amiga. Es la verdad.*" My high school Spanish wasn't impressing the man any-more than my English. "This is *very* important," I repeated for the third time in a row, resorting to body language for lack of a better tack.

"*No se. No se,*" he insisted, backing up, holding his hands in the air.

"Please?"

He shook his head, turned, and headed into the house. *Damn.*

"Hungry?" I asked Oliver, climbing back in the truck.

"We just ate, didn't we?"

"*You* just ate. I'm famished."

Oliver cruised the neighborhood, finally settling on a very crowded taqueria, a mile or so from the Morales home. We headed inside and took our place at the end of a long line. This was solid latino territory, turning Oliver and me into fish out of water. I asked Oliver to order me a cheese enchilada and a beer while I made use of the public phone in back.

I placed a call to St. Teresa's Church.

"I think I've found something," Cardez said, the moment he came on the line. "A number with an Orange County area code. We received three collect calls from this number, two at the end of November, and a third—this is the clincher, Sarah—on the very night that Jim died. Frannie knows nothing about any such collect calls and neither do I. They could only have been taken by Jim."

"Were these long conversations?"

"Twenty minutes, one. A bit shorter, another. The call the night of his death, only a couple of minutes. I tried the number this morning, but it came up disconnected. Any chance this Drug Agent friend of yours might be able to help us in tracking the number down?"

"He might," I said, passing over the question of whether or not I would be able to track down my 'Drug Agent' friend. "Listen, Enrique. I need your help this afternoon. I've located another person on the list—a Carlos Morales. Only he wasn't willing to cooperate with me. Didn't even want to talk. I was thinking that—well the fact that you speak Spanish, and that you're a priest—I might have better luck gaining his trust if you come along."

After conferring with Frannie for a few minutes, Cardez agreed to help me out. We arranged to meet at the Morales address a few minutes before three p.m.

"I thought you weren't hungry?" I said, joining Oliver in a booth by the window. My enchilada had arrived. So had Oliver's super chicken burrito and bottle of grape pop.

"Yeah, well . . ."

"As long as we're here, right?" I said, grinning at him—this guy was beginning to grow on me—and taking a long sip of my beer. Setting the bottle down again, I glanced sideways at the three men in camouflage fatigues who had just settled into the booth kitty-corner to ours, exchanging neutral once-overs with the only other 'gringo' in the place, a hefty gentleman wearing mirror sunglasses and a Chicago Cubs baseball cap. I continued to study the man out of the side of my eye, while biting into my enchilada, finding something familiar there. But what? The moment came when the man twisted around to pick up a napkin from the floor, and that was when I spotted it: the deep-purple birthmark that oozed out of his collar and up around his right ear. The same crawly birthmark I had seen in that blowup of the cop's face, seven days ago.

"Oliver, what do you say we take this stuff 'to go'?" I suggested, my hands shaking visibly as I wrapped tin foil back around the plate, grabbed up the check, and jumped to my feet.

"Huh?"

I headed over to the cash register, paid, and walked straight out the door, giving Oliver little choice but to follow suit.

"What's the big hurry?" he said, slipping behind the wheel with his burrito in hand.

"No hurry," I said, tossing what was left of my enchilada into the trash can just outside the truck. "We're going to wait right here until those three men sitting next to us come back out again."

"The ones wearing veggies? What for?"

"We're going to follow them, all right? Think you can handle that?"

"Who are they?"

"That's what I hope to find out."

"You're one crazy lady, you know that?"

"Yeah?"

"Yeah."

We sat there for almost an hour, eyes glued to the restaurant door. Or rather, I sat there, while Oliver squirmed and fidgeted without letup, at my side. Flipping the radio on and off, wrestling with the steering wheel, developing an unnatural interest in the mesh of wiring sprouting from under the dashboard.

"Here they come, Oliver," I said, grabbing his shoulder as the three men strode out of the restaurant door and down the steps.

"Shit," Oliver muttered, whacking his head on the steering wheel as he reared back up.

"Get her started, for God's sake."

Without incident, we followed them out of East L.A.

"You're too close," I warned, jotting down their license plate number as we trailed them down the highway. Then suddenly, we were too far away. For a moment, I thought we had lost them. But they turned up again at the traffic light, waiting out the green to make a left turn. We followed them onto the freeway heading south.

They proceeded to dart in and out of traffic, going ten to fifteen miles over the speed limit. Oliver did a damn good job of keeping up with them.

The bobbing and weaving continued for another twenty miles. When signs for San Fernando Valley came up, they shifted over to the right lane and took the 'Boris' exit, passing through the town and turning west on Highway 78. Now we were in hill country, and things were getting tricky again. The road being deserted except for our two pickups, one trailing the other by some thirty yards.

The road began running abreast of a stockade-like fence, topped off by a line of barbed wire.

"Watch it," I murmured, as the truck's brake lights flashed on and off. They took a left turn, through a gate and past a couple of armed guards in military attire. The sign above the gate read CAMP WILLIAMS. And under that:

> Federal Government Property—No trespassing
> Order of the Defense Atomic Support Agency

"So what the heck was that all about?" Oliver asked, a mile or so further down the road.

"You know anything about that place?"

"Nope. Never been around these parts before."

"What do you say we swing back through Boris. See what we can pick up."

Back in Boris, we took a slow cruise down the main street.

"How about a haircut, Oliver?" I suggested, checking out a barbershop that sported one of those old-fashioned candy-striped posts in its front window.

"I don't need no haircut."

"Then how about a shave?"

Oliver parked the truck in front of the shop and we got out. Two elderly gentlemen were seated inside.

"Howdy," said the one wearing the white coat and thick spectacles. "What can I be doing for you folks?"

Oliver and I looked at one another.

"You wanted a haircut, didn't you honey?" I suggested, nudging Oliver in the ribs.

"Yeah—guess so," he said, scratching at his neck.

"*Guess so?* What kind of an answer is that, young man?" the barber demanded, raising his eyebrows at Oliver. "Either you do. Or you don't."

"Yeah—well, I guess I do."

"Well then, you just go on and take a seat right over there. And you, Ma'am. Just help yourself to any of the reading material that perks your interest. You folks passing through?" he asked, taking an electric razor to the back of Oliver's neck.

"Actually, we're thinking about building down here," I said. "A summer home."

"That so? Now that's a switch, isn't it Ben?" he said, turning to his friend. "Been no building around here for some time."

His friend 'Ben' turned and asked me a question.

"Excuse me?" I said. The man had no teeth, false or otherwise. I hadn't understood a word coming out of his mouth.

"He's asking where you're planning on building this home of yours," the barber spoke up.

"We inherited a little piece of land from Grandpa. About 30 miles west of here."

"That so?"

"But the fact is, we hadn't realized it was going to be so close to that military camp."

"You're talking about Camp Williams, are you?"

"That's right. Has it been there long, that camp?"

"Lord, yes. Near thirty years now. Gotten so the townfolk don't even think about it anymore. It's just there."

"Problem is—our property is no more than half a mile from the place. Is there some kind of underground testing going on?"

"There's testing, all right. Least, that's what they told us. That's about all they told us, isn't that right, Ben? But they promised the testing wouldn't have nothing to do with any bombs, atomic or otherwise. And nothing's transpired out there to make us think any differently."

Ben mumbled something, looking from the barber over to me.

"That's right. Nothing but them buses moving in and out. Plain old army buses. Only they always got the windows blacked out. You can't see in. And I suspect you can't see out, neither. But I reckon everybody's got a right to privacy. Even the Army."

Ben mumbled on again, more excitedly this time around. Something about an airport?

"Something happened at the airport?" I asked.

"Well now, that's a fact, isn't it?" the barber said, clipping around Oliver's ear. "Near forgot there ever was such an incident out there at Carnac. 'Course, that was near six, seven years ago. Ben don't forget a thing," he added, looking over at me. "Got the memory of an elephant."

"What incident is this?" I was finally obliged to ask.

"Well now, we heard it from Sheriff Bill Benson, who heard it from Lenny Johnston. But Lenny's no longer with us. Died of one of them asthma attacks a few years back. 'Course, there're some people saying he just plum died of a broken heart, isn't that right Ben? Due to the fact that his wife walked out on him, see? Took most of what savings they had in the bank and just walked out."

"And this incident you're referring to? The one at the airport?"

"Well now, Carnac isn't much of an airport, to speak of. Mostly used by a couple of them aviation schools they got out there. So one morning, Lenny—he used to run one of them schools I'm talking about—Lenny and a couple of his instructors were just moseying around, see? Enjoying their wake-up cup of coffee. When who should come along but this jeep-load of M.P.'s armed to the gills. And these M.P.'s start playing pretty rough with the boys, forcing them back into their hangar and locking the doors shut after them, see? And Lenny, he's thinking he's in the middle of a military coup, is what he's thinking, which is why he got Sheriff Benson on the line. But even though Lenny and the boys were locked inside the hangar, they could still see out the window, see? And what they seen is one of them blacked-out buses I been telling you about. They seen it roll right up to an airplane parked out there, and then they seen these 15 A-rabs get out of that bus and embark in that plane. Then the plane took off, just like that. So did everybody else, Army-wise I'm speaking. The place just cleared out. Leaving Lenny and the boys just standing around scratching their navels and asking themselves what in the name of Jupiter that had been all about. Which was when this Lieutenant Colonel stopped by the hangar and now it was *his* turn to play rough. He just lined them right up against the wall, with their hands up above their heads, and forced them to swear on the Bible that they wouldn't be telling nobody what they'd saw. They got bullied with everything from jail to trials for treason for just so much as peeping a word about it. And that's all there is to it. The local papers got wind of the incident a day or so later, tried to dig something up. But the Army wasn't talking. Soon enough they apologized to Lenny and the others for using their strong-arm tactics. But that's all they would say. Nothing about that busload of A-rabs. And nothing about why they was acting so doggone cloak-and-dagger about it. What's the big mystery about 15 A-rabs getting out of a bus? Not a totally normal event. But not a totally un-normal event neither. Am I right? How's that, young man?" he added, stepping back from his work for a little perspective.

I had been so intent on the barber's story, I hadn't taken note of his progress with Oliver. With his red hair clipped so short and oiled down the way it was, he looked something like a ten-year-old kid with a serious thyroid problem.

"Kind of on the short side, isn't it?" Oliver suggested, grimacing into the mirror.

"Well now, I suppose that depends on your frame of reference, don't it young man?"

"I think it looks just fine," I said, getting to my feet and going into my purse. "What do we owe you, sir?"

"Well now, seeing as you're going to be neighbors in the near future, I'm going to give you folks my special rate. Ten dollars and we'll call it even. How does that sound to you?"

"Just fine," I said, glancing over at Oliver, who was muttering under his breath as he headed out the door. "And I want to thank you for the information on Camp Williams. Though I must admit, I'm still not sure how I feel about moving next to a place like that."

We both turned as Ben started to speak.

"Excuse me?" I said, smiling from Ben back to the barber, when the man had finished what he had to say.

"Not a bad idea, Ben. Might be just the ticket to set this young lady's mind at rest. He's recommending that you go have a word with Nick Hershey. Been running Hershey's Bar & Grill for the last ten or so years now. Ever since his Pa passed away. The place is just a few miles east of here on Highway 78. A number of the fellas from the camp frequent the place. Kind of the local watering hole for those boys. We reckon if there's anybody that can tell you what it's like having Camp Williams for a neighbor, Nickie can. Just tell him that Henry and Ben sent you. But if you want my opinion, Miss," he added, following me to the door. "The only problem you might have with a summer home in these parts, aside from a bit of unusual traffic now and again, is the dust. Gets bone-dry around here, come June and July. 'Course, some people take to that kind of climate. Say its good for the soul."

"Yes, well, thank you again, Sir."

"My pleasure, Ma'am. My pleasure."

When I climbed back in the truck, Oliver was still muttering under his breath and boxing the dashboard.

"Oliver, you look just fine. Really, you do."

"I look like a drowned rat is what I look like. So don't go trying to tell me anything different. I got two eyes, don't I?" he added, slouching in the seat.

"For God's sake, Oliver. Put this on and who's to know the difference," I said, scooping his baseball cap out of the back and jamming it on his head. "Now what do you say we stop by this Bar

& Grill down the road and have ourselves a little liquid refreshment? The treat's on me."

This was definitely pickup country. There were at least five of them parked in front of Hershey's when we swung into the lot. The time was 1:25. We headed into the restaurant and settled at one end of the bar. I ordered a beer. Oliver ordered an orange pop.

"What is it?" I asked. Oliver looked a little green around the gills. Maybe it was the light.

"You're looking for Howie, right?" he said, scratching at his neck.

"That's right."

"Well, your looking days are over, lady. Howie's right over there."

"What?" I murmured, grabbing his arm, resisting a strong impulse to hit the deck.

"I'm saying that Howie's right over there with that bunch of fellas, playing pool."

I took a quick look.

"Has he seen you?"

"Nope."

"Then let's get the hell out of here," I said, slipping off the stool and walking straight back out the door.

"Thought you said he was in Panama," Oliver said, climbing back in the truck.

"Just get us out of here!" I hissed. "Then we'll talk."

"Thought you wanted to talk to *him*," Oliver said, a few miles down Highway 78.

"What do you expect me to do, Oliver? Walk right up to the man and ask him if he killed Diana? This is the kind of thing that's got to be worked out. Which one was he, anyway?"

"The one wearing sunglasses and a baseball cap."

"Oliver, they were *all* wearing sunglasses and baseball caps."

"White moustache. Floppy ears."

"You're absolutely sure it was Howie?"

"Sure I'm sure. Howie's got a way about him. Kind of a swagger. Like he's King of the Castle or something. Know what I'm saying? You can't miss him."

By the time we had arrived back in East L.A. I had worked out a feasible game plan for my next encounter with Howie. A bit on the outrageous side, my plan. But wasn't that precisely what an encounter with a man like Howie Kelsey AKA Howie Townley AKA Cowboy demanded?

As Oliver took the corner at Ramona street, I caught sight of the familiar yellow van I had seen parked in St. Teresa's driveway on my previous visits to the Church. Cardez had arrived.

"You want me to wait out here, or what?" Oliver asked.

"That would be fine. And keep an eye out, all right?" I added, climbing out of the truck. "See anything unusual, then let us know immediately."

"Hop in," Cardez suggested, when I greeted him at the window of his van.

I got in. Cardez was looking very 'priestly' this afternoon, white collar and all. Just as I had hoped.

"So what's the story with this guy?" he asked, nodding at the bungalow at the end of the street.

"All I know about him is what I told you over the phone. A Nicaraguan. A contra, I assume. Arrested a year and a half ago for drug trafficking in California. That's about it. It was his brother who I talked to this morning. To be honest, Enrique, I can't even be sure they'll be here, this afternoon."

We discussed what information we hoped to get out of Morales and a viable approach, then headed up to the house. The place felt deserted. I knocked on the door—there was no bell—and knocked again. To my relief, there were footsteps inside, and then the brother—the one whom I had spoken to earlier today—answered the door.

He stood there a moment, looking from me back to Cardez, then started to shut the door again.

"*Uno momento,*" Cardez said, his hand on the door. A rush of Spanish—explanations—came out of his mouth. And introductions—*Senorita Calloway, una periodista*—was one of the few things I picked up. The brother—his name was Manuel—listened, wary and silent. And at last, let us into the house. In the living room, which seemed to be doubling as the man's workshop, another round of introductions took place. After which Manuel led us into the kitchen, settling us down at the kitchen table as he quickly extinguished a lighted cigarette and swept both ashtray and cigarette into the sink.

"*Cerveza? Café?*

I suggested coffee. But when Cardez opted for beer, I changed my mind, asking for a beer as well.

Manuel set three bottles of Dos Equis on the table and joined us there. Immediately, Cardez directed a question to Manuel in Spanish, something to do with the neighborhood, I believe. And in no time at all, the two men were off and running, rapping away like old friends. I sat back, marveling at the rapport Cardez had managed to establish with the man. Night and day from my own experience, earlier in the afternoon. The common language obviously had something to do with it. And the fact that Cardez was a priest. But there was something else working there, as well. A certain talent. A certain charm. The same charm he had turned on me to such good effect, at our first meeting, three or four days ago.

Where was Carlos? I wanted to ask, but didn't. Leaving the pace of this particular interview completely in Cardez's hands.

We had been in the kitchen for over thirty minutes, into our second round of Dos Equis, when the door opened across the hall. A young man stepped out of the bedroom, closing the door after him and crossing into the kitchen. Had he been waiting in there, all this time? The man nodded at Cardez and myself, and again, the introductions took place. Carlos had the same slight build as his brother. But it was his eyes that set him apart. Large and liquidy. Like Omar Sharif, I thought, getting to my feet.

Manuel offered his brother his chair, then stepped behind us, settling on a wooden crate by the kitchen door. Cardez and I took our seats again. Carlos remained standing, saying something to Cardez in a rapid-fire Spanish and nodding at me.

"Senor Morales wishes to see some identification, Sarah. He also wants you to tell him exactly why you have come here today."

I brought out all the identification I had on me, which wasn't much. My driver's license, a Visa bank card, my business card, and spread them before him, laying all my cards on the table as it were.

"I come here as a reporter," I said, talking directly to Morales as he looked from me back to my ID's. "But as I explained to your brother, I also come as a friend. In the hope that we can help each other out."

I had the distinct impression he had understood every word I had said. But he turned to Cardez for a translation, all the same.

"*Como puede usted ayudarme?*" he demanded skeptically, turning back to me.

"You know a man named Benny Conway?" Cardez asked in Spanish.

Morales glanced from Cardez to me, settling into the chair and leaning back on the rear legs, studying us.

"*Es posible.*"

"You're aware of the testimony he gave at his trial? His defense?" Cardez asked, translating for me as he went along.

"*Es posible.*"

"That he had been set up by the CIA because of his unwillingness to go along with some contra/CIA plot to kill the American Ambassador? An assassination they had planned to blame on the Sandinistas as a pretext for invading Nicaragua?"

"This is not new," Morales said with a shrug. "Your country looks for an excuse under every rock for such an invasion, yes? And sooner or later, they will find this excuse. I guarantee this. For it is a veritable passion with these people. This shameless desire to enter Nicaragua. To violate her. To deflower her, until there are no flowers left but the flowers that cover our graves."

"A poet among us?" Cardez suggested a bit sarcastically, upon translating Morales' last few words. "But as a contra yourself," Cardez added, turning back to Morales, reverting to Spanish once again. "You also invaded Nicaragua. Isn't this true?"

"It is true that I was a contra, yes. But people can change. Can begin to question. To ask why. I tell you, this is the reason why men such as Benny Conway and myself, why we have been set up. Why we have been convicted of these crimes, these crimes that everybody is guilty of. The CIA detests independence. It wants only lackies. Only yes-men. To ask questions, that is to become dangerous in their eyes. And so, they strip us of our danger by throwing us into prison, ruining our reputations, our credibility. Who is there to believe us now?"

"If a jail term ruins your credibility, renders you powerless, strips you of your danger, as you have just implied—then why are all these people being killed?" Cardez asked.

Morales looked from me back to Cardez.

"I do not understand."

"You're not aware that Mr. Conway died of a cocaine overdose three weeks back?"

"What?" Morales' chair dropped back to the floor.

"And there are more," Cardez added, holding his hand out for my notebook.

I opened it to the list of names I had scribbled out for Ronnie Wilkinson the night before, and set it down on the table. Morales sat there, very still, eyeing the pageful of names as beads of sweat formed on his forehead. Briefly, in a matter of a few sentences, Cardez explained how I had gotten my hands on the list. Howard Kelsey AKA Townley came into the explanation. As did the two Stevens women and the names of the other two men who had already been killed.

"*Mano Blanca,*" Morales finally murmured, rising to his feet and pacing across the room, pulling his hands through his hair. Suddenly, he turned and pointed an accusatory finger at us, fuming on in Spanish. More than once, Cardez tried to intervene, but Morales wasn't listening.

"*Mano Blanca?* The White Hand? Latin American death squads?" I confirmed. "That's what's behind all of this?" I asked Cardez.

"According to *Señor* Morales," Cardez murmured, as Manuel exchanged a few words with his brother, making an effort to calm him down. "These Cubans out of Miami—the veterans of the Bay of Pigs invasion—*are* the Latin American death squads. Or at least, make up the core of these squads. Apparently some of the military strongmen down there got together and hired them on to do their dirty work. Formed them into a roving band of hired guns. When they're not working for the CIA, they're working for the Latin Colonels. And hit lists are their area of expertise."

I started to ask another question, but Cardez stopped me, his eyes and his attention focused back on Morales, and his voice maintaining that same fluid, soothing ebb. On and on, the two of them talked, often simultaneously, the one nervous and intense, the other measured and low-key. The moment finally came when Morales retook his seat and the conversation continued at a lower decibel.

"Well, Sarah," Cardez said at last, turning back to me. "It looks like we've found our leitmotif."

"Our what?"

"With the exception of Jim and Dr. Juarez, every man listed here has apparently taken part in some dirty tricks unit set up by some of these White Hand Cubans as an adjunct to the contra network. The Enterprise, they called it. Used the unit as a funding arm of the contra network. According to *Señor* Morales, the unit moved between Central America, Miami, and California, smuggling drugs into the country, smuggling arms out, and cooking up any number of assassination plots, the majority of which never panned out. Or so he says." Cardez turned back to Morales. "Were there other men in this unit aside from the ones listed here?" he asked.

"Many more. At times, nearly fifty different men in the group at one time."

"And who made up the membership? Mainly Nicaraguan contras such as yourself?"

Morales shrugged. "Contras. Cuban-American lackies. American drug smugglers. Paramilitary 'volunteers.' The CIA's usual pack of liars and thieves."

"And it was Cuban-Americans out of *Mano Blanca* who led this unit?" Cardez confirmed.

"That is correct. You must understand something about these men. They are what I would call very hard-core. I never see a sign of a conscience with these people. Never. Never a sense of what is right and what is wrong. Never a sense that there is even a difference between one and the other."

"But out of the fifty or so men who made up this—this Enterprise," I interjected, after Cardez had translated Morales' last few words. "Ask him why these particular thirteen are being weeded out? More to the point, why would these Cubans out of *Mano Blanca* be killing off some of the very men who have been working for them all these years?"

Morales didn't appear to have an answer to that one.

"These men are not perhaps the loose tongues you spoke of earlier?" Cardez suggested. "The ones who have begun to question? The ones most likely to reveal damaging information about the contra network—this dirty tricks unit—given the chance?"

"Some, yes. But there are others here who count among the CIA's most loyal drudges. Why they should want these people dead, I do not understand."

Cardez asked Morales about Howard Townley, whom Morales apparently knew as 'Captain Red.' According to Morales, Townley had been a familiar sight down in Central America, both in and out of this dirty tricks unit. "Wherever *los Cubanos* go, Captain Red is never far behind."

"And Ronnie Wilkinson?" I asked through Cardez. "You worked with him often inside this unit?"

Morales shook his head, explaining to Cardez that he had only met *Señor* Wilkinson on a single occasion. At a meeting held at a Howard Johnson's motel in Miami, almost a year ago. Having said this, Morales looked from Cardez, to me, back to the list. Then picked up the notebook, his lips moving silently as he re-scrutinized every name.

"I think I see," he murmured, getting back to his feet, pressing his hands together in front of him as he paced across the room. "Yes," he added, turning back in our direction. "*Señor* Tiagas attended this meeting. As did every other member who has been included on this list!"

"*Señor* Tiagas?"

"The Panamanian defector. And it was at this meeting that *Señor* Tiagas discussed Noriega's tapes. I am sure of this."

"What tapes?"

Once again, and for an extended period, Morales talked on excitedly with Cardez.

"It seems," Cardez finally explained, turning back to me. "That General Noriega of Panama picked up a few pointers from President Nixon along the way. He's been amassing an impressive collection of taped conversations in his library."

"Conversations with?"

"Members of the U.S. Intelligence community. In particular, according to *Señor* Morales, who heard it from Tiagas at this meeting, conversations with a few key Cuban-Americans—White Hand people—who had been training contra troops down in Panama over the last seven years. Apparently Noriega is planning to use these tapes as collateral, should the United States renege on the Panama Canal treaty; try and take it back."

"But what would be the value of such tapes?" I asked. "What kind of collateral could they be?"

"*Mano Blanca!*" Morales answered for Cardez, as if those two words alone could answer any and all of my questions.

"According to *Señor* Tiagas," Cardez went on. "Certain of these Cubans, unaware they were being taped, were imprudent enough to have bragged to Noriega about many of the deeds they have carried out over the last thirty years. For the CIA, and for others. Indiscretions and crimes of extremely embarrassing and damaging proportions. Their connection to the cocaine trade, details of kidnapping rings they set up throughout Central America, their involvement in so many of the death squads down there."

"And this is only the drop in the bucket," Morales insisted to Cardez. "Assassinations all over the world they are responsible for."

"Like who, for example?"

Morales shrugged, crossed the room. "Like your Kennedy brothers, for one. Like them."

"President John Kennedy?"

"*Pero, si!* They never forgive him or his brother for not giving them air support when they attacked Cuba in '61. *Never.* From that day forward, John and Robert Kennedy are much hated men among the *Brigadistas*."

"This couldn't be true?" I murmured to Cardez. "They couldn't have gotten away with killing *both* Kennedys without us knowing about it?"

"But it is true!" Morales insisted in Spanish, having understood my words. "I can say it was this that bothered them the most. The fact that *Mano Blanca*'s connection to the Kennedy assassinations got onto one of these tapes. It made them a little crazy, I can say."

"Made who crazy?"

He shrugged. "Two American officials sitting in on the meeting. They were not introduced. This much I know—they were not happy that we should be hearing all of this. It had not been planned this way. How could it have been planned? The existence of these tapes took everybody by surprise. Even these officials," he added, recrossing the room. Cardez and I exchanged looks.

"What do you think?" Cardez murmured.

"I think it's incredible. And damn scary . . . How is it possible they'd get away with some of this stuff?"

"I tell you, Miss," Morales said in Spanish, pointing his finger at me again. "It makes no difference whether or not you believe what I say. What I say is the truth."

Cardez asked Morales something about McNally again, and again, Morales confirmed that he had never heard of the man.

"Well then, *Señor* Morales," Cardez said, getting to his feet as he checked out the time on his watch.

"Enrique, wait."

"I have a mass to get back to, Sarah."

"Yes, of course. But—what other government officials might *Mano Blanca* have assassinated?" I asked in English, turning back to Morales.

"Many," Morales answered in Spanish. "*Señor* Tiagas ticked them off his fingers like so many fleas. Even in Panama they have killed. General Torrijos, the leader before Noriega. Him too, they killed. And for no better reason than that he was too friendly to Cuba. For these *Brigadistas,* there is no sin so terrible and unforgiveable as showing a friendly face to Castro. Many, many people have died for this reason alone. I tell you, most countries around the world have felt the bloody reaches of the White Hand."

"And most of these exploits have been documented on these tapes?" Cardez confirmed.

"So *Señor* Tiagas has said."

"Sarah," Cardez murmured, prodding me to my feet.

"And Sweden?" I asked. "Swedish Prime Minister Olaf Palme? Do they have any responsibility for his death, as well?"

"*Pero, si.*" Morales said, nodding in Cardez's direction.

"Only one of many jobs they have done for General Pinochet. The White Hand is very mixed up in the Chile secret police."

"Well, *Señor* Morales. We must thank you," Cardez said again, offering his hand. "For your cooperation, this afternoon."

"Enrique, ask Senor Morales—ask him if he would be willing to speak with us again."

Morales answered in the negative. His plan now was to return to Nicaragua as soon as possible, to try and make his peace. What other chance did he have, he suggested, poking at the list?

The two men exchanged a few more words in Spanish as Morales walked us to the door. His last piece of advice, spoken to Cardez but directed at me, was not to be so foolish as to try and print anything he had told us today. To mess with the White Hand would mean only trouble for me and my magazine. And on that unpleasant note, our conversation with *Señor* Morales came to an end.

Back outside, I walked Cardez back to his van. We exchanged few words, the two of us in varying degrees of shell shock.

"It's deadly business," Cardez muttered again, shaking his head as he got behind the wheel. "And after all this, we still don't understand why Jim was dragged into it, do we? I have no idea how he might have learned about these tapes. You'll give that D.E.A. agent the telephone number I passed you? See what luck he has in tracing it back?"

I promised I would do my best. And we made plans to get back in touch first thing, the following day.

On the drive back to San Rodino, Oliver and I exchanged few words. He had tuned into a basketball game on the radio. I was madly scribbling out notes, racing through all the details of our conversation this afternoon. It was Morales' allegations concerning the death of the Kennedy brothers that astounded me the most. I had heard plenty of rumors down through the years linking President Kennedy's death to Cubans. But the rumors referred to Cubans from *Cuba*, Cubans under the direction of Castro, not Cubans under the direction of Anti-Castros in Miami! Assuming that what Morales had said held water, that meant that all the conspiracy freaks down through the years were in fact, dead on target. That in fact, there *had been* other gunmen, as so many witnesses and investigators had always insisted. Other more expert marksmen than Lee Harvey Oswald behind John Kennedy's death. Or Sirhan Sirhan, behind the death of Robert Kennedy, five years further on.

Before I knew it, Oliver was turning into the parking lot behind the Parkside Motel.

"This isn't really enough, Oliver," I suggested, handing him over the fifty I had promised. "Considering how much you've helped me out today. You did half the work. More than half . . . You'll forgive me the haircut?"

"Yeah," he said, smiling sheepishly as he stuffed the money into his pants.

"And tomorrow? You'll be available if I need you?"

"Yeah, I guess. You going to see Howie tomorrow?"

"Maybe. But Oliver, I have a rather large favor to ask of you. Will you be speaking with your brother tonight?"

"I don't expect so."

"If by any chance you do, it would be best not to tell him anything about today. With the kind of friendship Danny and Howie seem to have, it might—well, the fact is, I'd rather that Howie know nothing about me. At least, until I get a chance to speak with him. All right?"

"Like I said—I can keep my mouth shut."

"Fine," I said, moving out of the truck.

I waited until his pickup disappeared around the corner, then headed into the room, entertaining vague hopes that Nystrom had returned in my absence. But no such luck. Not even a clue this time that he had stopped by the place in the hours since I'd been away. But no sooner had I shed my sweater, kicked off my shoes, and poured myself a healthy dollop of vodka, than there came a rap at the door. I checked out the window. It was the elderly gentleman who'd been watching over the motel.

"Yes?"

"I have a message for you, Sarah. From Mr. Nystrom."

I opened the door. The man smiled, light blue eyes set in a grandfatherly, crinkled face, and offered his hand. "Charlie Palmer. We were hoping to take advantage of your perspective again this evening," he said, stepping deferentially into the room. "On the possibility that one or another of our suspects may be turning up at a gathering this evening. Mr. Carlotti's usual mix of pleasure and business."

"At his house?"

"On his yacht."

"His yacht? And where is Mr. Nystrom?"

"Otherwise detained at the moment. He will be there this evening, of course."

"Yes, I see." I hesitated, not sure just how much I should be telling this man. The truth of the matter was, that considering everything I had seen and learned today, we no doubt had much more reliable means of tracing down our assassins than the chancy strategy of running into one or another of them at one of Carlotti's midnight soirées . . . But then again, Nystrom was there and I was here. If I wanted his help in this thing—and I did—then I needed to see the man again. And at the rate things were going, this might be my only chance.

"I have time for a shower, I assume?"

"Take your time, Sarah. I'll be waiting in the car."

He stepped out and closed the door after him. In a matter of minutes, I had showered and dressed, once again making use of Cory's slinky ensemble.

"Where is this yacht of Carlotti's?" I asked, joining Charlie in the car.

It was in Newport, a good ninety-mile drive. If I never set eyes on another Southern California freeway again, it wouldn't be too soon. We rode in silence for the major loop of the trip, while my mind raced here and there, having taken in far too much, too fast.

"Mr. Palmer," I finally said, loosening the seat belt and shifting in the seat so as to face the man directly. "Peter tells me you're one of the disillusioned. Disillusioned what?" He turned my way, then back to the road. "Or would you rather not discuss it?" I asked.

"There is nothing secret about it. I was a former case officer for the CIA."

"I see."

Again silence, as Palmer concentrated on the road.

"What can you tell me about *Mano Blanca?*" I asked.

The question obviously took Mr. Palmer by surprise.

"You are speaking of the Miami boys?"

"That's right, yes."

"I believe you are the first reporter ever to ask me such a question. What is it that you wanted to know?"

"Is it a well-known terrorist group within the Intelligence community?"

"Certainly. *Mano Blanca* is your ultimate terrorist group. Creme de la creme. You've seen the film 'Manchurian Candidate'? Well then, imagine if you will, two or three hundred Manchurian Candidates let loose on the world, and you have a fair idea what these fellows are all about."

"Are they still with the CIA?"

"Officially, no."

"And unofficially?"

"Unofficially, they remain a rather irresistible resource. They also remain what is euphemistically termed a 'disposal problem.' Having trained these boys in every terror tactic imaginable, the question has remained of what to do with them, once the anti-Castro campaign fizzled to a halt. The fact is, we still don't have an answer to that one. Cutting them off the Company's payroll certainly didn't solve anything. Quite the contrary, as a matter of fact. They found plenty of other means of supporting themselves."

"Like their work in the death squads?"

"For one. And of course, their deep involvement in the drug trade. The Colombians are the ones we are always hearing about. But it was these Cuban-Americans—the *Brigadistas*—who first got the cocaine trade off the ground and pouring into Miami. They're the ones who showed the Colombians the ropes. It's what I call the boomerang effect," he added, after a pause. "And a very common phenomenon within CIA operations, I might say. We train a group of men to wreak havoc in some foreign land. Whether it be Cubans, or Vietnamese, or Laotian hill people, or today, our Nicaraguan contras. And sooner or later, when and if our operation fails, we are obliged to allow our 'warriors' to immigrate into the States. Where—trained as terrorists—they continue to act like terrorists. Only now, on the streets of America rather than in some foreign land. The chickens come home to roost. Who are the real victims of *Mano Blanca?* Cubans in Cuba? Not at all. It is Cuban-Americans living in Miami who must bear the brunt of their vicious ways. It is the same for the many Vietnamese communities in our cities today, at the mercy of the paramilitary terrorists we trained back in the sixties and seventies over in Vietnam. What goes around, comes around—yes?"

"But I can't understand how something as devastating as *Mano Blanca* can stay out of the news the way it has?"

He looked at me again, then again to the road. "The CIA has tremendous influence over the flow of information in this country. As a journalist, you must be well aware of that."

"But all the same . . ."

"How do you think the American people would react to the idea that the most terrible of terrorist groups—far more destructive than a Red Brigade or a Black September—was created by our own people, right here at home? It is my guess that the Iran arms scandal would pale next to a revelation such as that."

More silence, as he shifted into the near lane and took the first Newport exit and I weighed the pros and cons of broaching *Mano Blanca*'s connection to the Kennedy assassinations and the existence of Noriega's tapes.

"This is it?" I asked, when Palmer eased the car up to a pier—one in a series of piers fronting a series of marinas. Although in this particular instance, it was not a marina but a single boat, a very large boat, that waited at the end of the pier.

"This is it," he said, turning off the engine. "And now, we await our friend . . ."

"So there really exists such a group as DeWinkey?" I asked, turning to face the man again. "Defectors from the White Male Killer Establishment?"

He turned, smiled. "Damn right."

"What do you do, exactly? Help out the other side? People like Mr. Nystrom? Or—?"

"When the need presents itself, yes. But primarily, we see ourselves as an educational forum. Too few Americans are aware that these coups and backroom machinations synonymous with the CIA are patently unconstitutional. The Central Intelligence Agency—as its name implies—was created as an intelligence gathering operation. Nothing more. It's high time we reined that Agency in, or the next democracy we lose may well be our own."

"So . . . So Mr. Nystrom—he's part of your group? DeWinkey? Or—?"

"He's with Swedish Intelligence. He's never spoken of this?"

"Yes, he has, as a matter of fact."

"Mick's an excellent agent. One of the best. And one of the few I've run into who can keep the bigger picture in mind."

"If he's so good at keeping the bigger picture, then why is he working with a man like Carlotti?"

Palmer turned, gave me an appraising look. "Yes, well we all have to make compromises somewhere along the line. A hazard of our profession. And as drug dealers go, let's say that Carlotti isn't any worse than the next one. And certainly better than most . . . And there's our friend," he added, nodding through the window.

And there was Nystrom, approaching the car and opening the door.

"Good luck in there," Palmer said, as I stepped out of the car.

Nystrom helped me out, holding tightly onto my arm as he ducked down and exchanged a few words with Palmer. Then righting himself again as Palmer moved the Volvo further down the road. We stood there a moment, eyeing each other in silence. All the things I had wanted to say—that *had* to be said—upon seeing this man again, seemed to be trapped somewhere at the base of my tongue.

"So where the hell were you last night?" he asked, his hand moving up my arm.

"I was about to ask you the same question. We have to talk, Peter," I added, my voice sounding very strained to my ear.

He nodded, smiled. "I know. Later," he said, as two couples brushed past us and down the pier. "Charlie told you the rules?"

"What rules?"

"That yacht is one self-contained wiretap. So we keep anything important to ourselves until getting away from here. All right?"

"You don't understand, Peter. I think I learned enough today to make this whole thing superfluous," I said, nodding in the direction of the yacht.

He stared down at me, considering my words while another group of party-goers headed past us.

"Interesting day, Calloway?"

"Very."

"That's good. Meanwhile, I have some business to take care of in there. So do you. All right?" he repeated a second time.

I hesitated, considering the desirability of blurting out a few tidbits right here and now, ultimately deciding against it.

"All right. Fine," I said.

"Good," he murmured, his thumb massaging the hollow at my throat as his gaze trailed off my face, undressing me in casual, unflinching fashion. "What's that you're wearing, Calloway?"

"Same dress I wore the other night."

"I mean the perfume."

"It's not exactly perfume."

"Smells damn good, whatever the hell it is," he said, taking my arm again and steering us onto the pier.

"Peter?"

"Yep?"

"Aren't you even going to kiss me hello?"

He turned, gave me that half-smile, bent over and kissed me. Or maybe it was I who reached up to kiss him. But what started as a fairly innocent gesture, certainly didn't end that way. I found myself thinking some pretty disorientating thoughts, as we headed down the pier.

One of Carlotti's ubiquitous armed guards was waiting for us at the bottom of the ramp. He nodded at Nystrom as if he knew him. Then ushered us onto the yacht.

Compared to the New Year's Eve bash, things were fairly tame this evening. People were sitting around in small groups, sipping their favorite poisons, and actually talking to one another. A few couples were dancing to the piped-in saxophone music on the front deck. Nystrom seemed to know more people tonight. Or maybe I was in a better position to observe him this evening: the nods passing back and forth, the handshakes, a couple of slaps on the back. And always, the sliding of the eyes from Nystrom to me, checking out this chick Nystrom was hanging out with.

We headed downstairs and into a sitting room of sorts. The dimmed gas lighting, the leather walls, the plush furnishings, gave the place a rakish ambience. A group of men were making use of the pool table in one corner of the room. I noticed Nystrom observing me observing the others. But nobody here looked any more familiar than anybody else.

Nystrom went over to a self-service bar and fixed up a couple of iced vodkas.

"Hey, Skipper!"

It was the Fat Man from the other night, calling to Nystrom from the staircase.

"Okay, kid. Think you can take it from here?" Nystrom said, handing me a glass.

"Let's keep this short and sweet, all right?" I suggested. "Like I said, I have a *lot* to talk about."

"Sure thing," he said, his gaze already moving on to his big-bellied friend. Right.

Glass in hand, I headed up a back staircase and onto the rear deck. More couples dancing. A poker game in progress. One of Carlotti's sentinels moving about, checking everybody out. Including myself. I headed down another staircase and landed in a darkened video room. As far as I could make out, the place was deserted, except for the naked bodies cavorting on the screen that covered a near wall. I started back up the stairs, then turned right around again upon catching sight of my Latin sleazeball from New Year's Eve, standing at the top of the stairs. Back in the video room, I ducked under the screen and took a seat on a sofa pushed to one side of the room.

This was no porno flick. Too grainy and unembellished. Too real. Some middle-aged, pot-bellied Latin man being entertained by two very young girls, neither of them a day over thirteen. I was simultaneously fascinated and repulsed.

Suddenly, the film flicked off and the room went totally dark. I stayed in place, finishing my cigarette and considering my next move. A match flared up from across the way. So I wasn't alone, after all. My companion got up from his seat and crossed the room, turning on a wall light. He was a tall, thin man, with sharp features and very dark eyes, dressed entirely in white.

"Good evening," he said, smiling, composed. "Allow me to freshen your drink."

Without waiting for a reply, he swept my glass off the table and brought it over to the cabinet tucked behind the screen. "Vodka, I assume?" he suggested, bringing out a bottle of Stolichnaya. "Like the Swede?" He smiled again, sending shivers down my spine as he set the glass back down on the table and stood there, eyeing me from above.

"Who are you?" I asked, shifting in place, knowing damn well who he was.

"Your host," he said with a slight bow of his head, smiling again. "And I ask myself," he added, settling into the chair opposite, crossing one leg over the other, folding his hands in his lap. "I ask myself why this Swedish privateer is taking time out for a steamy affair with an American divorcée? Such a risk, yes? So unlike this man."

"Not that it's any of your business, but we're not having an affair."

"Ah, but I beg to differ with you. You see, I witnessed an

embrace the two of you shared before embarking on this yacht. To be frank, that is when my questions first began." The smile stayed on his face. I got to my feet.

"Please. You will forgive me?" he said, waving a hand at the sofa. I didn't sit back down. But I didn't leave the room, either. "And you enjoyed my little entertainment?" he asked, nodding at the empty screen. I said nothing, leaning up against the wall, drink in hand. "Certainly you recognized the star performer, yes? General Noriega of Panama? An interesting collector's item, would you agree?"

Noriega—again?

"You and the General are friends?" I suggested.

He smiled. "The best." Silence.

"So tell me," I finally said. "These rumors in the paper about four American administrations turning a blind eye to the General's drug smuggling—is there much truth to it?"

He shrugged. "Manuel Noriega has profited greatly from the drug trade passing through his country. That much is true. It has bought him his lovely home in France. It has bought him many other lovely things, as well," he added, waving back at the screen. "But then, that was the understanding, yes?" he added, getting to his feet, crossing the room to straighten out a painting of a nude young male hanging on the opposite wall. He sat back down again, carefully reinforcing the crease of his pant leg as he recrossed his legs.

"What understanding?" I asked.

He spread his arms to express the obvious. "The one between your government and his. That he could pick up on the drug trade where General Torrijos had left off. Providing, of course, that he agreed to be Washington's boy."

"And you, Mr. Carlotti? You have a similar understanding with our government?"

He smiled. "You Americans are shocked by such understandings? But they are rather to be expected, are they not? If your CIA wishes to deal with the people in power around the world, with the people who hold the reins, then they must deal with the likes of us. It is a fact of world politics which one can run with, or run away from. Long ago, your CIA decided to run with the situation. To run with the ball, as you say," he added, flashing me the smile. He turned toward the stairwell as one of his bodyguards entered the room. The man approached Carlotti, bent down and muttered something in a clipped Spanish.

"You will excuse me?" Carlotti said, getting to his feet, bowing slightly in my direction. "And my regards to our common friend."

He followed his man upstairs. I sipped my drink in place, while pondering the breadth and duration of Nystrom's 'friendship' with this man. Could Carlotti possibly know Nystrom as well as he implied when he used the phrase 'So unlike this man, yes?'

I put the empty glass aside and got to my feet, finding I needed to put a lot of effort into walking a straight line out of the room and up the stairs. I needed some food in my stomach and fast.

Once on deck, it was no small surprise to find we were at least a half a mile from shore. I hadn't even felt the boat move. It was that big. Or I was that drunk. With Cory's heels in my hand, I made my way up one side of the deck and down the other, dutifully checking out every male face I passed. Then I returned to the bow, where things were more subdued. Deserted, in fact, save for a woman relaxing in a lounge chair to one side of the deck. I settled into the lounge next to hers, not aware until too late that the woman was having herself a good old-fashioned cry.

She turned when I settled down, smiled, wiping at her face. "That saxophone. It—" Another sniff and an embarrassed laugh.

"Mood music," I said.

"Yes."

Her head dropped back on the cushion. I closed my eyes. Then fell asleep. For how long, I couldn't be sure.

"So this is where you've been hiding out?"

I opened my eyes to find Nystrom standing above me, smiling.

"Business taken care of?" I asked, scooting up in the lounge.

"Yep."

"No luck," I said, in answer to his questioning look.

He nodded, settling onto the other lounge—the woman had disappeared—and taking out a cigarette.

"You smoke too much. And how long are we going to be stuck out here?" I asked, waving towards the shore.

"What's up, Calloway?"

"What's up, is that we have a hell of a lot to talk about. That's what's up. And it seems we're always in a situation where we can't talk."

"Is that it?"

"What?"

"Something else on your mind?"

"You're always asking me that. What else could *be* on my mind, for God's sake?"

I dropped my head back on the cushion, checking out the moonless sky, the constellations jumping out at me, and aware that I was feeling slightly strange—squishy and high—and wondering vaguely if Carlotti had dropped anything into that drink.

"I met 'The Man,' by the way," I said, glancing over at him, then back overhead. "He wanted to know why some Swedish racketeer would be taking time out for a steamy affair—his words, not mine—with some American divorceé? Was that the best you could do, Peter? All the careers you could have given me, and I wind up a divorceé?"

He laughed. I turned on my side, observing Nystrom as he lay there, smoking his cigarette, trying to get under the surface of this man. Who was he? *What* was he? A hard-nosed, cold-blooded intelligence agent? A part-time arms dealer, on the side? How could a man who came across as tender and unaffected as this man did at times, still be dealing with the likes of a Roberto Carlotti? Did I really know this man at all?

"What's up?" Nystrom asked, for what seemed like the zillionth time tonight, his hand floating up my arm.

"Just thinking how funny life is, that's all."

"Such as—?"

"Among other things, that you and I grew up in the same city. For all we know, might have passed each other on the street."

"If I had passed you on the street, Calloway. I'd have remembered it."

"Yeah, right."

"So tell me, Calloway. What were you like back in Detroit?"

"As a kid? Kind of a ballsy little brat."

He laughed, looked over. "Haven't changed much, have you?"

"Guess not."

I turned on my back again, beginning to enjoy myself. A minute passed, maybe more.

"*Are* you divorced?" he asked, the hand floating back down my arm.

"Nope . . . Never married."

"Too ballsy?"

"Or too bratty. Take your pick."

He laughed again. This man was becoming an easy mark.

"So, how do you take to it?" he asked.

"To what?"

"The single life."

"It feels okay. More than okay. For me . . . How about you?" Silence.

"Guess I've seen better days," he finally said, flicking his cigarette overboard.

"You miss your wife? Your kids?"

"Not sure just what the hell it is I miss. If it's the wife and kids, why was I such a bastard when we were still together?"

"You were a bastard, were you?"

"So I've been told."

"Yeah? Well, as far as I can figure it, most husbands are bastards. Seems to go with the territory."

"It's a question of expectations, Calloway."

"Yeah?"

"Yeah . . . And this man you've been seeing back in San Francisco. It's serious?"

"Serious? It was very nice, if that's what you mean."

"Was?"

"Is . . . He's a journalist. He went off on assignment for a number of months."

"I see. This is none of my business, really."

"Why not? If you were married, I sure as hell would want to know about it."

"But you're not married," he reminded me.

"No. I'm not."

"In the mood for a little privacy?" he asked, swinging his legs over the chair and getting to his feet.

"Some place we can talk?"

"There's no place in this goddamn boat where we can talk. Come on," he added, reaching out his hand, helping me to my feet.

He yanked open a hatch in the middle of the bow and started down the ladder.

"Coming, Calloway?"

"Where the heck is this going?"

"Trust me, kid."

I threw him my shoes and climbed down after him, landing in a kitchen galley. Behind it was a pantry. Nystrom pushed aside a table and opened a trap door, climbing down a second ladder. I followed, my bare feet hitting thick carpet just as Nystrom flicked on a lamp over the sofa. It was a small room. Nothing more than a sofa, a TV, and a bar. Nystrom stepped back on the ladder and locked the trap door.

"What do you think?" he asked, loosening his tie as he looked around.

"How did you find this place?"

"Like it?"

"It's—how did you find this place?" I asked again.

"Just what the hell are you getting at?" he asked, pulling me close, squinting down at me.

"You haven't used this room before, have you?"

"Hey. I'm a one-woman man, Calloway. Didn't I ever tell you that?"

"That's what they all say."

"That so. . . ?"

He was smiling as our lips met. It was a slow, dream-like kiss—bottomless—that went straight to the pit of my stomach.

"I feel funny," I murmured, leaning my head against the wall, smiling up at him.

"Good funny? Or bad funny?"

"Good. Very good. Incredibly good."

"That's good."

Very slowly, we helped each other undress. And very slowly, we made love, the pulse of our lovemaking dictated by the smoky rhythms of that tenor sax.

Contrary to all expectations, I didn't want this stupid yacht returning to shore, I realized, staring down at him, drinking him in. Because when it docked, we would have to get very serious again. When it docked we would have 'to talk.' When it docked, we would have to deal with the terrible real world, once again . . . But the yacht did return to shore. And we managed to slip away from this evening's gathering as discreetly as we had two evenings before.

It wasn't until Charlie had dropped us back at the motel and we had settled into the room, that I began filling Nystrom in on all the news. Some of it *was* news for Nystrom, much of it wasn't. He had known about the existence of Camp Williams, as a secret CIA training camp. But he had not yet learned that Townley was back in the States. He had heard rumors over the years to the effect that *Mano Blanca* was tied into the two Kennedy assassinations, as well as into many other critical assassinations, including—via their connection to General Pinochet of Chile—the assassination of Olaf Palme. But he had heard nothing about Noriega's alleged tapes.

"Peter, you're saying you've suspected Pinochet's complicity in Palme's death all along?"

"Let's say he's always been one of the prime suspects," Nystrom said, staring into his glass, then back to me.

"But why?"

"You recall Palme opening Sweden's borders to American draft-dodgers during the Vietnam era?"

"Of course. Looking back at it now, I realize he was one of the heros of our time, not only for his stand against Vietnam, but his work for nuclear disarmament. For world peace. He was a great man . . ."

"Yes. And what he did for young Americans in the sixties, he did for Chilean exiles in the seventies and eighties. Thousands of them who fled Chile after the Pinochet coup. More to the point, he never missed an opportunity when speaking at the U.N. to take a jab at Pinochet. I mean, hell. That guy's another Hitler."

"Yeah, I know. And we put him into power. Not something to be terribly proud of."

"Hey look, Calloway. That's what you people are best at. Putting fascist crackpots into place all over the goddamn planet and then looking the other way."

It wasn't Nystrom's words that surprised me, so much as the tone. The bitterness there. He swung his legs over the bed and got to his feet, heading into the bathroom. The man was tired. Very tired. I still hadn't learned what *he* had been doing over the past day and a half. But I had to wonder how much—if any—sleep he had fit into the last 36 hours. There was something in his manner when he stepped back into the room—the bone-weariness—that echoed of that first night he had spent here, the night that he'd been shot.

"You saved my life that night, didn't you?" I said.

"What are you talking about?"

"The night Mrs. Stevens was killed. You saved my life. And I never thanked you for that, have I?"

"You've thanked me, Calloway. You've thanked me," he muttered, settling back on the bed.

"You know what astonishes me about all this?" I said, moving to the edge of my bed. "What scares the heck out of me? That these guys—*Mano Blanca*—can actually get away with these kinds of heinous crimes! It's mind-boggling!"

“Let’s face it, Calloway. They wouldn’t be getting away with this stuff if there weren’t a hell of a lot of people up there looking the other way.”

“I know. That’s what I find the scariest of all. That some of our most popular leaders—men who are truly loved by millions of people—men who are badly needed—can get knocked off like that—murdered—because why? They’re too liberal? Too peace-loving? Too what? Anti-business? Anti-war? What? And the perpetrators get away with it because somehow it suits the powers that be? Even in Sweden, yet?”

“The Palme assassination is *not* going to get buried like the rest of them,” Nystrom said, putting aside his glass. “Not if I have anything to say about it.”

But do you? I wondered to myself, looking over at him. *Do you* have anything to say about it?

“I’ve been thinking, Peter,” I said, getting to my feet, pacing across the room. “Assuming that Townley brought back Noriega’s tapes—a long shot, I realize—but he *has* been down in Panama these last few weeks—and assuming that the White Hand and Pinochet’s connection to the Palme assassination is on these tapes, among God knows what other grisly details, what do you think are our chances of getting our hands on these tapes?”

“Probably zip. A lot of the CIA’s top secret operations get their walking papers at that Camp. There’s got to be damn heavy security down there. Besides, Calloway. As you pointed out, we have no idea if Townley brought the tapes back, do we?”

“True. So, why don’t we start with Townley? Or rather, why don’t *I* start with Townley?” I suggested, settling on the other bed, my drink in hand.

“What are you getting at?” he asked, giving me that look.

“I’ve been working this plan over in my head all afternoon, so give it a chance, all right? First of all—tell me, Peter. What are your chances of digging up some kind of listening device by tomorrow afternoon? Some kind of bug? Preferably, one that doubles as a fountain pen?”

He stared at me, at my question.

"It's in the realm of possibility," he finally said.

"Okay. So let's say I hang out at that bar tomorrow afternoon. Engage the man in a little conversation. And before parting ways, manage to plant the pen on his person. After which—we may assume—Howie heads back to that Camp with the fountain pen AKA bug intact. Stands to reason we might learn a hell of a lot, doesn't it. . . ? What do you think?"

"Sounds damn tricky, Calloway."

"Why?"

"For starters, just how are you going to approach the guy in this bar without raising his suspicions immediately. He's no dope, Townley."

"That's just it. I'm *not* going to approach him. He's going to approach me. And he's going to approach me because I'm going to walk into that bar looking the spitting image of Diana Stevens. Obviously, Townley will know I'm not Diana. I mean, Diana's dead. But let's say I look enough like her to spook the hell out of him, right? And certainly get his attention. I could start from there. This is with the assumption, of course, that I have you or one of your friends for backup. So? What do you think?"

He smiled, shaking his head. "I think it's fucking crazy, is what I think."

"But not all *that* crazy, right. . . ?"

January 3, 1988

I called Cory at 8 a.m. And she showed up at the motel by ten, a large leather bag in one hand and her daughter Tammy in the other.

"This is sounding a little on the hairy side, if you ask me," she said, stepping into the room.

"I'm not talking a carbon copy, Cory. Just enough of a resemblance to get the guy thinking. That's all."

"Well now," she said, sinking down on the bed, studying my image in the dressing table mirror. "I'll have to dye your hair, for starters. Maybe kind of frizz it around the edges. And Di had these, you know, these eyebrows." She circled around the chair, now studying me head-on. "Maybe a few freckles across the nose. Some rouge. Di was real big on rouge. Till the end, when she gave up on makeup all together. Had this real palish skin. Red cheeks. Her dark hair. Sort of like Snow White, I used to think."

In short order, Cory drenched my hair in a temporary dye, snipped it around the edges, set it, and dried it, while filling me in on her decision to quit her job at the Interlude Salon.

"It was Diana—what happened to her—that got me thinking. Know what I mean? It's like—I remember one day, she and I talking about what we were going to do with our lives when we—you know—got it all together. And she talked about wanting to raise up a whole bunch of kids. At least six of them. And she talked about it like she was really going to do it. Like she really believed it was going to happen. And now—well anyway—it just got me thinking, that's all. 'Cause I could wind up no better, right? I mean, we all could. I mean, we all *will*, come sooner or later. So what the heck am I waiting around for? If I'm going to change my life, I better start right here and now. While I still got the will in me to do it.

"So, I've been thinking," she said, hauling out a bagful of cosmetics. "There's this dress design school there in Rodino. It'll mean a year out of my life. But what the heck, right? I mean, I got the money saved up, what better way to spend it, learning a trade. Giving myself a chance to earn money doing something I *like* to do," she added, laying the white powder on my face. The eyeliner. The mascara. "Something I can be proud of. Something my kids can be proud of, if you see what I mean," she added, threading some large gold-hoop earrings, shades of Mrs. Stevens, into my ears.

Eyeing myself in the mirror, I couldn't say I looked like Diana, having no clear idea of what the woman looked like. But I couldn't say I looked like myself anymore, either. Cory was certainly impressed enough with her work to assure me that the resemblance was there. Which was enough assurance for me.

There was a rap at the door. Then Nystrom stepped into the room.

"Jesus Christ," he murmured, looking from me over to Cory, shaking his head at my transformation.

"What do you think?"

Nystrom chose to reserve further comment.

"You remember Cory? From your visit to the Interlude?"

As Cory proceeded to pack up her array of cosmetics, a few words were exchanged, primarily between Nystrom and Cory's daughter. There seemed to be a natural affinity there. By the time Cory was packed, Tammy was holding on to Nystrom's hand. I accompanied her and her daughter back out to the car.

"How are things progressing between you and Cutie-Pie in there?" Cory asked, lifting her daughter into the car seat in back.

"Someday Cory, I'm going to tell you the whole bloody story."

"Yeah? Well, I'm not holding my breath," she said, getting behind the wheel, shutting the door.

"How can I thank you for all the help you've given me over the last couple of days?"

"Come on, girl. Anybody'd have done the same. Besides, I wasn't just doing it for you. I was doing it for Diana. Say good-bye, Tammy," she added, securing her daughter's seat belt, then her own.

"I owe you and your kids a night on the town. Soon. All right?" I suggested, bending through the open window and giving Cory a peck on the cheek.

"Sounds okay by me. Sound okay by you, Tammy?"

Tammy nodded, smiling shyly.

"You be careful now," Cory added, starting up the car.

With her and her daughter waving through the open window, they headed down the drive. I returned to the room just as Nystrom slammed down the phone.

"Townley just showed up at the bar," he said, grabbing up his jacket and keys.

"Already?" It was 12:35 p.m.

Nystrom headed across the street to pick us up some lunch. I changed into the getup Cory had lent me—a red sequined cardigan and a pair of black velvet pants—and joined Nystrom in the car.

"Keyed-up?" he asked, some time later, when I put aside the ham sandwich without taking a bite.

"I don't know. Maybe it's just the reality of finally coming face to face with this guy, that's doing it."

"Everything's going to be fine," he assured me, smiling over at me, patting my thigh. For a guy who had considered this whole scheme to be 'fucking crazy' less than twenty-four hours ago, he certainly had come around. While I, on the other hand, was beginning to entertain some serious second thoughts.

"Here's the prop we talked about," he said, going into his pocket and passing me the electronic bug, masquerading as a fountain pen. Which was *exactly* what we had talked about. I tried it out on my notebook. It wrote just fine.

"Is the bug part already working?"

"Yep. Mind telling me just how you plan on planting that thing on Townley?"

"No problem, Peter. Trust me," I added, relishing a chance to use Nystrom's favorite line.

"Calloway—"

"*Trust me*."

"Have it your way. But this guy wasn't born yesterday, Calloway. Keep that in mind. My advice—if you're interested—is to play it totally straight with the conversation. Right down the line. No funny questions. At least, not at this first meeting. It will only be counterproductive, set him on edge."

"I wasn't born yesterday either, Peter. All right? Now where exactly are you going to be?"

"Setting things up at a trailer park, just outside the Camp. About five miles from the bar. Charlie's already in the bar itself. And

Butch, he's parked outside, in a blue Monte Carlo. If anything goes really wrong, don't bother taking this car back. Just hop into Butch's, and he'll take it from there. All right?"

"I guess." But why did I suddenly feel so goddamn on edge? "You have any—you know—downers, Peter? Something that will take the edge off for me. Calm me down?"

He swung the car into the trailer park, turned off the motor, and took my chin in his hand.

"You're sure you want to go through with this, Calloway?"

"Sure I'm sure."

"All right then," he said, leaning across my lap, going into the glove compartment, bringing out a small vial of pills and shaking a couple of small yellow pills into my hand.

"What are these?" I asked.

"Don't tell me you've never had Valium before?"

"Nope. I'm just an old-fashioned girl."

"Yeah, well it's the old-fashioned girls who eat this stuff like candy."

"So these are relaxers, right?"

"That's right. Take them now and wait until they kick in. And you better put something in your stomach, while you're at it."

But I could no more have eaten that sandwich than an entire roasted pig.

"When I'm through I'll just head straight back to the motel?"

"Right. I asked Butch to follow you back there, okay? Just to make sure you get back safe and sound. Anything else?"

"And you're going to be. . . ?"

"Like I said, setting things up."

"Right . . . So, I better head off, right? Wouldn't want to miss the guy, after all this."

"You're going to be all right?"

"A piece of cake," I said, sliding over the gear shift and behind the wheel as Nystrom got out of the car.

"Calloway?"

"I'm *okay*, Peter. You take care of this end, I'll take care of mine.

All right?" With a last look passing between us, I started up the engine again and headed back out on Highway 78.

By the time I arrived at Hershey's Grill, the butterflies had settled somewhat. But whether the Valium had 'kicked in' or not, as Nystrom had put it, I couldn't say. I parked the car, downed half a sandwich, rechecked the location of the pen in a side pocket of my bag, and headed inside. The juke box was playing 'Don't it Make Your Brown Eyes Blue.' I settled at the far end of the bar and ordered a sweet vermouth on ice from the bartender, an older man who registered mild surprise at seeing me there. Apparently few women—if any—ever set foot in this bar.

When my eyes adjusted to the light, I realized it was Charlie sitting at the other end of the bar, feigning interest in the ballgame playing on the TV overhead. The same group of men from yesterday, in baseball caps and sun glasses, were huddled around the pool table in back. And they too had taken notice of my presence, as one by one they began sending furtive glances my way. I lit a cigarette, sipped my drink, and imitated Charlie's interest in the game.

"How about a dance, honey?"

I turned to find a gangly young man with bad teeth grinning at me, as he leaned precariously against the bar some three stools down.

"I'd rather not, thank you," I said, smiling briefly and turning back to the TV.

"Aw come on. I got a wee bet going with the boys. A little turn around the floor isn't going to hurt anybody?"

"No, really. I—"

"This is our song, honey," he said, swooping in.

"Ease off, Freddie." A second man had come up behind 'Freddie' and put a hand on his shoulder, proceeding to gently shepherd the young man back across the room.

I turned back to the TV, aware that the second man had already returned, and was making no bones about checking me out, leaning up against the bar just where Freddie had been before him.

"Yes?" I said, turning, smiling vaguely.

With a bit of a flourish, the man removed his baseball cap and sunglasses and smiled back. Grey moustache. Iron-blue eyes. Snow-white hair. Ruddy cheeks and the build of an ox. So *this* was Howard Townley. . . ? But then, what had I been expecting? The Prince of Darkness himself?

"Nick," he said, waving his sunglasses at the bartender. "Set this young lady up with another drink."

"Why, thank you."

"Don't mention it. And you excuse my young friend there. They've been going through a bit of a dry spell these last couple of weeks. Doesn't put them on their best behavior."

I nodded, smiled, turned back to the TV. He continued to stand there, checking me out.

"What is it?" I asked, still smiling, giving him a questioning look.

"Nothing. It's just a crazy . . . Nothing. Well now, Ma'am. You have yourself a good one, all right?"

"What are you drinking?" I asked, as he turned to go.

"Me?"

"What's his drink?" I asked, turning back to the bartender.

"Howie's a Jack Daniel's man, aren't you Howie?"

"Fine," I said, tapping the open space beside me on the bar and looking back in Townley's direction. "Care to keep a lady company for a few minutes?"

"Well now," he said, rolling the cap in his hand, looking from the bartender back to me, smiling. "Isn't often I get an invitation as sweet as that one. No siree," he added, straddling the stool next to mine.

The bartender returned with a second vermouth and a bourbon straight-up.

"Thanks, Nick," Townley said. "And thank *you,* Miss—?"

"Rosie."

"Here's to you, Rosie," he said, lifting his glass in a toast, taking a good swallow, smacking his lips. Then turning to study me again, his eyes moving down my face. "It's uncanny," he said, looking into his glass, then taking another swallow.

"What's that?"

"You. It's just—well now, you ever wake up in the morning with a feeling in your bones? A feeling that this day is going to be different than other days. That ever happen?"

"Sometimes," I said, going for my cigarettes.

"Shouldn't smoke, Rosie. If you don't mind my saying. A pretty lady like yourself. Takes the prettiness right out of you, seeing one of those cancer sticks hanging from your lips. Besides the fact that the Lord didn't put us here just so we could turn around and start abusing ourselves like that. Isn't that a fact?"

"Now that you put it that way," I said, dropping the pack back in my bag.

"You a native of these parts, Rosie?"

"Passing through, actually."

"So, I figured. Where're you from, if you don't mind me asking."

"Here and there."

"Here and there?" he repeated, smiling, cocking his head. "A gypsy? Is that what you are, Rosie?"

"In a manner of speaking."

"Gypsy Rose Lee?" He nodded to himself, still smiling, staring into his drink, then back to me. "So tell me, Gypsy Rose. You any good at telling fortunes?"

"Fortunes?"

"No gypsy's worth her salt who can't tell a man's fortune. Isn't that a fact, Nick?" he said, winking at the bartender as he held out his hand.

I took it, turned it palm-side up.

"So what's in my future, Rosie? Tell me all."

"Right now, I seem to be seeing into your past."

"That so?" he said, shifting on the stool and sending Nick another wink. "So what's it say there about my past?"

"Looks to me like there's been a great deal of adventure there. Derring-do. You're a risk-taker, aren't you, Howie?"

"Well, yeah. I guess I am. Adventure, huh? Hell, I sure have seen my fill of them in my time. What else you see there?" he asked, bending in closer, his moustache brushing my cheek.

"I see a trail of broken hearts. You're hard on the ladies, Howie. Don't try to deny it."

"Well now, I don't know about that. Show me where you read that, Rosie. The part about the broken hearts."

My finger followed a line that went off his palm and into a vein on his wrist.

"That one there?" he said, grinning, his gaze moving from my finger to my face, looking me in the eyes. "I'm sweet on the ladies, that I wouldn't be denying. But I'm no heart-breaker, Rosie. No, siree. So you put that thought right out of your head."

I leaned across him for a napkin, put it in front of him, and went into my purse.

"Write something on that," I said, bringing out the pen, uncapping it. "Anything. Your name—whatever."

"What for?"

"Go on," I said, pressing the pen into his hand.

"You read handwriting too? Is that it?"

"That's right."

He gave me a look, a trace of wariness bleeding into his smile.

"Well now, maybe I'd be opening myself up too much, wouldn't I? Putting myself out on paper like that, for you to see."

"You have something to hide, Howie?" I said, smiling, searching his face.

"Hell no. It's just—"

"Well then?"

He grinned, shook his head. "What the hell," he muttered, jotting his name out on the napkin. Howard Kelsey, in a blocky script. Then pushing the napkin over to me. I picked it up and had a good look.

"Well now, Rosie. Let's hear it. What do you see?"

"I see a man who tends to see the world in black and whites."

"Yeah?"

I looked from him back to the napkin.

"A man who isn't particularly interested in the finer shadings of life. A man who likes life straightforward and simple."

"Like my women," he said, winking at Nick again, nudging his glass to the edge of the bar.

"A man who's not afraid to stand behind his principles," I added. "To fight for what he believes in. And that's where the adventure comes back again. But I see—yes—there's the tiniest of doubts beginning to creep in, as well. You can see it in the way you wind up the 'd' and 'y.' Just the slightest suspicion that the world isn't quite as you see it, after all."

He pulled the napkin back, had another look.

"You're reading all that in the way I close off a lousy 'y'?"

"Handwriting's the mirror of the soul," I said, smiling at the man.

"That a fact? All right, Rosie. You take a turn," he said, turning the napkin over and handing me back the pen.

I jotted out the sentence—I fancy you, Howie Kelsey—and pushed the napkin back in his direction.

"So what does that tell you?" I asked, leaning on my elbows, watching him. He shook his head, grinning again, his natural ruddiness getting ruddier.

"It tells me a hell of a lot, Rosie . . . Where's that drink, Nick," he added, a trifle on the nervous side. "And another for the lady. That's my man," he added, as the bartender set up the two drinks. "You've got the gift of gab, haven't you, Rosie? What do you do?" he added, passing me the vermouth.

"Do?"

"You know, for a living."

"Divorce," I said, bringing the glass to my lips.

He squinted at me, smiling crookedly. "You're kidding, right?"

"Sort of."

"Divorce? What kind of profession is that?"

"Works for me. On my fourth, at the moment."

"Fourth divorce? God bless, you do get around, don't you angel?

All right, so this divorce business aside, what else do you do?"

"This and that."

"Here and there. This and that. You're beginning to sound like a dangerous woman, Rosie."

"Let's call it adventurous."

"Yeah?"

"You find it in your ways, I find it in mine."

"And what ways would you be referring to?"

I smiled.

"You're a real tease, aren't you Rosie?" He picked up my hand, running a finger along my knuckles and sending goosebumps up my arm. It was all I could do to stop from yanking my hand free and high-tailing it right out of that bar.

"What's going on over there?" I asked, referring to the raised voices around the pool table.

"Just the boys. They're getting a little hard to handle these days. Don't run away now," he said, squeezing my hand and setting it back down on the bar. Then heading back over to 'the boys.'

I exchanged quick looks with Charlie, and continued to nurse my drink, while working out an exit plan that would be smooth and painless, and still be leaving him with the damn pen.

"Excuse me, Ma'am. But haven't I seen you somewhere before?"

I swiveled around on the stool to find myself staring straight at that purple birthmark. Like a snake, I thought, my eyes moving up to face-off with the brown eyes of that San Rodino cop.

"Haven't I seen you somewhere before?" he repeated, more or less fencing me in as he leaned against the bar.

"Not that I can recall," I mumbled, swiveling back around and grabbing up Townley's drink by mistake, taking a quick sip.

"I'm not one to forget a face," he said, slipping around, leaning his back up against the bar, holding my chin in his hand.

"Yes, well I'm afraid you're quite mistaken this time," I said curtly, pushing his hand away and moving down one stool.

"Why don't you leave the lady alone?" Nick suggested, strolling slowly toward us.

"Yeah. Sure thing," the man said, shoving off the bar and giving me one last speculative look before heading back across the room.

Charlie and I exchanged another look.

"Jack giving you any trouble?" Townley asked, retaking his seat.

I shrugged, set down his glass. "Thought he had seen me before, that's all."

"Maybe you're that kind of woman, Rosie," he said, brushing at his moustache.

"What kind is that?"

"The kind that reminds a man of other women. Women that came before."

"Do I remind *you* of other women, Howie?"

"Now that you mention it. Yeah, you do," he said, looking down the other end of the bar, wiping his hands on his pants.

"Howie?"

When he turned back, I could swear there were real tears swimming on the surface of those iron-blue eyes.

"You want to talk about it?" I asked.

"About what?"

"About this—well, this woman I seem to remind you of?"

"Nope."

He finished off his bourbon with a final toss. Then pulled a wallet out of his back pocket. "Have a look-see," he said, flipping a snapshot onto the bar. It was a picture of Townley in camouflage fatigues, standing in front of a helicopter.

"You fly helicopters?" I said, stating the obvious.

"Damn right. Rotor-heads, the whole bunch of us," he said, nodding at the pool table crowd. "This here's a helio," he added, flipping out a second photograph, showing Townley and a fellow pilot, standing on either side of a small prop plane. "You can land that baby most anywhere. Don't even need a landing strip to speak of, if you're good. I'm good," he said matter-of-factly, tapping the photo with his finger. "Helios are damn fast machines. But tricky son-of-a-bitches to fly. Light in the tail, see? Give me a Pilatus Porter any day," he went on, dropping a third photo onto the bar.

"My personal favorite. Built by the Swiss for mountain flying, see? For landing on glaciers and that kind of shit. It's a slow craft, but damn trustworthy. And I'll tell you something else about these babies. In a high wind, you can zero land them. Can zero take-off, too, if the occasion calls for it. Like your landing strip is a chimney or something, you get the picture? And this here's a C-47. The real workhorse of the stable. Carries the big loads. Soft rice drops. Hard rice drops. Whatever."

"And you can fly all these different planes?"

"Damn right. And that's just for starters. End of Show-And-Tell," he added, shuffling the photos together, slipping them back in his wallet.

"You're a talented man, aren't you Howie?"

"In my way."

"What did you mean by soft and hard rice drops?"

"Did I say that?" he said, cocking his head, smiling slightly.

"Yes, you did," I said, returning his smile.

"Well now, the difference is—hard rice isn't rice, see? It's—let's say guns or ammo or whatever other shit we're supplying the friendlies with. Only we call it rice 'cause, well 'cause usually the weapon drops are kind of unofficial business, if you get my drift. Thanks man," he added, as Nick served up still another round of drinks.

"Not for me," I said, pushing mine aside. "No, really Howie. I have to hit the road. An appointment with my lawyer."

"Aw, Rosie. We're just getting acquainted here, aren't we?"

"Will you give me a call?" I suggested, scribbling out the name of a motel on the napkin. "Anytime tomorrow, all right?" I added, capping the pen, rolling it up in the napkin, tucking the pen into his shirt pocket. "You won't disappoint me now?"

"Not a chance in hell."

"Tomorrow then?" I said, flashing him one last smile before slipping off the stool and making my way self-consciously across the room and out the door, into a blazing sunlight. God, it was bright. I got into the Dodge Dart, started her up, then checked the lot, sighting the blue Monte Carlo just a few cars down from where I had parked. I couldn't see inside the vehicle—too much light reflecting off of glass. But I waved anyway and headed on my way.

By the time I got back to the motel, the sun had set. It was 6:35. I turned into the lot and eased the car into my usual parking space, just under the balcony, got out and looked for evidence of the Monte Carlo somewhere behind me. Nothing. I headed up to the room.

Everything was going to work out, I assured myself, settling down on the bed. I suspected it was the Valium talking. But all the same, I felt it in my bones. Everything was going to work out. We were—one way or another—going to get our hands on those tapes. I was going to have myself one hell of a story, as if I didn't already. And Nystrom was going to have enough solid evidence in his possession to force Swedish Intelligence to re-direct their investigation into Palme's death. Which—as I had learned last night—had been his principal reason for coming over here in the first place. And that hadn't been the only news I'd picked up last night. Among other things, Nystrom had told me that he and his friends had managed to trace back nine out of the thirteen names. As could have been predicted, everyone of them, with the exception of McNally and Juarez, had a history of drug and/or gun running, and had been dabbling in a paramilitary career. As could have been predicted as well, every single one of them, with the possible exception of the last three men on the list, was already dead . . .

Only minutes after returning to the motel, I fell into an early evening snooze, waking up with a start sometime after 7 p.m.

The place was empty. Soon enough, I was back in a fitful sleep. When I awoke again, the room was pitch dark and everything felt slightly out of synch. Where the hell was Nystrom? I leaned across the bed to check out the time again. 9:20. I was damn thirsty. Also a little woozy, I realized, getting to my feet. I sank back down on the bed, going over my conversation with Townley. And jumping ahead to tomorrow afternoon, and the possibility of speaking with the man again.

There was a rap at the door. I flipped on the light and waited.

"Calloway?"

It was Nystrom. With Charlie right behind him.

"What's happened?" I asked, the minute they stepped through the door.

"It's going great," Nystrom said, squeezing my shoulder as he headed past me and across the room, grabbing up the phone.

"Like a charm," Charlie added, giving me a wink as he settled into the rocker by the door.

"It is?" I said, sinking back on the bed. "So Townley's still wearing the bug?"

"Wouldn't be surprised if the bum takes it to bed with him," Nystrom said over his shoulder. "You hooked him, Calloway. But good."

"We're picking up quite a bundle of information," Charlie said, leaning forward in the chair. "At the moment, they're buried in a poker game. But dinner was a windfall. They were briefing some fellow out of the U.S. Council for World Freedom."

"U.S. Council—?"

"A right-wing funding organization based out of Phoenix. The timing couldn't have been better," he added, looking over at Nystrom, who had started speaking—in Spanish?—to someone at the other end of the line.

"So what have we learned?" I asked.

"For starters, looks like your friend Morales was right on the money about those tapes of Noriega's."

"And Townley has them now?"

"Doesn't look that way. Apparently, they're in the hands of a couple of members of the Colombian cocaine cartel."

"Oh?"

"Or should I say, that is what we're assuming from what we picked up tonight. Seems as if some American officials, or possibly a couple of the Miami boys, made a deal with the cartel a few months back. Assuming the Colombians could get their hands on these tapes, the CIA would return the favor by ousting Noriega and putting someone in his place more amenable—or, shall we say, less expensive—for the cartel. Apparently, Noriega has been charging the Colombians what they consider to be offensive fees for using Panama as a country of transit."

"You mean to say we're agreeing to put someone in Panama who will make it *easier* for the cartel to push its cocaine?"

"That seems to be the case, yes. Although it's possible that our side is only bluffing. That we have no intention of doing any such thing, once we get our hands on those tapes. Certainly the Colombians seem to suspect just that. Which is why they've switched the game around. Aren't agreeing to hand over any tapes until *after* Noriega is out and someone who meets their approval has been put in his place. Then again, they *also* may be bluffing. Possibly it's Noriega who still has the tapes. In which case, they'll never get him out of Panama."

"These tapes are as important as all that?"

"Think of it this way. If anybody's been in a position to pick up classified information over the years, it is Manuel Noriega. Panama's the nerve center for the CIA's entire Southern Command. All of Latin America is kept in check through secret stations set up in that little country. At least eight CIA stations at last count, and an additional three National Security Agency spy laboratories. Then there's the School of the America's down there, which happens to train most of the security forces throughout Latin America, as well as the United States' own Special Forces. There's no limit to what might have gotten onto those damn tapes. At any rate, that's all these fellas could talk about tonight. How to smoke Noriega out. Get him off the throne. As usual, they're talking about going at it in the most lame-brained fashion."

"Like what?" I asked, one ear tuned to Palmer. The other tuned to Nystrom, winding down his conversation on the phone.

Palmer shook his head, shrugged. "To judge from this evening's conversation, we plan to announce to the world that Noriega is no longer legitimately in power in Panama, and leave it at that. Then begin freezing Panamanian funds. The consensus seems to be that Noriega will somehow take it all quite meekly and step down."

"And you don't believe this will happen?"

"No, I don't believe it will happen. Not unless we're holding something over his head that I don't know about. But on the contrary, it seems that Noriega is the one holding something over *our* heads, doesn't it? To make matters worse, we've apparently persuaded Noriega's underling—President Delvalle—to go along with our efforts, and step into Noriega's place. Leave it to the State Department to come up with someone like Delvalle, essentially our puppet's puppet, to be our representative for this damn switch. That man has about as much credibility with the Panamanian people as a muddied doormat," he muttered, looking over at Nystrom as he hung up the phone. Then getting to his feet. "I'll spell Butch around ten?" he suggested, turning to Nystrom.

"I'll take over tonight, Charlie. You can pick it up in the morning."

"Well, Sarah," Palmer said, extending his hand. "You've helped us out mightily today."

"Yes, well the feeling is mutual," I said, returning his smile, hoping I would have the opportunity to speak with the man again. Nystrom walked Palmer onto the balcony, where they exchanged a few words. Then he returned to the room.

"You're all right?" he asked, holding my chin.

"Fine."

"You were dynamite this afternoon, you know that, don't you?"

"Yeah? To be perfectly honest, I think the Valium deserves a share of the credit. Tell me, Peter. Why are you so concerned about continuing this tap on Townley, when we already know he doesn't have the tapes?"

"But who does?"

"Charlie said something about the Colombian cartel?"

"That covers a lot of territory, doesn't it? We need some names. Some places."

"And given the names and places, has Carlotti agreed to help you get your hands on these tapes?"

"It's in the works, yeah."

"But why on earth would these guys hand something so valuable over to a man like Carlotti?"

"We wouldn't be bargaining for custody, Calloway. Just a chance to hear them through. Re-tape a few relevant pieces."

"I see. Like any pieces *of* Palme, for instance . . ."

Nystrom headed over to the dresser for the bottle of vodka, pouring a bit into both glasses, passing me one, and settling back on the bed.

"Peter?"

"What's that, honey?"

The warm and casual way he said that made me suddenly wish things were very different than they actually were.

"What kind of 'deals' do you have to make with men like Carlotti, in order to get his—his sponsorship, shall we say?"

He looked up, smiling slightly. "This and that . . . How about some dinner, kid? I owe you one. I owe you more than one."

"I don't think I'm hungry."

"Come on," he said, getting to his feet again, picking up the phone. "You have to eat sometime." He ordered a meal for us from the Vietnamese restaurant across the street.

"What's up?" he asked, patting the space beside him on the bed.

"I don't know. Maybe just coming down from those pills."

"Calloway, you don't 'come down' from something like Valium. They're not a hell of a lot stronger than aspirin."

"Yeah? Well, I guess hangovers are more my speed."

"What's up?" he asked again.

"When are you heading off with Carlotti?"

He squinted up at me.

"I overheard the conversation, Peter. A *little* Spanish I understand."

"As soon as he can arrange it. The transport. The necessary groundwork in Panama . . . Is that what's bothering you, Calloway? That I'm taking off?"

"Can't say that it thrills me."

"We knew this was in the cards, right? That I wasn't going to be hanging around here forever."

"Yep. It's just that . . ."

"What's that?"

"Nothing."

"Say it, Calloway. I want to hear you say it."

"Say what?"

"That you're getting a little attached. That *I'm* getting a little attached. More than a little. That this thing has taken on a lot more importance than we ever thought it would."

We stared at each other from across the room.

"If you *do* manage to get your hands on any of those tapes, Peter. Would you consider passing them along? If not the tapes themselves, then their contents?"

"It's a deal."

"Promise?"

"Promise."

"Good. 'Cause I'll be counting on that. I mean it."

"Hey look, Calloway. I owe you that much. More. We worked this thing as a team. And a damn good one."

"Tell me something, Peter," I said, settling down on the bed. "If somewhere down the line I wanted to get a clear picture of you in my memory—you know, for nostalgia's sake—should it be Mick Nystrom I'm remembering? Or is that an alias, as well?"

His hesitation said it all.

"I kind of figured that," I said, getting back to my feet.

"Come here, Calloway."

"Nope."

"Hey look. See it from my angle for a minute, all right? For all I know, I'm going to wind up in one of those goddamn books of yours."

"*What?* So you know about my first book?"

He nodded, tossing down a bit of vodka.

"Since when?"

"Since back when I was trying to get a handle on you, Calloway. After the Stevens funeral."

"As far back as that? And you never thought to mention it? You're a funny man, Peter. No kidding . . . I'm going to make *you* a promise . . . All right?" I said, sitting back on the bed. "You tell me your honest-to-God real name, and I swear, with every bit of heart and soul that I've put into our friendship, that I won't be using it in any other book I might write . . . Okay?"

He smiled, shook his head. Then drew me closer, his lips somewhere between my right ear and the nape of my neck as he told me his 'real name.'

"The whole truth and nothing but?"

"Cross my heart."

It was the knocking on the door, first soft, then a great deal harder, that brought us back to the surface.

"Yeah!" Nystrom called out, swinging his legs over the bed and getting to his feet.

"Mick, it's Butch!"

"What the—?" he muttered, heading to the door. "Are you telling me that Charlie's trying to handle it?" Nystrom said upon opening the door.

"I think the game's up," Butch said, stepping into the room, looking from me back to Nystrom.

"What are you talking about?" Nystrom said, as Butch tossed a tape onto the bed, followed by a small machine. "This isn't everything?" he asked, picking up the tape.

"That's the last tape I got."

"The last?"

"See if you can figure it out. Whatever the hell happened, I don't think we're getting anymore information out of Townley."

Nystrom set the recorder up on the dresser. Then put in the tape and started it up. There was the sound of typing in the foreground. And behind that, the scratchy recording of an ancient Brenda Lee hit:

> You tell me—mistakes—are a part of being young,
> But that don't right, the wrong that's been done.

"Mind telling me what this is all about?" Nystrom asked. Butch held up his hand. The tape played on.

> For love is blind, and I was too blind to see.

Then came the sound of Howard Townley's voice, speaking to someone as a chair scraped across the floor.

"Well, I'll be a monkey's—what storm brought you in from the cold, buddy?" Silence. "How the hell did you get in here, anyway?"

"Why'd you do it, Howie?"

"Oh my God," I murmured, looking over at Nystrom as he flicked off the machine. "That's Danny."

Nystrom turned the machine back on, rewound the tape a round or two:

". . . do it, Howie? Why'd you do it?"

"Look, buddy. I wouldn't lie to you, would I? I had *nothing* to do with it. The boys, they—see, well she went and did something that wasn't real smart, see? Something she had no right to have done. Started taking things into her own hands, see?"

"And that's why you killed her, Howie?"

"Come on, sport. Diana was my woman. I was nuts about her. Almost as nuts as you were. Yeah, buddy. I knew what was going on. Think I didn't know you were falling for her? But hell, she was carrying my child. You think I'd kill my own child. . . ? Hey!

What are you—crazy? One word from me and there'll be forty of my men crawling all over your ass."

"One word and you're dead, Howie. I mean that."

"Jesus, buddy. Don't go and do something you're going to regret. We go back a long way, you and I. A long fucking way."

"What was with the list, Howie?" Danny asked, his voice quieter now, but closer to the mike. "That list of names?"

"Damage control, buddy. You know how that works. With these damn committee hearings and lawsuits popping out of the woodwork, the shit's going to hit the fan unless we work up a little containment here. It's a question of national security, man."

"It goes back to your damn Cubans, doesn't it? You've wasted your whole fucking career covering for those bastards."

"And it's been worth it. You know it. And I know it. They're the best goddamn band of commie hunters we got around."

"You know, Howie. I've had about enough of your bullshit over the years. Just about enough."

"Don't do it," Howie murmured, tripping backwards over something, the chair?

I found myself murmuring the same refrain. Don't do it, Danny. Please. But it didn't work. One gun shot rang out, loud and clear. And then another. And then, the sound of a body crashing to the floor. A third shot pierced the silence. Followed by—what?—a gun being tossed to the floor? Or a second body? It was impossible to tell, as everything was suddenly drowned out by the rush of voices and scuffling as at least two or three men broke into the room. Then silence, as the tape too went dead.

Nystrom turned off the recorder and the three of us stood there, staring at one another. The phone rang. Nystrom picked it up, mumbled something into the receiver, then passed it to me. I knew who it was before even hearing his anxious voice over the wire. Oliver.

"You're going up there *tonight?*" Nystrom asked, after I'd hung up the phone.

"He's panicking. Doesn't know who to turn to. Seems that Danny left some kind of strange note in his letter drop. Something about everything being up in the cabin."

"Calloway, it's almost midnight."

"What can I do? And the poor guy's blaming himself for all this. Apparently he told his brother about Howie's return, early this morning . . . My blood runs cold at the thought of telling him what we just heard on that tape."

"Who was that guy on the tape, anyway?" Butch asked.

Nystrom answered him. I went over to the tape recorder and played through that last segment, over and over again. Trying to piece it together. Or rather, to take it apart. That third shot. Had Danny killed himself tonight? Or had that been meant to finish off Howie? Did it even matter anymore?

"He warned me he would do it," I told Nystrom, when he came back into the room. "Actually told me he would 'exterminate the son-of-a-bitch'—those were his exact words—if he ever found out Howie was responsible for Diana's death. How was I to know the guy was serious? How could I have guessed? Jesus, what a mess!"

"Hey, come on," Nystrom said, pulling me to my feet, wrapping his arms around me.

"What a goddamn awful mess."

It was with heavy heart that I climbed into Oliver's pickup an hour later. And with heavier heart still, that I climbed back out again, once we had reached our destination, some miles down a logging road in a hilly, heavily wooded area in the middle of San Rodino State Park. We continued on foot for another mile or so, Oliver's flashlight leading the way, until Danny's cabin came into view, set into the side of the hill.

"Danny?" Oliver called out. "Danny, it's me. Oliver!"

"Doesn't look like he's here, Oliver," I suggested, leading the way up to the cabin door. It was unlocked. We stepped in. Oliver swung the flashlight around the room. There was a gas lantern sitting in a corner. I lit it and held it in the air to give us a better picture of the situation.

The cabin appeared to be just this one large room, with a bed pushed against one wall and a couple of chairs and a table pushed against another. A small, wood-burning stove sat in the middle of the floor. I took a closer look at the table. There were three neat piles of what I took to be Danny's special possessions set out on the table. On the pile nearest to me lay an envelope addressed to 'Mom.' On the middle pile, an envelope addressed to 'Pop.' And on the third pile, an envelope addressed to 'Ollie.'

"Oliver," I said quietly, holding the lantern over the table. He walked up, stared at the three piles.

"Oh shit," he mumbled, sinking into the chair nearest the table, his head buried in his arms. He sat there, rocking back and forth silently, for what seemed like a very long time before he got back up and picked his envelope off the pile and opened it. He read it in the light of his flashlight, shaking his head back and forth as he read, the tears rolling down his cheeks. Putting the letter aside, he picked up the fishing rod his brother had left him, carressing it as if the thing were alive. Then he sank back in the chair, the fishing rod held across his knees, his eyes shut, rocking once again.

"Oliver?"

He didn't answer. I waited a few more minutes, then stepped over to the wood stove and built up a fire from the large supply of dry kindling Danny had left there. In minutes, the stove was crackling and the room was beginning to warm. Oliver didn't move. I brought the second stiff-backed chair closer to the fire and sat there, staring into the flames and struggling to make some sense out of everything that had happened. The next time I checked Oliver out, he was fast asleep, his chin resting on his chest, the fishing rod held tightly in his arms.

January 4, 1988

Oliver and I passed the morning packing up what was left of Danny's possessions and loading them into the truck. The ride back to the motel was a very melancholy one. But at least we could finally talk about it. About Danny. About what had happened. And at least we had come around to the point where we were no longer blaming ourselves for the tragedy that had occurred.

By the time Oliver dropped me off, it was two p.m. Nystrom's Dodge Dart was still parked under the balcony, a very welcome sight. As usual, I waited until Oliver had backed his way out of the lot before starting up to the room.

"Peter?"

The room was empty. No Nystrom. And what was worse, no bottle of vodka. I went under the bed for my suitcase and yanked it open, finding what I knew I would find there. His note:

> Calloway,
>
> I don't like cutting out on you like this. But there seems to be no other choice. Plans got shoved ahead and out of my control.
>
> Seems like there are a hell of a lot of things I never got around to telling you. Like how my little girl is as nuts about peanut butter as you are. Every time I saw you chowing down, I thought of her. Now I suppose that every time I see Scooter with her paw in the jar, I'll be thinking of you. Life works like that, right?
>
> I'm not saying good-bye, because my gut feeling tells me we're not a closed chapter. And I'm never going to forget that face.
>
> Soon,
> M. R.

I read the note over a second time, put it back in the suitcase, took up the car keys he had left me, and headed back out, taking a drive down to Riverside and St. Teresa's Church.

As usual, it was Frannie who answered the door, informing me that Father Cardez was not yet back from his rounds. I told her I would wait for him back in the church, then headed down the walk and around to the basilica. I settled into one of the back pews, staring at a candle burning under a statue of the Virgin Mary, wondering who among Cardez's black-veiled parishioners had lit it. And for whom. A husband long dead? A daughter or son?

Inevitably, my thoughts drifted back to Oliver, to the image of him reading that letter from his brother last night. And then suddenly, the dam broke and the tears came. At last. Tears for Oliver, and Danny, and Diana, and Maude Stevens, and Ronnie, wherever he might be. And for Peter. Never had life seemed so ridiculous and confused.

"Sarah?"

It was Cardez, his hand on my shoulder.

"Hi. I—" I wiped at my face, brought out some Kleenex and blew my nose.

"What is it, Sarah?" he asked, settling down beside me.

"Nothing. I—well, everything. Including the fact that I didn't get any sleep last night. Which must have something to do with it," I added, going on to tell Cardez about what had transpired at Camp Williams the night before. "And now, Detective Ray—*he's* gone—before I even got a chance to ask him to trace back that number for us."

"That's all right, Sarah. Maybe it's just as well that we never know . . . How about coming upstairs? Joining me in front of the fire?"

"Sounds wonderful," I admitted, getting to my feet, feeling thankful that he was here to turn to.

Cardez built one of his fires, we sipped sweet vermouth, and we talked. Not so much about the present, as about the future. And the past. One thing led to another, and I learned—not entirely to my surprise—that Cardez had seriously considered leaving the priesthood in recent months. But that was before Jim died. Now things were different. Now, for inexplicable reasons, he was feeling more committed than ever, to the priesthood and the Church.

"What about you, Sarah?" he said, settling back in his chair.

"Me?"

"What happens now?"

"Looks like I finish one story. And start another. *This* story.

Problem is, all my sources seem to have been killed off or have disappeared back into the woodwork. I have to ask myself *what*—if anything—has been accomplished here?"

"You've gotten to the bottom of it, haven't you? Dug up the truth?"

"But what good is digging up the truth if you can't do anything with it? At least there's a good chance my magazine might pick this up. Which could mean that my investigation down here has only begun. You haven't seen the last of me, Enrique."

"Could this be the begining of a beautiful friendship?" Cardez suggested, doing a pretty lousy Bogart imitation.

"I guess it could," I said, unable to keep the smile off my face.

At nine p.m.—after a round of pizza and coffee—I took my leave, having made up my mind to be back in San Francisco and in Eddie's office tomorrow morning, as promised. There was a hell of a lot of catching up to do.

"Sarah," Cardez said, halting my progress toward the door. "Let me give you something. A little memento of these past few weeks."

I waited at the bottom of the stairs, while Cardez headed back up to the library, coming back down with a copy of Father McNally's book in his hand.

"I think you'll appreciate this, Sarah," he said, handing it to me.

"Yes, I think I will," I murmured, opening the front cover, re-reading the inscription there. Struck by how differently the words of the Guatemalan poet read to me now.

> . . . think as well
> that in this battle
> between animals,
> the beasts died
> forever
> and humanity was born . . .

Jean Warmbold is a freelance journalist who lives and works in San Francisco. Her current passions are researching and writing Sarah Calloway political thrillers, and walking in the countryside. She has written two other thrillers featuring Sarah Calloway. Virago will publish one of these, *Dead Man Running*, a mystery about the origin of the AIDS virus, in 1991.